DARK DESIRES

Marrianne looked at Stephen, her eyes wide, her body trembling. 'Please . . .' she whispered.

'What else can I do?' he asked reasonably. 'You've been warned before. It's as if harsh words aren't enough. Sometimes I think there's only one thing you'd respond to. Sometimes I want to . . .' He stopped, suddenly aware that he'd said too much, gone too far.

'What? Do what? I'll do anything, you know I would,' she said earnestly.

She was beautiful. Even the tears in her eyes and the anguish on her face was seductive. His heart was racing. He had said too much. 'Nothing. Forget I said anything,' he said apologetically.

'Please Stephen, what were you going to say? You owe me more than that.'

'I was going to say that sometimes I think you'd only respond to being properly punished. As in smacked on the backside and told to behave.'

'Yes,' she agreed quietly. 'That's what I thought you meant. Perhaps I do want to be punished like that.'

Stephen breathed deeply, his hands were trembling. 'Remove your stockings,' he said, his voice almost hoarse.

A NEXUS CLASSIC

DARK DESIRES

Maria del Rey

This book is a work of fiction.
In real life, make sure you practise safe sex.

First published in 1996 by
Nexus
Thames Wharf Studios
Rainville Road
London W6 9HA

This Nexus Classic edition 2001

www.nexus-books.co.uk

ISBN 0 352 33648 X

Typeset by TW Typesetting, Plymouth, Devon

Printed and bound by
Omnia Books Ltd

Contents

Versions of these stories have appeared previously in *Forum*, *Erotic Stories*, *Februs*, *Scorpion* and *Sapphire*.

My thanks go to Elizabeth Coldwell, Paula Meadows, Delaney Silver, Josephine Scott, Kerri Sharp and the editors of *Scorpion* and *Sapphire* magazines.

Marianne

Stephen stood up and went to the window. The sky was a uniform milky grey, leeching the colour from the day and leaving everything dull and flat. He stood for a moment, looking out across the fields to the thin line of trees on the horizon, the thin green plumes pointing to the hazy white disc that was the wintry sun.

'If we're going to do this then we have to do it properly,' he had said earlier in the bar. She had agreed readily but had avoided his eyes, looking instead into the roaring flames crackling in the brick fireplace.

The air felt heavy, the atmosphere was already very tense, filled with an expectation that was almost tangible. He returned to the desk and buzzed Marianne, jabbing a finger forcefully at the intercom.

'Yes sir,' she responded breathlessly. He could imagine her sitting on the edge of her seat, waiting for his call, her legs crossed so that the tight skirt revealed the perfect shape of her thighs.

'I want your personnel file please,' he said clearly, managing to conceal the tremor of emotion with an air of cool formality.

'My file?' she asked with a note of genuine surprise.

'Yes please,' he said, and cut the phone off, her quizzical note still hanging in the air.

He leaned back, sinking into the welcoming comfort of the leather chair, and waited for her to come in. The Sullivan account file lay on the desk in front of him, the buff folder containing the full details of the most important account the company had. It was the first file he had asked for when they had both arrived that morning. He remembered the nervous look in her eye as she handed it over, as if she wasn't sure that she wanted him to see it. But the account had been lost and he had to see the file.

Marianne entered and smiled coolly. It was an efficient smile that managed to conceal whatever feelings she had, yet managed not to look false. 'My file,' she said, carefully handing him the blue folder with her name neatly stencilled on the cover.

'Thank you, Marianne,' he said, deliberately placing it next to the Sullivan file.

'Is there anything else?' she asked, hovering in front of the desk nervously.

'No thank you.'

He looked down at her file, not bothering to wave her away. She hesitated for a second, standing in front of the desk, one leg crossed in front of the other, hands together, fingers locked tight. It was only when she turned to walk away that Stephen looked up again. She was wearing a smart navy skirt and jacket, with black seamed stockings and black high heels with butterfly bows on the heel. Her skirt was tight and her hips swayed slightly with each step, emphasising the constraining tightness of the skirt and the elegant curves of her body.

She lingered at the door for a moment and he felt sure she was going to say something, but if she was she changed her mind. She closed the door gently and he felt a sigh of relief. These situations were always so difficult, so very tricky. He skipped through her file, flicking through the pages, not even pretending to read through it. He knew all that he had to know, but he was stalling for time, wanting just those few extra moments to think things through. He leaned back in his seat once more and looked around at the comfortable office, at the framed certificates on the wall, at the book lined shelves, at the painting by the door, at the drinks cabinet in the corner. Success – everything reflected the success of the company and of the people who worked there. Until now.

He buzzed Marianne again. She responded too quickly, her voice just a little too loud and a little too eager. 'Marianne, I'd like to see you for a moment, please,' he said, as calmly as he possibly could. His heart was thumping and his throat had gone impossibly dry.

'Yes, Stephen,' she said when she came in. Her smile was more nervous than it had been a moment earlier, as if she realised that things had finally come to a head.

'This is going to be very difficult,' he said, playing with a pen nervously, finding it easier to look at that and not at her. 'Very difficult,' he repeated softly, 'for the both of us. You've been with us a long time now and sometimes that's not a good thing.'

'It's about the Sullivan account,' she said quietly, barely whispering, her sharp blue eyes suddenly filling with tears.

'Yes. The Sullivan account.' He paused and exhaled heavily. 'But that's not the first time, is it?'

'But it wasn't my fault,' she whispered, her lips trembling.

'I'm afraid it was,' Stephen said softly but firmly, hoping that she wouldn't make a scene. 'You were late with the tender documents. We missed the deadline for the contract and they lost the job. They lost a major contract because of us, and it was our fault. Your fault. They were our biggest client and now they've gone. This was the third time, Marianne, the third. We've given you chances before, too many perhaps. We just can't go on like this.'

'Please, I'm sorry,' she said, the anguish etched miserably on her face. Her skin was pale, making her red lips more prominent, pouting, alluring.

'I'm sorry too,' he said closing her file and pushing it towards her.

'Please Stephen, I'll do anything . . .'

He shook his head sadly and exhaled slowly. 'I'm sorry,' he repeated, looking up into her eyes for the first time.

She looked at him, eyes wide, her body trembling, then she looked away. 'Please . . .' she whispered.

'What else can I do?' he asked reasonably. 'You've been warned before. You've been given chances. What can we do? It's as if harsh words aren't enough. Sometimes I think there's only one thing you'd respond to. Sometimes I want to . . .' He stopped, suddenly aware that he'd said too much, gone too far.

'What? Do what? I'll do anything, you know I would,' she said earnestly.

He looked at her. She was beautiful. Even the tears in her eyes and the anguish on her face were seductive. His heart was racing. He had said too much, letting the tension and the emotion get the better of him. 'Nothing. Forget I said anything,' he said apologetically.

'Please Stephen, what were you going to say? It's not fair, you can't do this to me. You owe me more than that.'

He nodded. 'I was going to say that sometimes I think you'd only respond to being properly punished.'

She looked up sharply. 'What do you mean?'

'I mean treated like a naughty child. Punished with more than just sharp words.'

There was a moment of tense silence and he regretted ever opening his mouth. It hadn't been a smart thing to say and it was going to make a difficult situation impossible.

'Yes. Maybe you're right,' she said very quietly, her face flushing pink. Her eyes were fixed on the ground, avoiding his own questioning look.

'Pardon?'

'I said maybe you're right. Maybe I do need to be punished.'

'No, I don't think you understand. I meant punished as in smacked on the backside and told to behave.'

'Yes,' she agreed quietly. 'That's what I thought you meant. Perhaps I do want to be punished like that.'

Stephen breathed deeply, his hands were trembling. 'Remove your stockings,' he said, his voice almost hoarse.

Marianne's face was burning red, her embarrassment clear to see, yet she obeyed. She turned her back to Stephen and pulled her skirt up at the front. She reached under and fiddled with her suspenders. Stephen stood up and walked round to the front of the desk, his eyes fixed on her long elegant thighs. She looked away from him but made no effort to cover herself. Her stockings were dark against her soft white skin, and when she rolled them down he felt the heat rising within him. It was like a dream, something he could hardly believe was happening. She slipped her shoes off and pulled the stockings off completely.

'Bend over the desk,' he said, putting a hand to her shoulder to stop her picking up her stockings.

She stepped back into her high heels and then went to the desk. She bent over at the waist, pressing herself flat against the smooth leather-topped desk, pressing her face against the cool surface, her hands up by her face.

Stephen stood behind her, enjoying the sight of her skirt pulled tight over her backside, pulling the buttocks apart slightly. Very gently he took the hem of her skirt and lifted it high, up and over her waist. Her long legs were smooth and straight, the knees locked tight so that every muscle and sinew was stretched taut. Her snow white panties were pulled tightly between her thighs, deep between her rounded bottom cheeks. The darkness between her thighs was unmistakable, the outline of her sex clearly visible.

5

'I'm going to smack you six times,' he said, his voice trembling. 'I don't want you to scream or cry. If you do I'll punish you for that as well. Is that clear?'

'Yes,' she said, her voice as nervous as his. 'Yes, sir,' she added, twisting round to look at him, her eyes sparkling with fear and excitement.

Stephen hesitated, eyeing her lovely long legs and beautiful rear. He reached over to the desk, to the photograph of happy laughing children and turned it over.

The first smack echoed in the room, a sharp sound of flesh on flesh. Marianne moaned softly, her hands pressed hard onto the desk, her eyes half closed. Stephen waited a second then smacked her again, a hard slap on the other buttock. He stopped to admire the imprint of his fingers, marked deep red on the soft white flesh of Marianne's backside.

'Does it hurt?' he asked softly.

'Yes, it stings horribly,' she replied quietly, her eyes still half closed. She was breathing hard, though Stephen couldn't tell how she was reacting. Her feelings were closed off from him, obscured by her silence and her half-closed eyes.

He spanked her again, two quick strokes in rapid succession. Each time she tensed and then exhaled slowly, the breath escaping from her glossy red lips like a sigh.

'Oh, it stings. It's like a fire spreading . . .' she whispered, as if talking to herself, telling herself what it was like.

Stephen's prick was hard, throbbing. Marianne's beautifully punished backside was the most erotic thing he had ever seen. He wanted to stop and touch her, to slip his fingers under her panties, to part her buttocks and stroke her there, to press a finger between the inviting lips of her sex.

Marianne moaned again. She was opening and closing her eyes slowly, breathing hard and deep, almost

6

gasping for breath. He saw that her panties were damp, and that the wet heat was spreading. The look on her face seemed to hover between pleasure and pain, her lips parted, half smiling, half scowling. He smacked her again, a hard stroke directly between her gorgeous arse cheeks.

'Oh Jesus . . .' she moaned, her body tensing momentarily, her eyes flaring open. Another hard smack in the same place and she cried out, an animal cry that could only be interpreted in one way. She had climaxed powerfully, the heat from her reddened backside spreading deep into her sex.

'Don't move,' Stephen ordered sharply, stepping away from her.

Marianne opened her eyes and twisted round to look at him but he had retreated to the back of the office. He poured himself a drink from the glass cabinet and then turned back to her. He could see that her skin was patterned red with his finger marks, that even the white panties couldn't obscure the evidence of punishment. But it hadn't been enough. She had found pleasure in the pain, joy in her punishment and finally release.

'Don't move, not until it's over,' he warned.

'Yes sir,' she responded, so softly that he hardly heard her. He downed his drink and then stripped off quickly. It wasn't what she was expecting, but then neither had he expected her to climax while he spanked her.

'What . . .'

'Quiet!' he snapped, banging the bottle of whisky down in front of her. 'You haven't been very honest with me,' he said grimly.

'I don't know what you . . .

'Quiet! Now I'm going to punish you properly.'

Marianne screamed when the heavy leather belt fell across her buttocks. She tried to move away but he held her in place and beat her again with the belt, striking hard at the top of her thighs. The office resounded to

7

the rhythm of the belt and Marianne's cries of pain and moans of pleasure.

'Oh please – please . . .' she whispered, sounding close to hysteria.

'Please what?' he asked coldly, his own nervous feelings swept away by the wave of excitement.

'Fuck me! Hit me with the belt and fuck me . . .'

Roughly, Stephen pulled her soaking panties down to her knees. Her sex was hot and wet; he felt her respond when he pressed his fingers into the sticky heat.

He raised the belt and brought it down swiftly between her arse cheeks and she climaxed again, arching her back and crying out deliriously. He picked the bottle up and poured the amber fluid over her smarting skin, watching it cascade down between her thighs, droplets glistening like jewels in the raw pinkness of her sex.

At last he took her by the waist and pressed his raging hardness into the velvety heat of her pussy. She was hot and receptive, raising her punished backside up to meet the hard thrusts of his cock. She rode with his rhythm, moving with his body, eyes closed and a look of ecstasy etched on her face. She was beautiful, sexy, the most fantastic lover he'd ever had. He fell over her, covering her body with his own, pumping hard, crying out with her, then sharing an explosive climax as one.

Marianne was waiting when he emerged from the office. She was trying hard to look cool and composed, but her eyes were glowing and she still looked a little dazed. He knew that her bottom must still be smarting; it would be marked for days, an eloquent reminder of her punishment.

'Thank you,' she said quietly, counting the money at the same time.

'Will we ever do this again?' Stephen asked hopefully.

She shook her head. 'I think not,' she smiled.

Stephen nodded sadly. That was how it was, he had

known all along that it would never happen again, but in the shared excitement he had hoped that Marianne would change her mind. He took the money from her and stuffed it into his pocket. They shook hands and then she disappeared back into the office. Stephen waited a second in the Saturday morning silence, hoping that she would relent. He looked at the door for a moment, at the name plate that said: MARIANNE HUGHES, MANAGING DIRECTOR. He wished it would open but there was no point. He shrugged, then turned and left.

Aptitude

Peter checked himself in the mirror at the top of the stairs, slicked a hand through his hair and then walked down as casually as possible. It was going to be a big day, a big couple of days in fact, but he knew that it mustn't show.

The receptionist who had checked him into the hotel was still at the front desk. 'The Churchill Lounge?' he asked her.

'Yes sir, the second down along the corridor, you can't miss it.'

He thanked her and moved on. If things worked out well, and he knew they would, then he could kiss his old life goodbye. A lot was at stake; a strategic career move, a near doubling of salary, and excellent future prospects.

The Churchill Lounge was less impressive than its name suggested. He looked around, at the armchairs and coffee tables, at the morning's newspapers spread out on a table in the centre of the room. But no waiting personnel manager. The only other person in the room was an attractive blonde sitting in the corner, reading a magazine, her long legs crossed, showing a length of stockinged thigh.

Peter glanced at his schedule again. *Informal meeting with Mr C. Nash, Senior Personnel Officer, 8.30.* The clock on the wall made it 8.25. He crossed the room and picked up a newspaper. He turned to look at the clock again and saw the woman looking at him. She turned away, returning to her magazine, but for an instant their eyes had met. Her red lipstick matched her shoes and contrasted with her short black skirt and stockings. He waited and she looked up again. This time she held his gaze for just a second longer and then turned away again, a smile flickering on her glossy lips.

'Excuse me,' Peter said, walking over to her. 'Have you got a light?'

She looked up, as if surprised by his approach. 'No, sorry,' she said, and her voice was soft and husky, almost breathless.

'That's OK,' Peter said, 'I don't have a cigarette.'

It was a corny line but she smiled. He sat in the seat next to her, absently glancing at his watch. 'Are you a guest here?'

'Yes, I've been here a couple of days now. And you?'

'Just got here,' he said. 'Alone?'

She paused and smiled. 'Not exactly,' she admitted, leaning closer to him, her skirt rising up a fraction so that he could see more of her shapely thighs. 'I'm here with my boyfriend, but he's disappeared. Again.'

He smiled, noting the exasperation in her voice. 'Peter May,' he said, putting his hand out.

'I'm Chrissy,' she said, letting him squeeze her fingers for a second.

'Look, maybe we'll bump into each other later. For a drink perhaps?'

She smiled again, showing brilliant white teeth and widening her grey-green eyes. There was something about her smile, something very very sexy. 'Perhaps,' she agreed. 'Look, I'd better be going, my boyfriend'll be wondering what's happened to me.'

Peter got up when she did. The boyfriend? He couldn't amount to much, neglecting her like that, especially in a hotel full of men. Together they walked out of the lounge and towards the front desk.

He stopped and watched her go up the stairs. As she

got higher he could see that her skirt was slit at the back, revealing the black band of her stockings and then a glimpse of white thigh. He could imagine the feel of her smooth skin under him, of his lips between her soft white thighs. The thought made his prick harden.

'Yes sir, can I help you?' the receptionist asked, appearing from the back office.

'Yes, I was supposed to see a Mr Nash in the Churchill Lounge at eight thirty, but he hasn't turned up. Could you check things out for me?'

'It's Mr May isn't it? I think there was a telephone message just now,' she said, picking out a handwritten message. 'The message is from Mr Nash. He apologises for not being able to make it, but wishes you every success in the selection process.'

He felt both relieved and disappointed, and also regret that he hadn't spent more time with Chrissy. He was going to see her again, there was no way that he was going to let a woman that beautiful and that classy get away.

With sessions called CORPORATE CULTURE, APTITUDE, LEADERSHIP and A TEAM PLAYER, the selection process betrayed its American origins. Peter's first instinct was to laugh it off as so much grand verbiage but he latched on to the significance very early on.

The first session was on corporate culture. It began as a rather flash introduction to the history of the firm, from its founding in New York to its global expansion. All presented with an array of snazzily captioned slides and charts. Peter was unimpressed and he felt bored by it all. His thoughts kept wandering to Chrissy, to her glossy lips and long elegant thighs. Her voice had been low and breathless, every word was a sigh, spoken as if his prick was sliding deep and hard into the warmth of her pussy.

Peter caught sight of someone from the firm sitting in

12

the back row. A young guy who kept looking up and making notes, eyeing each of the applicants in turn. They were being watched and their responses noted. The other applicants looked as bored as he did, eyeing the clock or gazing out of the window. He started taking notes straight away, scribbling things down in a pad, trying to look as interested as he possibly could.

The lights came up and then the questions began. No one had expected that, and he watched the others stumble through their answers. When it was his turn he had the answers down on paper, he spoke confidently, quoting verbatim and then adding his own comments to the answers.

At lunch the other applicants conspicuously gave him the cold shoulder. He sat down alone to eat, scanning the restaurant for Chrissy, but there was no sign of her. Someone else noticed that he was alone; the man who'd been asking the questions joined him. They talked business and Peter knew that he had done well, much to the annoyance of the other applicants.

The afternoon session was different from the first. They had to play games and pretend to be different characters. All very American and very strange, but treated with the utmost seriousness by the team of assessors. It was a breeze. Peter felt that he could do no wrong. It was a game and he was good at games, always had been.

The evening meal passed off in stony silence. He ate quickly and left, going straight to the bar, hoping that Chrissy would be there. She wasn't and he felt disappointed.

He went to his room and watched TV for a while before deciding to get some sleep. He felt good; he'd made a mark straight away and he knew just how important first impressions could be. The knock at the door was so quiet that at first he thought it was imagination.

'Oh, sorry ... wrong room,' Chrissy said, backing away when he opened the door.

'Hi, I was hoping to see you again. Didn't think my luck would be this good though,' he laughed, opening the door fully.

'I was looking for Mark, my friend. He met up with some other people down in the bar and said they were going to play cards. I thought this was the room number ...'

'No, no cards here. You don't look very happy about all this, do you want to go down for a drink?'

She hesitated, her eyes nervous and tearful. 'No, I don't want a drink.'

'A chat, come on, you could do with someone to talk to,' he said, taking her by the sleeve and pulling her gently into the room.

She bit her lip anxiously. 'Mark will go spare if he finds out about this.'

'Well, he won't find out, will he?' Peter said, leading her over to the bed. 'Don't worry, we can just chat if you want. Tell me about Mark if you like.'

'No, why talk about him?' she said bitterly. 'Ever since we got here I've hardly seen ten minutes of him. First it was a drink with some friends, and after he sobered up he went and found himself a poker game.'

'He needs his head examined,' Peter said softly. He moved closer to her, breathing her subtle fragrance. 'That's no way to treat a woman, no way at all.' He put his hand on her knee, resting it there a second, feeling the warmth of her skin under her stockings. She didn't resist. When he looked into her eyes she was on the verge of tears. He moved towards her and she parted her lips instinctively.

'Please, don't do this,' she said softly, pulling her lips from his. But her eyes told a different story, the tears were gone, and in their place was a look of desire; a look of desperation and longing.

14

He kissed her again, and she responded, throwing her arms around him and her head back so that he kissed her under the neck. He moved a hand up the knee and over her thigh, sliding easily under her skirt. His fingers passed from the silkiness of lycra to the smoothness of her skin.

'Please no,' she said, stopping his hand going further.

'But you want this,' Peter said breathlessly. 'We both do.' He took her hand and placed it between his thighs, letting her feel his raging prick. She stroked him lovingly, her fingertips moving up and down.

'Yes, I want to,' she admitted sadly. 'But it's my time of the month . . .'

'I see,' Peter said. That explained it – why her boyfriend was being so neglectful. The game of cards sounded less likely now, and he was amazed that Chrissy had fallen for it. He suddenly felt sorry for her and he pulled her close and kissed her again.

Chrissy carried on playing with his prick, running her fingers up and down. She slipped out of his arms and knelt down between his thighs. She looked up at him and smiled, carefully pulling down the zip to his trousers. He stood and in a second he was naked, his long prick standing stiffly before her. The feel of her fingers made him sigh; he closed his eyes to the exquisite sensation. Her lips were on his prick, kissing him softly on the very tip.

'I love this,' she whispered taking his prick deep into her mouth. She sucked and licked, her tongue toying with him, making him shudder and moan with pleasure. He began to buck and writhe, forcing his hardness deeper into her mouth, her head moving with the same urgent rhythm.

She moved her hair back and smiled over his prick, letting him watch her lovingly caress it with her lips and tongue. His prick was smeared with lipstick and the beads of fluid that poured from his glans. He moved

15

more urgently, faster and faster. Her fingers cradled his balls and carefully she inched a finger between his buttocks.

Her finger entered him from behind and then he cried out. She moved back a little and thick cream spurted out onto her lips and face and into her hair.

'That was really . . . really . . .' Peter said eventually, struggling to find the right words. He was lying on his back, lazily stroking her thigh.

'You don't have to say anything,' Chrissy said huskily, brushing her hair back over her shoulders.

'I'm just sorry I can't do anything for you in return,' he said dreamily. She had showered afterwards while he had dozed, but now he felt desire flare up again.

'There is something,' she said, and she sounded nervous. 'Promise you won't think badly of me.'

'Of course I promise.'

She reached out and switched off the bedside lamp, plunging the room into darkness. She lay down beside him, flat on her stomach and then took his hand and slid it very slowly up her thigh and then pressed his finger between her buttocks.

'Don't touch me any lower, please,' she said softly. 'Let me feel your lovely cock over my backside, rub it between by bottom cheeks, let me feel it on my skin, please.'

It was a strange request, uttered in a strange tone of voice, but Peter kissed her on the neck, running his hands down over her lovely round arse cheeks. He felt her reach for her bag and she explained that she had some hand cream, which she smeared between her buttocks.

He moved over her, taking her waist, his thighs stretched over her back. Her fingers were slippery with hand cream and he gasped when she smoothed it over his prick. She guided him towards her, holding his prick

16

lovingly until it was pressed tight between the perfect flesh of her arse-cheeks.

'This feels so good,' he whispered, surprised at how pleasurable the sensation was. She was tensing and re-laxing her body, clutching at his hardness with the softness of her backside. He was pumping hard, rubbing himself between her globes, feeling her bottom pressing sexily against his abdomen.

'It feels huge, lovely . . .' she said dreamily. She sighed and pressed herself up, arching her back. He held her tightly and moved faster, his thighs pressed tightly over hers, his prick rubbing smoothly over her skin.

She writhed madly, her cries becoming more urgent, her voice was deeper, whispering wordlessly while he fucked her as hard as he could. She climaxed, her body freezing and then shuddering, a last strangled cry escap-ing from her beautiful lips. He climaxed a moment later, letting his spunk jet out over her behind.

He rolled off her and she lay still for a moment. 'That was lovely,' she murmured and then sat up to wipe away his semen. In the darkness he could make out the out-line of her body as she fixed her skirt.

'Will I see you again?' Peter asked, still a little dazed by the experience, more erotic and blissful than he had ever imagined.

'I hope so,' she said. They kissed gently on the lips and then she was gone.

The second day of the selection process was much like the first. The highlight was a test of creativity that went like a dream. They were each given a tray of lego and told to build a bridge that would take the weight of a man.

For a while Peter watched the others building compli-cated and intricate structures. He was thinking about Chrissy when the idea came to him. He turned the bricks over and built a long flat structure, very simple but with lots of supports along the surface. It looked too simple and the others smirked at his design. When they were finished the structures had to be tested, an assessor stood on each in turn. Only Peter's avoided instant collapse.

After it was over he tried to find out about Chrissy at the front desk, but no one claimed to know anything about her. No one had seen her, and there was no Mark or Chrissy in the register. He shrugged it off, people did all sorts of things at a hotel. It was a shame really but that was that.

Days later the letter arrived. He felt a rush of adrenaline as he ripped open the embossed envelope, eager to read of his success. The disappointment was a hammer blow. How could it be? Everything had gone his way, he had scored the highest in everything.

He called the firm immediately. He was livid, the job was his, something had gone wrong. A mistake, that's what it was. The people he spoke to were apologetic, understanding, but they stood by the decision. Eventually he was put through to Mr Nash.

'I'm sorry Mr May but you failed the most important test of all,' Nash said after a considered delay.

'Which test?'

'Observation.'

'There was no observation test. I've got the schedule here, there was no such thing.'

'But there was Mr May,' again a painful silence. 'It was so important that it wasn't even marked on the schedule. I'm sorry but you failed it.'

'How? Tell me that at least.'

There was another pause, and then a sigh. 'You were very nice, Peter,' Nash said, and this time his voice was different. 'Chrissy liked you a lot, but you didn't notice . . .'

Peter let the phone fall from his grasp, Chrissy's voice still in his ears.

Pact

I used to think the devil would be cloven hooves, horns
and halitosis. And then, after Fay Weldon, I thought
he'd be suave, sophisticated and totally convincing.
What I never expected was the librarian in front of me,
thin, balding, weedy, his watery eyes blinking at me
through round schoolboy spectacles.

'Let me get this right,' I said, unable to stop myself
smiling. 'This is the actual "sell my soul to the devil"
contract we're talking about.'

He nodded. So I had the choice of anything I wanted:
wealth, fame, power, anything and everything all available in return for a small consideration on my part.
Wealth, fame, power – my needs were more basic than
any of these.

My smile grew broader. 'Anything?' I repeated, for
perhaps the twentieth time.

'Anything,' he agreed.

'There is one thing.'

'Yes,' he said, though I couldn't tell whether his tone
indicated exasperation or expectation.

'It might seem a bit unusual,' I said, hesitating. I
mean the devil knows all about sin, but the librarian in
front of me looked totally innocent and naive.

'Might it?' he asked, though I guessed then that nothing
would sound unusual to this squinting emissary from hell.

'It's a fantasy I have,' I started, trying not to sound
too embarrassed. 'It involves two sisters . . .'

'Twins?' he interrupted, flicking open his notebook, as

if he were going to jot down the title of a Barbara Cartland novel that an old age pensioner was asking for.

'No, not twins,' I said. I'd tried that, and it had failed miserably, the twins seemed more interested in each other than in me. 'Just plain sisters would do fine.'

'Plain sisters,' he said, writing it down.

'No, not plain sisters. No, I don't want them to be plain. They've got to be stunning, absolutely beautiful, long dark hair, pert fine breasts, long elegant thighs. Absolute stunners.'

He exhaled forcefully and looked at me over his round specs as if I was being an awkward customer. He scrubbed out what he'd written and scribbled something else. 'Anything else?' he asked.

I wanted to say the latest Jeffrey Archer, but held back. I don't think he would have seen the joke, and there was no way I was going to sign my soul away for a Jeffrey Archer. 'Yes, just one thing. They've got to be in uniform, French maids' uniform, both of them.'

'Satin, rubber or leather?' he asked without batting an eyelid. I realised just how mundane this was to him. My ideal fantasy scenario meant nothing to him, a man, no a devil, who, by the look of him, probably got his kicks sniffing out old library books.

'Satin. Black satin,' I mumbled. 'Oh, and add some champagne, and plenty of ice.'

He scribbled that down too and then looked up, ready to end our little meeting. I wanted to laugh at that point, because if it was a joke then the punch line had passed, his whole ridiculous manner was as far from devilish as you could possibly get.

'What about the get out clause?' I asked.

'Get out clause?' he repeated in bewilderment, as if I'd refused to pay the fine on a stack of overdue library books I'd returned.

'Yes, you know, the chance I get to cheat the devil.'

'I see,' he repeated, sitting back down and flicking

open the notebook. 'And what exactly did you have in mind?'

I suppressed the smile. 'How about . . . how about . . . how about the deal's off if I can spend the whole night with these women and not come?'

'Not come where?'

I couldn't help myself this time, I laughed till it hurt, and the more I looked at the incomprehension and confusion in the chinless face, the more I laughed. 'What I meant is that I don't orgasm,' I finally explained, catching my breath. 'No ejaculation.'

He nodded, tapped the pencil between his yellow teeth. 'OK, if you can spend the night with these two women, engaged in frenzied sexual activity, and you do not ejaculate by dawn then the devil will have no claim on your soul. Is that acceptable?'

I wiped the tears from my eyes, trying hard to hide the triumph I felt. 'Yes, that's acceptable. Where do I sign?'

He opened his battered brown briefcase and pulled out the contract, neatly printed out on computer paper. I was disappointed, I'd expected something more dramatic: a faded parchment, the contract in a thick gothic script in red ink. I gulped, some of my self-assurance ebbing away when I read the contract, precise in every detail, including the black satin and the champagne. How could he have known in advance?

'Please sign at the bottom,' he urged, glancing at his watch.

'Don't I have to do this in blood or something?' I said, trying to joke away my sudden nervousness.

'Oh please, this is the twentieth century,' he said, smiling for the first time.

I signed in plain old blue ink, my hand shaking just a little. He took the contract and stuffed it in his case before I had a chance to change my mind. He stood up and shook my hand, his palm cold and flabby, not at all how a devil's hand should feel.

'When will it happen?' I asked, opening the front door for him.

'My secretary will be in touch,' he said, sounding more like an insurance salesman than the timid librarian he so much resembled.

After he went I poured myself a stiff drink, and then another. I had done it, I had stitched a deal with the devil which I just couldn't lose. What he didn't know was that I had the best prick control of any man alive.

I was the envy of my mates, and more than just a little popular with the ladies. I could make love for hours without losing control, without losing strength, without losing interest. And the best part of it was that I climaxed time and time again without losing that precious fluid that marked a halt to the entertainment. I would enjoy moments of intense physical and mental pleasure, moments of heightened awareness when my body felt as if it was floating, every pore screaming with blissful pleasure – but no spurting of bodily fluids.

I had no idea where my particular talent came from, I just thanked my lucky stars that I had it. It meant that no woman would go unsatisfied with me, and for those lucky women who were multiply orgasmic I could match them climax for climax, until our bodies screamed for us to stop. It was a rare and beautiful talent, and I made sure that it was enjoyed to the hilt, at every possible occasion, and with every possible permutation of bodies. And always, at the end of a night's frantic sexual gymnastics, at the height of our pleasure, I would allow myself to come, showering my partner, or partners, with a wet creamy reward.

The devil had no idea of this. I was going to make my dream come true, two lovely sisters in uniform, for hours on end, and while I would ache with pleasure I wasn't going to spurt away until the sun was high in the sky. I knew I couldn't lose.

* * *

I had to hand it to the devil, he'd done a brilliant job. There was a knock at the hotel bedroom door and then they entered, two lovely goddesses in shiny black satin. They stood there, back to back, eyeing me intently, their dark oval eyes running over me greedily. Two beautiful West Indian goddesses, smooth dark skin, long black hair falling over bare shoulders, sensuously glistening red lips, naturally parted over pearl white teeth. Legs long enough to give me vertigo, balancing on six-inch black high heels, and clad in black seamed stockings, the suspenders peeping from under the frilly white skirts of the maids' uniforms.

I wanted to climax there and then. He'd done a good job; I swear any other man would have creamed just watching them there, back to back, sensuously rubbing their shoulders against each other. One of them passed the tip of her tongue over her lips and I felt my heart doing somersaults. He wanted my soul bad and he meant to get it. These sisters meant serious business. It was going to be a contest, but I knew that I was up to it, and when I threw the covers aside so did they.

They moved on air, gliding across the room with a feline sexiness that had me gasping for breath. They were beside me, their breasts straining against the constricting tightness of the uniform. The soft rustle of silk and satin was accompanied by the breathless sound of the air escaping from their lips. They were all over me, their mouths devouring me, their thick sensuous lips passing butterfly kisses up and down my body. One of them took my prick in her mouth and flicked her long tongue all around it, making me dizzy with sensation. It felt so incredibly good, I felt strung out, every inch of me alive with surges of passionate energy. Nothing had ever felt this good before.

I breathed hard and knew that I was going to have to call on my secret weapon. I had to do it, the end had never been so close before. I shut my eyes tightly, but the feel of two delicious mouths on my prick made me open them again. Could any man take this for one whole night? I shut my eyes again and brought the secret weapon into play: 0.301, 0.477, 0.602, 0.699 ... I recited the logarithms in my head until the danger point had past. I opened my eyes and saw the sisters looking at me strangely, their dark mysterious eyes edged with confusion. No man had ever resisted the twin play of their mouths on his prick, no man had been able to take the supreme pleasure without shooting into that inviting warmth.

They moved round. One of them straddled me, and I moaned as I pushed my prick into the red heat of her sex. She moved down, forcing her gorgeous round backside onto my belly. Her sister kissed me on the mouth, sucking away my resolve before straddling my face also. I looked into the moist pinkness of her pussy, knowing that it was something to die for. I kissed her, slowly, reverently, worshipping her sex as it had never been worshipped before. They moved together, up and down, round and round, screwing me so that they could attain maximum pleasure, knowing that I would be unable to resist it for long. Waves of pleasure pulsed through, blinding white pleasure that was orgasm in every way but one.

They climaxed together, again and again, forcefully riding my hard prick and aching tongue. At the peak, when I teetered on the edge the numbers came back to me: 0.778, 0.845, the logarithms to the base 10 as God and John Napier had intended.

The sisters, and they were close enough to be twins without being boring, looked askance, utterly perplexed by the way I carried on. All three of us were bathed in sweat, our bodies glowing from the blissful ecstasy. I had lost track of time, but I knew that I had gone farther than they had ever imagined. I was still hard, my prick wet with their honey juices which I licked from my fingers.

They hadn't spoken a word. The only sounds that had emerged from those quivering red lips were the echoes of pleasure, the sighs and moans of orgasm that they couldn't suppress. But they could communicate without words; perhaps they could read each other's minds, or they had planned it all beforehand. They retreated to the edge of the bed and began to undress each other, pulling each other out of the thrilling tightness of the French maids' outfits. They kissed and sucked, exploring each other, making sweet sensual love all the time. Those lovely round breasts, smooth as chocolate, were tipped with deep red cherries that were sucked and played with.

I watched intently. They were a tangle of legs and arms, breasts and buttocks. One was sucking the other's back hole, pressing her pink tongue into it, while the other reciprocated by drinking the sweet nectar from her sister's pussy. I'd seen women making love before, but never this intently or this beautifully. I closed my eyes and felt the flash of passion but I held back, the numbers only just managing to postpone the flood that was building so surely in my balls.

They looked exhausted, their bodies weak with exertion, glistening with sweat, their hair bedraggled. They paused, their eyes fixed on my bulging hardness that had yet to fountain its load. I hadn't seen them bring any props, but suddenly one of them held a wicked looking riding crop and she approached me with an angry look in her eye.

In an instant I was on my hands and knees submitting to this dark beauty, kissing her incredibly high heels while her sister pinned my back with her heels. I've always liked a bit of SM, and I couldn't help but wonder how in the devil they knew. I shrieked when the first stroke came down on my bare backside. The sharp pain was soon burning through me, a white heat that made me cry out with a sudden orgasmic sensation. Each stroke, hard and sharp, was licking at my balls, trying to force out that thick white come that would spell my doom.

The numbers in my head were no longer ordered, the sequence had gone, replaced with a mixture of fear and ecstasy. My eyes were rolling in my head as I submitted on my hands and knees to this strict goddess. I sucked at her heels while she beat out her anger and confusion on me. My prick was wet with glistening fluid, but somehow, miraculously, I kept it back.

The beating stopped and the two sisters, those terrible demons of pleasure and pain were standing over me. I had survived; my body was latticed with vivid red stripes, my mouth filled with the taste of patent leather, but the delirious and blissful feelings had not produced that shower of come.

I looked up, out of the hotel window, hardly able to believe my eyes. My gamble had been won, the distant horizon was tinged with brilliant white light. The darkness of the night was retreating, the day was breaking and with it my victory over Beelzebub. The sisters looked at one another and then at me with something like panic in their eyes. I half expected them to wrench my prick off with frustration.

Instead one of them put her heel on my shoulder, pinning me neatly into place. I looked up at her lovely pussy, ringed with jet black curls of hair, speckled with drops of white cream, her pink bud nestling between her kissable, suckable pussy-lips. I gasped suddenly, as the light broke on the horizon. Unexpectedly a golden trickle of water poured from her sex, raining down on me, washing me away. It trickled down my shoulder and over my chest, warm rivulets passing over me, washing away all my resolve, all my power. I climaxed, jetting thick white come all over the floor. I looked down at the puddle between my thighs, thick drops of come floating in the yellow sea. It was something I had never expected to see, something I had never planned on.

That's when it ended. The deal was for my soul, not my body. I had sort of imagined, if the worse came to the worse, that there would be some decent delay between giving up my body for my soul. Forty or fifty years at least. What I hadn't counted on was keeling over with a massive coronary. I watched my body lying in the sea of piss and come, covered in red stripes and the lovely thick cream from the sisters' hot pussies. It hadn't been a bad way to go, but it wasn't much consolation.

I used to think hell was all fire and brimstone. And then, after Jean-Paul Sartre, I used to think it was other people. But old Jean-Paul was wrong. As I sank down, down into hell, the only thing on my mind was a simple sequence of numbers: 0.301, 0.477, 0.602, 0.699 . . . repeating over and over again. Hell, I realised, is numbers.

The Mission

Alexandra waited by the window, lifting a corner of the heavy velvet curtain to peer suspiciously out into the darkness. The gaslight flickering in the street caught the flakes of snow falling from the black sky; orange particles were slicing through the night.

The grandfather clock in the study chimed softly, the twelfth hour marking the end of one day and the beginning of another. One day closer to the glorious revolution, Alexandra thought hopefully; one day closer to the end of Tsarist rule, one day closer to the dawn of the new age. It was a day that she looked forward to with a wild optimism, certain that all the evils of corruption and decay would be swept away as the people rose against their masters.

'Comrade Alexandra Panovsky?'

Alexandra turned, startled to find that she was no longer alone; that lost in her daydream someone else had entered the small study. He was a small figure, thin, short, unhealthy looking. She stepped closer to him and saw a pale face, a thick moustache, sunken cheeks. It was only the eyes that made him stand out – intense eyes, burning with a fervour that matched her own. 'Yes comrade,' she whispered, 'I am Alexandra Panovsky.'

'I have instructions for you, comrade,' he said, walking slowly towards her, holding his heavy black cap in his hands.

'You are cold, comrade?' Alexandra asked, suddenly afraid that this poor man before her was going to collapse. His voice gave him away; he was a working man, slaving all the hours of the day in a hellish factory, and then staying up all night to agitate among his fellow workers. Alexandra was filled with pity and yet her heart was glad that she and he were on the same side, part of the same struggle against autocracy.

'Thank you comrade Panovsky, but I must be brief. No one saw me come here but if the eyes of the *Okhrana* are upon you then they may catch me leaving.'

The *Okhrana*, the Tsar's dreaded secret police, scourge of the revolution. The very name made Alexandra justifiably nervous. 'Yes comrade, proceed,' she said, hoping that his fear was unjustified. Already two members of her revolutionary cell had been arrested and sent into internal exile, banished like common criminals to the depths of Siberia.

'What are your opinions on the female question, comrade?' he asked, as if he were still slightly in awe of her, aware that she was a fine young lady while he was just a poor worker, despite their common struggle.

'The struggle for the emancipation of women is one with the struggle for democracy,' Alexandra ventured tentatively.

'And the question of sexual relations?'

Alexandra blushed. 'Comrade,' she said quietly, 'may I ask why I am being questioned?'

'Because it has a bearing on your mission,' the man replied, evidently relaxing somewhat. 'We must be sure that your commitment is absolute.'

'My views on the question of sexual relations are already known. I subscribe to the theory of "free love", comrade. After the revolution male and female will be able to enter into sexual relations freely, without the false bourgeois morality that so enslaves the woman of today.'

'Excellent, comrade,' the man smiled. 'And in the cause of the revolution, you are willing to use any tactic?'

'Any tactic that does not run counter to revolutionary morality,' Alexandra replied, wanting to impress with the depth of her determination.

'Then we wish you to seduce an agent of the Tsar,' he told her bluntly.

Alexandra swallowed hard. It was not the mission she had expected. In the past she had smuggled weapons into prison to help free imprisoned comrades; she had helped to print counterfeit money to finance the formation of trade union groups. She had even hidden the proceeds of a bank robbery, but all that was nothing as to this. She sat down heavily in the nearest chair, her mind reeling from the sudden shock.

'It is vital that this is done, comrade Panovsky, we have no other choice,' the man told her quietly, sitting beside her. He touched her hand with his. Rough callused hands – hands that reminded her of the misery of the people, that reminded her of the system she had sworn to abolish.

'What is your name, comrade?' she asked, looking into his sad eyes, which blazed with an impossible intensity, as if his soul knew that he was not long for the world.

'I am Vano Isanovich. Will you accept the mission, comrade?'

'Yes, I must. The idea of it revolts me, but if it needs to be done then I will do it.'

'Good. You have heard of Colonel Zaspykin?'

'The torturer? Yes, I have heard of him.'

'We have information that he has decadent sexual tastes and that he seeks a mistress to satisfy these desires.'

Alexandra looked up sharply. 'What sort of urges?'

'You have heard of a book called *The Venus In Furs*? I have been given to understand that his perverse tastes are described in that book. It means nothing to me, comrade, but do you know it?'

'I have read the book, Vano,' Alexandra said softly. 'A product of the purest decadence, an offence against all that is dear to my heart. How will you ensure that I meet this vile creature?'

'Do you know old Natasha's place?' Vano asked, his face colouring with embarrassment. He turned away from Alexandra, unable to look her in the eye.

'The brothel? I am to meet him there?' Alexandra said bravely, trying hard not to let her feelings get in the way of her task. She had a mission and that was more important than anything else. More important even then her own fear.

'It is old Natasha herself who has informed us of Zaspykin's ways. We want you to do what is necessary to procure from him one vital piece of information.'

'And what is that, comrade?'

'The name of the *agent provocateur* who has infiltrated our group. We know that there is one among us who is in the pay of the *Okhrana*. We must find out before we all face Zaspykin in a prison cell. Be at Natasha's place on Friday, after eight o'clock.'

'I will do my best Vano,' Alexandra promised, managing a smile to hide her heavy heart.

'Good luck,' Vano said, kissing her fingers before getting up to leave, as quietly as he had come.

Alexandra had kissed mama on the cheek before going up to bed, feigning weariness to explain why she was retiring to bed so early. She had then slipped on a heavy coat, a fur hat and silk scarf and slipped out of the house into the thick snowy night. A carriage awaited her, the coachman hidden in shadow, and there, waiting inside the cab, was Vano.

'Are you afraid, comrade?' he asked, daring to look into her eyes properly for the first time.

'Yes Vano, I am afraid. But joyful too, certain that I'll be able to unmask the traitor in our ranks.'

'It is not my plan,' Vano explained softly. 'I wanted to capture the beast, to do to him what he has done to so many of our comrades. But I was told that it would not work. Why is that so, Alexandra?'

'Because he is a man that enjoys pain for its own sake,' she explained. 'The whip is his reward not his punishment.'

'But you . . . you are so pure . . .' Vano whispered, and Alexandra realised that he felt as disgusted by the plan as she did.

They fell silent, Alexandra pondering Vano's words. Was she so pure? Her life was the revolution, there was nothing else, everything else was a distraction. Yet sometimes she longed to forget, to just let a man take her in his arms.

'Remember, be careful, he is a very dangerous man,' Vano warned tenderly as the carriage rattled to a halt. 'You mustn't stop once you have the name of the informer. You must carry on till the natural conclusion of the rendezvous. On no account should Zaspykin's suspicions become aroused.'

'I understand, comrade,' Alexandra whispered, and then she leaned forward and touched her lips to Vano's, kissing him softly for a second before stepping down from the carriage into the thick snow. The carriage moved away, the horse's hooves muffled by the thick blanket of snow.

'Wanda? Is that you?' a voice from the shadows asked.

'Yes, it is I,' Alexandra said, accepting the name that she had been assigned. It was a good choice for a code name, it matched that of the cruel mistress from *The Venus In Furs*, the strange book that Zaspykin was obsessed with.

'Quick,' the voice whispered, 'follow me.'

Alexandra trudged through the snow, following the dark figure through the frozen alleys of the poor district.

She was concentrating hard on her mission and trying to put Vano out of her mind; trying to put away the image of his childlike face obscured by long black hair and the thick black moustache.

Natasha's was above an inn and, as Alexandra climbed the icy wooden steps, the sound of laughter and singing wafted out into the night. Drunken songs sung by men out of their minds from hard work and too much vodka. The dark figure pushed open the door and Alexandra stumbled into the warmth.

The dark figured unwrapped a thick fur coat and revealed herself to be a young girl, still in her teens, with the dark skin and oval eyes of a Georgian.

'Zaspykin is not here yet,' she whispered, her Russian heavily accented. 'Wait here and I will fetch Natasha.'

Alexandra waited, standing near the door, a little afraid to venture further into the house of sin. She was a revolutionary for certain, but in many ways she had the same moral outlook as her parents, much as she liked to deny it.

'Wanda my dear, follow me,' a woman cried, emerging from inside the house and taking Alexandra by the hand. She was past her prime, her tired face heavily rouged, her ample figure forced into corsets, but her eyes were still alive, and her voice too.

'Natasha?' Alexandra guessed.

'Yes dear, old Natasha, and if you do badly tonight it could be old dead Natasha,' she laughed. 'Be good, do as the lecher wants and I'm sure you'll get what you want too. And remember child, you are Wanda, his goddess, his mistress. Understand?'

'Yes. I'm not a child,' Alexandra complained, following Natasha into a bed chamber.

'Not a child?' Natasha laughed. 'Have you ever had a man? Have you ever had a hard prick between your elegant thighs?'

Alexandra coloured, her face flared scarlet with

shame. It was true, she had never made love with a man, never experienced the joys of the sexuality she ardently preached. The revolution had no place for personal pleasure, no place for diversions.

'Your costume is there.' Natasha pointed a painted finger at a neat bundle of clothes on the chair by the bed. 'Change quickly, he will be here soon.'

Alexandra waited until she was alone before looking at the clothes. It hadn't occurred to her that Zaspykin would require his mistress to dress up. She had assumed that she would be allowed to remain in her own clothes and for that reason she had selected long skirts with full petticoats. The clothes that Natasha had selected were very different: silk knickers, a black basque that was tightly ribbed, silk stockings and black ankle boots. Alexandra kept an eye to the door while undressing, afraid that Zaspykin would catch her in some immodest pose.

The silk stockings felt cool and soft against the thigh, delightfully sensual in a way that Alexandra had never imagined possible. The basque was tight-fitting, constricting, lifting her bosom so that it swelled voluptuously as she breathed. The ankle boots had high heels that seemed to dig into the unpolished wooden floor.

She stood before the mirror, looking at herself strangely, seeing herself as she had never seen herself before. Her body seemed to be different, moulded by the costume so that her femininity was emphasised, her breasts, thighs, bottom all drew the eye. She felt a swirl of emotions, anger and disgust that she should be forced to degrade herself before a servant of the old regime, yet also a sensual feeling, a delight that she should be so unexpectedly beautiful. She felt alive. Her body was tingling with excitement, her rosy nipples were hard and erect, and there was an exquisite heat rising from between her thighs.

'Wanda?'

'Colonel Zaspykin I presume,' Alexandra said calmly, turning to face the man who had entered without knocking. She fought the urge to cover herself, the instinct of modesty less strong then her dedication to the cause.

'It is true then,' Zaspykin said, stepping out of the shadow and into the light. 'The old hag Natasha did not deceive me, you really are a creature worth seeing.' He was dressed in a full grey military great coat. His face was hard and pointed with a sharp nose to match eyes that were cruel and clear, and thin lips that could smile brutally yet smother a woman with kisses.

Alexandra paused for a moment, studying him; was this soldier, this man capable of the utmost cruelty, really interested in her?

'Is that any way to address a lady, Zaspykin?' she sneered coldly, narrowing her eyes to glare at him disdainfully.

The effect was instant. Zaspykin threw off his heavy coat and fell to his knees before her. 'I am sorry mistress,' he begged, 'I have been unworthy. I am your servant, your slave, to be trampled underfoot.'

'Kiss my heels,' Alexandra ordered, swallowing hard. So it was all true, Zaspykin did desire to be dominated by an imperious and wicked mistress.

He obeyed at once, smothering her heels with lavish kisses, grovelling unashamedly at her heel. 'Enough of that, slave!'

'But I have been unworthy, mistress, I deserve only the cruellest of punishment. You must beat me, mistress, it is only what I deserve.'

'Silence you insignificant wretch!' Alexandra snapped. 'You bore me, vile insect. On the dresser, by the mirror, I have my dog whip. Undress and bring it here, with your teeth.'

Zaspykin's eyes were shining. He looked to be in ecstasy, his breath was coming hard and fast. He undressed quickly, throwing his uniform to the ground in a frenzy. In a moment he was naked. Alexandra watched him, unable to turn away from his handsome body. He was muscular, with thick biceps and a wide chest matted with dark hair. His thighs were heavy, muscled and from the dark ring of hair between them his erect penis stood proudly. He knelt on all fours and crawled across the room to retrieve the whip, taking it in his teeth and bringing it faithfully to her.

'What an obedient little dog you are,' Alexandra said. Her own words and those of the fantasy corresponding for the first time.

'I am your slave, mistress, to do with as you desire.'

'Is it true, Zaspykin, that you are the cruellest torturer in the Tsar's service?'

'It is true, mistress,' he admitted proudly, a smile crossing his lips. 'I serve my master completely, I am nothing if not his servant. I will punish without mercy all those that seek him harm.'

'And now you are my slave,' Alexandra reminded him. She raised the whip and brought it down with a loud snap of leather on flesh. Zaspykin seemed to freeze, his cry of pain strangled in his throat. She raised the whip and brought it down again and again, marking thick red slashes across his back and rear. He begged and grovelled at her feet, snivelling like a dog.

'Thank you, mistress, thank you,' he sighed, gratefully kissing her heels as the rain of blows marked his white flesh.

'Enough! You disgust me!' Alexandra spat angrily, stamping on his back with her heel. He fell back, clutching the wound, looking up at her with nothing but desire in his eyes. His maleness was hard, throbbing, flexing, drawing Alexandra's eyes inexplicably.

'Thank you, mistress. Truly you are the embodiment of Mother Russia herself, imperious, cruel, but deserving nothing but devotion.'

36

'Tell me slave,' Alexandra asked, standing before him, hands on hips, looking down scornfully. 'How is that you grovel before me as a slave yet you whip the revolutionaries mercilessly?'

'I dream of you, mistress,' Zaspykin admitted, massaging his wounds softly. 'I wield the whip and imagine that it is I who is being punished. I beat the degenerate rabble as I would be beaten by the cruel spirit whom I see before me.'

'A degenerate rabble? Who are they, Zaspykin? I am of noble birth, who are these people that would displace me?'

'They are degenerates all of them, imbued with nothing but a hatred of all that is pure in the world. They recognise no authority, neither church, nor the Tsar, mistress. That is why we must destroy them one and all.'

'But who, Zaspykin? How can you know who they are?' Alexandra continued, trying not to betray herself. The heat in her belly was spreading, it made her feel breathless, as if there were a hunger inside her waiting to be fed. The whip was still in her hand, and with every stroke inflicted on Zaspykin there had been a flame of pleasure that pulsed through her.

Zaspykin hesitated. 'That I cannot tell you, great lady,' he said.

'You dare talk to your mistress like that? A slave obeys without question. Without question!' She marched across the room, stamping her heels hard on the floor, aware that he was melting again, his eyes looking at her with nothing but desire and longing. On the dresser she found the metal cuffs that Natasha had placed there. She took them and marched back to Zaspykin who looked on abjectly.

'Will you beat me again, mistress?' he asked hopefully when she snapped the metal cuffs onto his wrists, behind his back.

'I'll beat you, then I want total servility, understand?'

37

He nodded and then she raised the whip high, her breasts swelling in the constraining basque. He shuffled round, bending low to kiss her feet again, so that she had a clear view of his masculine backside. Three quick strokes of the whip had him squirming on the floor, his backside patterned with lines that crossed from one side of his body to the next.

'Well, dog, how do you know who these filthy degenerates are?' she asked breathlessly.

'There is among them one that has a sound heart. A student from the seminary, he has told us who they are and what their plans are.'

Alexandra licked his back with the whip, anxious to keep him talking, yet enjoying a guilty pleasure at the same time. 'You mean there are many of these people?'

'Yes great lady, there are many. There is the doctor, Rabinovich, and the daughter of the lawyer, Panovsky, and the worker Isanovich, the old woman Frestinsky. But they are soon to make my acquaintance and, when they do, they shall find that the heart of Mother Russia is cruel and jealous, with no room for traitors.'

'Enough, slave!' Alexandra commanded. The *Okhrana* knew far more than she had feared, and they had been betrayed by the young seminarian Djugashvili, the one who had posed as the most ideologically pure. Now that Zaspykin had revealed all, it was time to end the scene; to finish it cleanly so that she could return to warn of the great danger.

'Is there something wrong, mistress?' Zaspykin asked, managing to sit up on his knees.

'No, nothing is wrong,' Alexandra assured him, her mask of cool disdain slipping. 'You bore me, that is all. You are not worthy. How can any woman love a man that grovels before her?'

'But I love you nonetheless, mistress,' he said softly, looking away from her.

'Silence! Or must I gag you too?'

'If you must,' he whispered, looking at her slyly, his eyes sparkling with delight.

Alexandra acted quickly. She took her discarded underclothes and pushed them into his mouth then tied her scarf around his face. He was before her – helpless, arms cuffed, mouth gagged, his body red and black from the whipping that she had inflicted. Yet he still longed for more and, strangely, Alexandra felt drawn to him. She sat over him, studying the whip marks on his skin, touching his shivering body with her fingertips. The heat between her thighs was insistent. She saw him looking at her hungrily, his eyes fixed on her silk knickers. She looked down at herself and felt her face colour with shame, a dark patch had appeared, wet and sticky.

Now that he was helpless, silenced, she felt in greater control. She touched his penis with her fingers, surprised to feel it hard yet pliant, the skin smooth and soft, the slit in the purple head crying a jewel of silver fluid. He moaned, the muffled breath escaping from under the gag. So that was what he wanted. Alexandra caressed his hardness again, enjoying the sensation greatly.

She stood up over him, again aware that his eyes were on the damp patch in her soiled knickers. She turned from him and touched herself, just to feel the hot stickiness, but the feel of her finger sent a tremor of sensation pulsing through her. She touched herself again, more insistently, rubbing herself over the knickers. A sigh escaped from her lips; the pleasure had been so great, so powerful.

'Is this what you desire, Zaspykin?' she asked, turning to face him, the crotch of her panties pulled aside to reveal the luxuriant dark hair and the fleshy pink of her sex. His eyes widened, and he moaned, jerking his body up, his thick hardness spearing the air.

She grabbed the whip and flicked it hard, catching his hardness so that he writhed in complete agony, yet still

39

he desired her. She whipped him again, then instinctively she straddled him and took his stiff organ into the wet heat of her sex.

She was out of her mind, the powerful and contradictory emotions merging together. His hardness speared her. She cried out. A long piercing scream of pain that turned to pleasure as the feel of his hardness inside her changed. She moved up and down, rubbing herself on his flat belly while his hardness moved like a dream into her sex. He bucked and writhed and she reflected his movement, thrashing her head from side to side, her hair falling over her face. It was bliss, a pure ecstasy borne from the squalor of their meeting. She arched her back and cried out once more from the white heat of pleasure as the hot semen poured from his burning shaft.

'Now slave,' she whispered, getting up unsteadily. 'Your mistress will leave you forever. By the time you are freed I will be away, fleeing Mother Russia to the safety of Europe. I am Alexandra Panovsky, one of the rabble as you so kindly put it.'

She dressed quickly, discarding her soiled clothes, kicking off the tight boots and slipping off the silk stockings, all the time keeping a wary eye on Zaspykin who was struggling to free himself. Quickly she marched out of the room, stopping to spit in his face, and even as she did so she saw his penis rising once more, aroused by the disgust he saw in her eyes.

'Nothing can stop us. The revolution will wipe away you and all your kind,' she hissed, looking back one last time. Proud words that she did not mean; something had changed. Alexandra felt dirtied, degraded, no longer the innocent that she had been only an hour before. Deep down she knew that the revolution could never succeed, because the sickness was now in her heart too.

Training

I had almost resigned myself to failure when I came across him sitting alone in a first-class compartment. He looked up at me and smiled before I had time to fix my hair or anything, but as soon as I saw him I knew that he was going to be the one. The train was rattling along, shaking from side to side as it picked up speed, making me feel a bit unsteady in my high heels. I struggled with the door to the compartment, hoping that the state of my hair and the way I was being thrown around by the train didn't give him the wrong impression. The last thing I wanted was for him to think I was drunk.

I heaved my case into the compartment and slid the door behind me, taking one last look in the corridor and glad to find it deserted. When I turned I found him with his face stuck in a book, reading it with the kind of fixed expression that you have to really try hard to achieve. He was deliberately ignoring me, doing his best to make me disappear, and the thought of it made me shiver with excitement. I got a good look at him; blond wavy hair, powerful build, clean shaven, quite good looking behind his glasses.

I stepped into the carriage proper, pulling my case in with me. His baggage was in the rack above him, so I turned to the seat opposite and heaved my case up. I stretched, really pushing the case up, standing on tiptoes to get the extra leverage. The reflection in the window was perfect: my short skirt had risen up, revealing the marble white skin at the top of my thighs, the black band of my stockings, the lacy suspenders and my back-side pressed out enticingly. The case seemed to be stuck, or rather I pretended it was stuck, so that I held the position for as long as possible, pushing up and down, my skirt riding higher and higher.

He turned to look in the window. I saw his eyes scan the crystal-clear reflection, travelling from my knees, up a full length of thigh, over my tight round backside, pausing at my breasts (the nipples poking against my tight red top) and finally stopping at my face. Our eyes met and for a moment I saw the hesitation, the sheer confusion in his baby blue eyes, then he turned away. The case slid into place and I relaxed, exhaling heavily, as if the effort had worn me out.

'It's a beautiful day,' he said conversationally, as I sat down opposite him.

'Yes, it's lovely isn't it,' I agreed, flashing him the sort of cold smile that I normally reserved for Jehovah's Witnesses or insurance salesmen.

He nodded, then stuck his nose back into his book, reading my smile the way it was intended to be read. I sat back in my seat, leaned my head back against the wall and exhaled heavily once more. My knees were crossed and from where he sat I knew that he could get an eyeful of my long, stockinged legs. I was balancing my foot on the high heel, surreptitiously pulling my skirt a little higher. Sure enough I caught him glancing up from his book, his eyes feasting on my thighs then furtively returning to the page.

'You're a priest aren't you?' I said suddenly, though with a dog collar, cassock, battered leather satchel and devotional book in hand he could hardly be anything else.

'Yes, that's right,' he smiled patronisingly, giving me a *what do you want, bimbo*, kind of look.

'You help people, don't you, Father?' I asked, making it sound as much like a demand as a question. My face was hard, my red lips glistening sexily, my eyes burning with a kind of fierce intensity. I was a lady with attitude, and I wanted him to know it.

'Yes . . . yes I do. Though you don't have to call me Father,' he said, taking off his glasses to get a better look at me.

'I want to call you Father,' I insisted. 'And you help anyone, right?'

He hesitated, but I wanted an answer. I was looking straight into those lovely blue eyes and I knew that he was hooked.

'If we can,' he agreed. His voice was slow and soft, very thoughtful, very mature. I sighed. He sounded so strong, as if he were middle-aged and not some young man of flesh and blood and still not thirty years old.

'Will you help me, Father?' I asked softly, turning round slightly, so that my skirt was pulled back several inches, the stocking top completely exposed. The breeze passing through the carriage grazed the smooth skin of my thigh.

'If I can,' he agreed, his eyes homing in on my thighs. He looked up from the bare flesh and our eyes met. His face flushed red, the colour burning on his pale skin.

I felt the pleasure pulse through me, but on the surface I remained calm and pretended not to notice his embarrassment, nor the fact that he couldn't keep his eyes off my legs. 'This is a sort of confession, Father,' I started, putting my face in my hands guiltily.

'But this isn't a confessional . . .' he interrupted.

'But I need this!' I cried, looking up at him with an expression of purest pain and anguish. My eyes were already wet with tears, I saw him through a blur, looking quite alarmed.

'As you wish . . . my child,' he stuttered.

Again I sighed, the excitement growing inside me, making my pussy begin to throb deliciously. 'There's something inside me, Father. Something that makes me

43

think evil thoughts and do sinful things. It's inside me
Father, and I can't help myself . . . Something shameless
. . .'

'I see, my child,' he whispered, raising his eyebrows
and fixing me with a look that had me squirming. 'What
sort of sinful thoughts and deeds?'

I hid my smile by taking my head in my hands, bending low to hide my pretend shame. He was hooked. And
now came the interesting bit. I uncrossed my legs, put
them down straight, very modestly, side by side, but
with my skirt pulled right back. He could see nearly all
of my legs; he could see the white flesh of my thighs on
both sides, and he was certainly enjoying the view.

'Everything you can think of, Father. Not just sinful
thoughts about having sex with men that I know. I'm
ashamed to say it, Father, but I fantasise about making
love to complete strangers, to men I have never met
before and will never meet again.'

'I see,' he nodded. 'And do you act upon these sinful
impulses?'

'Yes, Father,' I whispered, turning away from him. I
caught sight of him in the window, the dirty glass acting
as a perfect mirror. He was leaning forward, listening
intently, but not intently enough. 'There are other things
too, Father,' I added, realising that boring old promis-
cuity was not going to do it for him.

'Other things? Other sins of the flesh?'

'Yes, Father,' I half-sobbed. 'Other sins of the flesh.
In my mind I dream of other women, Father. I desire
sexual contact with other women. I dream of lying
naked in their arms, of being touched by feminine fingers, of being kissed by feminine lips. I dream these
things and my body grows hot, I grow restless, unable
to cope unless I touch myself. Is it wrong, Father?'

'It is very wrong,' he decided, and that made me feel
even more excited.

I loved being told I was doing wrong, it seemed to

trigger a signal deep in my sex. I was wet and I could feel my pussy growing deliciously moist.

'Do you act on these desires?'

Was that it? Did the idea of two women getting off on each other ring any bells for him? 'Yes, Father . . . I have made love to other women too. I know it's wrong. I tell myself I shouldn't but then the desire is too strong. I let myself be seduced; I enjoy the feel of another woman putting her hand under my skirt. I enjoy her fingers stroking my thighs, of touching me *everywhere*. And Father, I have allowed myself to be seduced by two women together. They made love to me, sharing me . . . I'm so ashamed.'

'Two women together?' he repeated, his face growing red. The idea seemed to appeal to him. He was leaning closer to me, his eyes fixed on my body, his hands together under his chin. He looked good enough to eat.

'Yes, Father, on a number of occasions. I couldn't help myself. I met one of them at a health club. She came up to me in the showers and began to soap my naked body. The feel of the hot water coursing down my skin and the feel of her fingers on my back soon had me aching with desire. Her fingers touched my breasts as if by accident but then I responded, I touched her back. Soon we were both making love under the jets of water, kissing, sucking, touching each other. I wanted to resist but couldn't.'

'And the other woman?' he asked hotly, sounding rather strained.

He crossed his legs and I cursed the fact that he was wearing a cassock. I couldn't see the size of his erection. Almost there, I told myself.

'We made love until I had climaxed and then she called to her friend. I was still feeling dazed as it had been a very violent orgasm and I hardly knew what was going on. Before I knew it I was making love with the second woman. She was exploring my naked body

45

under the rushing water. They took it in turns, making love to me several times. After that they took me whenever they felt like it. They would call me up and tell me to be at a certain place at a certain time and I would go. Sometimes they made love to me in turn, sometimes it was all three of us together.'

'I see,' he said, shifting round, trying to make himself more comfortable. 'You say they took you whenever they wanted. Surely it is correct to say whenever you wanted.'

'Are you blaming me, Father?' I asked, sounding appalled by the suggestion. 'I was weak, they took advantage of me. I couldn't resist. They only had to caress my body, touch me in my feminine places and I was at their mercy.'

'So there was an element of coercion involved? They forced you?' he asked excitedly.

Bang! That was the key. 'Yes, Father,' I said, and it took all my willpower to keep that miserable tone. 'They forced me, much as I didn't want to. And sometimes if I wasn't good they would punish me.'

He coughed, his eyes bulging dangerously. 'Punish?' he managed to ask, straining to catch his breath and appear calm.

'Yes, Father. On many occasions they physically punished me. It hurts even to talk about it.'

'Then it is good that you talk about it,' he insisted. 'If you bottle it all up then it does no good.'

'They would punish me like a naughty girl, Father. One of them would pull my knickers down and bend me over her knee. I'd beg her not to chastise me but it wouldn't do any good. She would pull up my skirt and then spank me several times on the bare bottom. It hurt me so much, I'd scream and sob but that only made her more determined.'

'How did she punish you? With her hand? A slipper?'

'It started with her hand. But then she moved on to

46

using the flat side of a hairbrush. She would smack me until my bottom was red hot. I could see myself in the mirror. By the end of a session my bottom would be patterned red and pink, all over my buttocks and at the top of my thighs, and even on my breasts sometimes.'

'Would you have to display yourself?' he asked eagerly.

Display myself? I didn't know what that meant, but I could tell from his eager expression that it was important to him. 'I'm not sure what you mean, Father?'

'Did she make you stand in a corner, displaying your chastised posterior?'

'Yes, yes. She would make me stand in a corner, holding up my skirt so that she and her friend could admire by smarting backside. It was so humiliating, Father. But the worst of it was that I enjoyed the humiliation; I enjoyed being spanked. Afterwards they would fuck me like a whore and I'd have the most intense orgasms of my life. I loved being degraded by those two women.'

He said nothing; his posture matched my own. He was leaning forward, face hidden in his hands. I could see that his hands were shaking and the colour had drained completely from his face. Outside it was raining, the world speeding past was a liquid blur. Had he read Freud? I wondered. Did the symbolism of speeding trains mean anything to him?

'Will you help me, Father,' I pleaded.

'What can I do, my child? Do you seek forgiveness for these wanton sins?'

'More than forgiveness, Father. I know I have sinned and I need to be punished. I need to suffer for all the wrongs that I have done,' I said evenly. The excitement pulsing in my veins was making it harder and harder to control myself.

'Punishment?'

Our eyes met and I saw the doubt expressed there. 'Yes, Father. Punish me.' I fell forward, to my knees, in front of him. He tried to sit back but I buried my face in his lap, pressing my tits against his thighs. My face brushed against his prick, its divine hardness buried in the thick vestments that were a mark of his ministry.

'As you wish, my child,' he whispered, his voice quivering, ready to crack. I sat up on my knees and rolled my skirt up, revealing completely my black stockings and suspenders. He sat back and I bent over his lap, lifting my backside up as high as possible. My panties were soaked through, the dark patch between my thighs clearly visible. He pulled my knickers down and I felt the breeze brush between my thighs.

The first smack sounded so unreal; a high-pitched slap of skin on skin that was almost drowned out by the rattle of the train. If the sound was unreal then the sharp dagger of pain that shot through me wasn't. It stung, but the pain was turned to pleasure, the red imprint of his hand connecting to the delicious excitement in my pussy. He spanked me several times, long hard strokes, moving from buttock to buttock, rouging my skin and building layer upon layer of exquisite pleasure.

'I've been a bad girl. So very bad,' I cried, wishing that he would chastise me verbally as well as physically.

'So very bad,' he repeated breathlessly. 'And now you are being spanked for it.'

The heat on my backside was delicious in itself, but I wanted more than just a sound spanking. 'But, Father,' I cried, 'this is how those sinful women treated me. It is the same pleasure I feel. You must show me how wrong I have been . . .'

'How child? How?'

I passed my hand over his lap, found his prick and squeezed it lovingly. We said nothing; we understood. I slipped from his lap and knelt against the seat where I had been sitting earlier, my backside raised up, smarting painfully, the juices from my pussy running down my stockings.

It took a second, but when I turned round I saw him

standing over me, his prick red and hard in his hand. I arched my back, opened my aching pussy with my fingers then guided his cock deep into me. The pleasure pierced me. I climaxed immediately, my cry filling the compartment. He thrust forward, fucking me quickly, going dèep into me, filling me with his lovely hardness. He was inexperienced, his rhythm rough and ready, violent, passionate. I climaxed again, enjoying the feel of his cool body against my burning backside.

His cry was muted, as if at the moment of his orgasm he remembered himself. He filled me with thick cream then withdrew quickly. I fixed my clothes slowly, slipping my panties off and stuffing them into my bag. He was already nosing through his book, his ashen face turned away from me, lips quivering tearfully.

We remained silent until the train drew slowly into the station. I reached for my bag and the skirt rose up. I knew he was looking at my uncovered backside, still stinging red.

'You know, Father,' I said, smiling guiltily. 'I tell a lot of lies.'

'I'm sorry?'

'All that stuff about the other women, it wasn't true,' I admitted.

'But why . . . For what reason?' he mumbled, looking askance.

'My real sin is seducing men of the cloth. Nothing turns me on more than sex with a young priest.'

The look of pain and confusion on his young face was pitiful. I sort of shrugged, grabbed my bag then went to the door. I turned and saw him still looking lost.

I stepped out onto the platform then turned back. 'It's all right, Father,' I assured him, putting my head back into the train. 'You're the sixth priest I've seduced this way. The others enjoyed it as much as you did.'

I watched him fall back into his seat, burying his head in his hands. He looked so sexy then, I almost climbed back into the train.

The Birthday Present

Ian cursed the traffic as it slowed down to a crawl once more. The light drizzle had turned into a heavy rain that drummed on the car as the wipers struggled to give him some visibility. Paradoxically the delay only served to heighten the feeling of excitement that had been with him all day, making his prick harden again. It was his birthday, and all he could think about was his wife Linda and the special surprise he hoped she had in store for him.

His colleagues at work had been very rowdy when he had left them earlier, half-drunk and angry that the birthday boy was walking out on them early. Then they'd laughed and joked, guessing the reason for his uncharacteristic eagerness to leave the pub on his own two feet. He knew that he was going to be ribbed about it for days but it only made him smile. They just didn't know what sort of surprises Linda could think of. They had no idea at all.

It had been his idea in the beginning. In the first year of their marriage he had bought Linda something just a little bit different on her birthday; something she had never expected. He could still see the look of surprise on her face, imprinted forever on his memory as if it had been yesterday. The party had been in full swing when he pulled her into the kitchen, surreptitiously dragging her away from family and friends. They had kissed passionately and then he made her close her eyes. The box was long and thin, and her guesses had been so far

50

off that he had to laugh. He laughed even more at the horrified look in her eyes when she tore open the box and saw the thick white vibrator, all nine long inches of it. The diamond earrings nestling under it paled into insignificance.

The family never did find out why the birthday party fizzled out so quickly. One moment it had been singing and dancing and the next they were being practically pushed out into the street. The wild look in Linda's eyes should have been enough to tell them what was on her mind.

Once they were alone they had torn at each other like wild things. She ripped the buttons from her silk blouse, pushing her lovely breasts into his face. He had slipped a finger under her knickers and found her soaking. Thick sticky cream pouring copiously from her hot sex. She screamed with pleasure as he forced the vibrator into her there and then, still standing in the middle of the room and surrounded by all the jolly trappings of a birthday party. Pressing the vibrator in to her like that had given her the first climax of the night, her cries of pleasure filling the room.

She climaxed again when he took her up to the bedroom and sucked her pussy clean, while making her suck her juices from her thick phallic birthday present. And again when he frigged her with it while she sucked his aching prick. Then he lost count. It went on for hours; hot, frenzied sex. In his mind he could still see her, arching her back, her eyes closed, face and chest flooded with colour.

His first birthday surprise had been as great as hers, simply because he had never imagined that Linda had a mind as devious as his own. If the fancy-dress party had been a great idea, her wearing a crisp white nurse's uniform had been positively inspired. All night she teased him, bending over this way and that, letting him glimpse her white cotton panties, the tops of her white stockings, her bust set to burst through the constricting tightness of the uniform. It was agony. Every time he had tried to touch her she had skipped from his grasp. At last, when the last guest was unceremoniously dumped in the garden, he had her all to himself.

They had fucked all night. He took her from every angle. From behind he had her bending over, making the uniform stretch tight over her backside before pulling her virginal white panties to one side and planting his pulsing cock deep into her silky wetness. All through the night, whenever he was tired out, she had paraded in front of him until he was aching for her once more. And the way she had taken his temperature had had him jacking warm salty come into her waiting mouth.

The traffic moved again, inching back up to speed. The rain was easing off too. If there was a God then Ian offered up his fervent thanks. As the cars sped forward he willed them on, faster and faster. The sky was clearing and the murky grey clouds parted to reveal a rich blue sky tinged with the fleshy pink of twilight.

There was a gap in the flow of cars and he accelerated out into the fast lane, ignoring the flashing headlights of the car he had cut up. He gave a one-fingered salute in time honoured fashion, and was gratified to see the driver of the car behind turn a spluttering purple with rage. Ian laughed and sped forward, now more than ever looking forward to his birthday present.

Linda's next birthday had not been as enjoyable as the first. But it hadn't been his fault, it had been a genuine mistake, a missed date in the diary that's all. He remembered the scene well, arriving home after a session with the boys, half-drunk and randy but without much idea why she was icy cold. She hadn't reminded him, she was stonily silent. It had been the cards on the mantelpiece that did the trick but by then it was too late. Women, he thought, too emotional that was their problem. The card and the flowers next day went straight into the bin, making him screech with anger and indignation over her petty-minded attitude.

By the time of his birthday though it had all been forgotten. There had been no fancy-dress party that second year, nothing quite so obvious. Again Linda's imagination had taken him completely by surprise. The meal in the restaurant had been far from exciting: the menu was in French, the waiter condescending and the prices mortgageable. In all, not the sort of night that normally sparkled in Ian's memory. Not until she decided it was birthday present time.

She kissed him on the lips lovingly, wished him a happy birthday then slipped under the table. He would never forget the dawning horror; his nervous glances at the other diners, the fear of capture growing in his mind. Linda was on her hands and knees, hidden by the table cloth, snuggling up between his thighs. She unzipped his fly but the fear and embarrassment kept his cock down. But once she went to work there had been nothing he could do.

Her tongue had lapped at his prick till it felt fit to burst. Sweet lips caressed him, making him struggle for breath. The agony was unbearable. The waiters were going back and forth, customers were laughing and joking, while his wife was giving him the best blow job he'd ever had. She had worked him so well, kissing, sucking, grazing his prick with her teeth. He had grunted loudly when coming, startling the old couple at the next table. A minute later she reappeared, delicately dabbing the come from her lips with a pink serviette, her fingers glistening with her own pussy cream.

It had been bliss of course, and he had fantasised about it more than once. But sometimes he couldn't help but wonder at Linda's motives. It had been bliss, but of a difficult kind, the kind that had him squirming uncomfortably in his seat.

The memories were making him more excited, his

prick was caught in his trousers, trapped in his fly but that only made the ache all the more delicious. He raced along the motorway, zooming past other cars with scarcely a glance over his shoulder.

It had been unfortunate missing Linda's birthday a second time, but he knew that she was an understanding woman and that it didn't really matter. Besides, he was certain that she didn't even have an inkling about Sally, the flighty young admin girl in the office. The problem was that Sally was a demanding sort of young woman who, apart from regular screwing, also wanted to be wined, dined and danced. Trying to explain to her that Linda's birthday was important was never going to be easy. Linda's birthday was simply not on Sally's agenda, so he didn't even bother trying. And the motel room she had booked for the night had satellite TV, so that when he hadn't been wrapped between Sally's deliciously long thighs he had watched other men wrapped in other deliciously long thighs on the box.

The excuse about work was still a good one. He used it sparingly and though Linda hadn't been Mrs Happy when he got home the day after her birthday she hadn't been Mrs Miserable-Cow either. She was good like that really. Next year he was going to give her a really big treat he promised himself.

At last the long journey home was over. The headlights cut through the darkness and swept across the house in a long white swathe. He caught a glimpse of someone at the bedroom curtain upstairs and he knew that Linda was ready. He was definitely going to make her next birthday the best ever, it was a promise he had made before but this time he was going to keep it.

She was at the door before he was, ready with a tumbler of whisky and a loving kiss.

'Happy birthday darling,' she whispered sexily, taking his hand and pulling him into the house.

'We're not going out then,' Ian said, pointing to the

thick terry bathrobe wrapped tightly around her. He was glad of course. Another semi-public blow job would have been too much to take. The bathrobe suggested something altogether more intimate.

'No,' she smiled coyly. 'This year I've decided we'll party at home.'

She stepped back and in one smooth motion let the bathrobe fall from her shoulders to the floor. She stood before him, perfectly posed, waiting for his eyes to pop back into his head.

'You look fucking brilliant,' was all he could say. She was wearing a tight black leather mini skirt, a leather bustier that lifted and separated her gorgeous breasts, the nipples open and suckable, and long thigh-high boots to complete the costume.

'You like it then?' she teased, knowing full well that one look at her had Ian's prick stiffly to attention.

'Like it? Like it?'

She laughed, her eyes glittering with delight. She skipped out of his clammy grasp and ran upstairs, her spiked heels exploding like gun shots on the stairs. She stopped at the top and bent over provocatively. The leather skirt was stretched around her backside, a tight black skin that was moulded to her body. He looked up at her. His eyes traced the sinuous line from spiked heels, up her long legs and under her skirt where a thin black strip of leather parted her arse cheeks.

She waited for just a moment then straightened up slowly, watching Ian ripping off his clothes in a frenzy. In an instant he was naked. His prick, jutting from between his thighs, was hard and already smeared with glistening fluid that dribbled from the opening. He chased after her, a man possessed, eyes feasting on her body with a hunger she had never seen before.

Ian burst into the bedroom, the flight of stairs doing nothing to reduce his fever pitch of lust. Linda was by the bed, smiling, flexing a wicked-looking riding crop between her hands.

'Let's play this game properly,' she suggested, running her tongue along her glossy red lips.

'What do you mean?' he asked, stopping in his tracks, an element of doubt passing through his mind.

'Just for tonight I'm going to be your Mistress, and you're going to be my . . .'

'. . . slave.' Ian finished the sentence.

It was an intriguing idea, not something he normally went for but it had its possibilities. And if it meant he got to screw her in her leather-girl from hell outfit then it was all to the good.

'On the bed,' she said, smiling excitedly, swishing the riding crop through the air.

He obeyed instantly, lying on the bed quickly, his greedy eyes fixed on Linda's delightfully hard nipples, cased in tight black leather. His mouth watered at the idea of having to suck them, forced against his will.

'On your stomach,' she told him.

She leaned across him and he felt the coolness of leather against his skin, a sensual tingle passing through him. He obeyed without question, nuzzling his face against her thigh-length boots, breathing in the scent of leather as if it were a perfume. Again he couldn't help feeling surprised at his wife's ingenuity; at her sheer inventiveness. Already it was shaping up to be the best birthday surprise of them all.

From nowhere she produced a pair of leather cuffs which she attached to his wrists, and then chains which she used to bind his wrists to the top of the bed. In a matter of a few seconds he was tethered face down on the bed, his leather-clad wife standing beside him, her smile even broader than it had been.

'What now?' he asked, forcing his head back to look up at her.

'One more thing I think,' she decided after a pause.

He watched her expectantly. She put one foot up on the bed, her heel close to his face so that he had a clear view up the length of her boots. She reached under her

56

skirt and very slowly peeled down the soft leather thong that was pressed tightly into her sex.

'I'm wet,' she smiled, teasing her pussy lips apart. The leather thong was slipped down and then she stepped out of it. He watched her silently as she screwed it into a tight bundle then forced it into his mouth. It fitted tightly, filling his mouth completely, the taste of leather and sex suffusing into his mouth and throat.

He hardly had enough time to get used to the improvised gag when the first blow landed across his bare backside. His body snapped rigid as the surging white heat of pain scored him. The cuffs on his hands were tight and the gag effectively silenced him. A second and then a third stroke followed the first, each biting intensely into his flesh.

'Did that hurt, darling?' Linda whispered, running her fingers over the burning tracks, making him wince again with pleasure and pain.

Ian nodded vigorously, fearing that in her search for authenticity she was going too far. Playing games and dressing up were one thing, being whipped was something else.

'I'm so wet,' she purred, 'so very wet. I need something don't I?'

He nodded again, his eyes lighting up at the prospect of finally getting to shaft his wife.

'What do I need? Do I need a man? A nice hard man to fuck me?' she teased, smoothing her hand down to tickle him under the balls.

'It's lucky I've got one then, isn't it?' she laughed suddenly.

Ian strained, managing to twist round enough to see her march across the room. The door opened and there was somebody there. He began to struggle, fighting hard against the chains that bound him tightly into position. The sweat was pouring from him, and as he fought for air every breath was perfumed with his wife's feminine scent.

Linda was by the bed once more, and with her a man. He was tall, muscular, blond, naked. Ian swallowed hard, his eyes fit to burst from his skull. She was kissing the man, pressing herself against him suggestively. He had his arms around her, slipping his fingers under her skirt and lifting it to reveal her glorious round bottom, his finger tracing a line between her buttocks.

'And let's not forget this,' she remembered suddenly, walking across to the dressing table and pulling something from the drawer.

Ian didn't know where to look. At his wife holding the massive vibrator in her hands, or at the naked man and his bulging hard-on.

'This is Gary,' she said walking back from the drawer, pausing to run her hand up and down his prick, her fingers stroking softly. 'You haven't met him, but I think you've met his wife, Sally.'

Ian caught his breath. He looked up at the man who was smiling now. Sally's husband.

'Gary's a fantastic lover. He's going to make love to me in a way you've never done,' Linda was saying. 'He's going to fuck me blissfully, till I scream with the ecstasy of it. And you're going to watch, Ian, you're going to watch him eat my pussy, eat my backside, fuck me in the mouth, in the cunt, between my tits, everywhere.'

'But we don't want you to feel left out,' Gary said, his voice a low rumble.

'That's right,' Linda agreed. She stepped forward and took hold of Ian from behind. Gary moved too, crossing the room to help her. Ian felt his backside being parted, Gary's hands holding the buttocks apart. Then Linda started to ease the vibrator into the tightness of the rear hole.

Ian pushed and struggled but the fight had gone out of him. The thick vibrator went deep into his rear hole. It filled him, searing him as if he were a virgin bride.

'That's to remind you of what Gary's going to give

you when he's finished with me,' she whispered, giving him one final slap across the buttocks.

Linda and Gary moved to the centre of the room, sucking at each other excitedly, ignoring Ian moaning softly on the bed. He was staring at them, wide eyed, unable to believe what was happening, unable to fully grasp what was going on. Unable also to understand why his prick was still achingly hard.

Our Little Secret

I was certain that she was doing it deliberately and in that certainty I found nothing but confusion and indecision. That certainty was reinforced when I looked up and saw Nicole coming into the room. She beamed me a smile and then carried on through the room to switch on the television. I half smiled back, trying to fathom the look in her dark brown eyes that seemed to be at once so innocent and yet so knowing. My eyes scanned her quickly. She was wearing a very tight T-shirt, the shape of her firm young breasts impressed on the cotton, her nipples protruding slightly, and her short skirt revealing just how long and smooth her thighs were. She flicked the television on and then sat down on the sofa, directly opposite to where I was sitting.

'What time's Jim getting home?' I asked her, forcing my eyes from the view of her shapely thighs, displayed to perfection by her skirt which was short and tight.

'He said he'd be late again,' she said with a sigh, for one moment an expression of sorrow clouding her eyes. She turned back to the television, perhaps wanting to hide her true feelings from me.

At first I had been sure that it was my imagination, after all I was probably spending more time at home with Nicole than Jim, who seemed to be putting in more and more hours at work. It could have been imagination but slowly I grew certain that Nicole was flirting with me. No, it wasn't flirting exactly, it seemed to me that she was playing a little game and enjoying every second of it. First it was her clothes: very short miniskirts, skin-tight tops, low-cut blouses. Then it was more obvious. The bath robe that would fall open accidentally, affording me a split second view of her finely shaped breasts, her nipples cherry-red against the whiteness of her skin, the bedroom door left open so that I'd see her as I walked past.

Never a word was said, never a hint of anything untoward, not even a silent smile of complicity. On the surface everything was entirely innocent and I'm certain that Jim had no idea that anything was going on. And perhaps there really was nothing going on, but then again every glimpse of her body, every look that was so innocent and so knowing, would set my heart pounding and body responding. Damn it, Nicole was a beautiful young woman and I found her presence very arousing sometimes.

'Are you watching this?' she asked, turning to me and breaking my train of thought.

'No, not really,' I mumbled, aware that she had been talking to me and I had been so wrapped up in my thoughts that I hadn't even noticed.

'Daydreaming again, Paul,' she sighed, a sad shake of the head transforming into a friendly smile.

'Sorry, I was miles away,' I told her, smiling back, all the time wondering what was going on in her pretty head. Her smiles could mean a million different things, always open and friendly, but occasionally I thought I detected something else, something much deeper and more dangerous.

'Do you mind if I turn this over?'

'Not at all. Is there anything else on the other side?'

She shrugged. 'Isn't there a film on tonight? Have you got the paper?'

I pointed to the magazine rack beside the television. Where was Jim? Such a pretty girl and yet he was neglecting her again, spending time at work or with his workmates in the pub rather than with her. I couldn't understand it. He and Nicole were the same age, just under twenty – half my age, and yet they were worlds apart in personality. She liked nothing better than to cuddle up close to him, or for them to go out dancing, whereas he had plainly decided that his career was number one.

Nicole dutifully dragged herself off the sofa and walked across the room to the magazine rack. My eyes widened as she bent over to retrieve the newspaper. She was standing with ankles together, bent over at the waist, her skirt rising up at the back so that I could see the full length of her gorgeous thighs. She flicked idly through the thick pile of papers and magazines, and as she did so she swivelled round slightly, making her skirt rise even higher. I could see the muscles of her thighs pulled taut, every inch of her silky smooth skin displayed and, at the top of her thighs the curve of her backside and the slight bulge of her buttocks. Her panties were a thin white strip of cotton that had been pulled tightly between her rear cheeks.

'Can't find it, you sure it's here?' she called, glancing round. I nodded silently, my eyes fixed on that rear view of her.

Was she doing it on purpose? I didn't know, and yet she was surely driving me insane. So sexy, so desirable, but still very distant and definitely hands-off. As she read the paper I caught her sneaking looks in my direction. Furtive little glances over the top of the newspaper and then a guilty smile. Or did I imagine that?

'There's nothing on,' she announced after a few minutes, as though that were a surprise to either of us.

'So, you don't know what time Jim's getting back tonight?' I asked her.

'No, I just know he'll be late. I'd better put this back,' she said, getting up to walk back to the magazine rack. She looked over her shoulder at me again, caught my eyes and smiled. I couldn't keep my eyes from her. She bent over very slowly, her black skirt rising inch by inch over her thighs until I could see the faintest outline of her white panties pulled tight into her crotch. She held the position for a few moments, wriggling from side to side to force the paper back into the overloaded rack, and incidentally allowing me a good long look, and then she straightened up.

She looked at me again, her eyes sparkling with excitement. This time there could be no pretence, I had to say something. 'Doesn't Jim mind you wearing those miniskirts?' I asked, managing a note of admonition.

'No, why should he?' she responded, smiling a smile of sweet innocence that made my prick throb dangerously.

'Well, they're so short,' I explained.

She laughed. 'They're supposed to be, silly, that's why they're called miniskirts.'

'Of course,' I agreed, smiling. Damn it! The moment had gone. I had been certain that there had been something beguiling, something alluring in her smile, but now that was gone and all I could detect was that childlike innocence that I found so effective.

'There's nothing on the box tonight,' she remarked, 'but you couldn't do me a favour could you?'

'Sure, what is it?'

'Well,' she said excitedly, 'Jim has promised to take me out to a club tomorrow night and I don't know what to wear. If I try on a couple of outfits would you tell me which one you like the best?'

'Me? I have the dress sense of . . . I don't have any dress sense at all.'

She giggled. 'It doesn't matter, you're a man. You know what you like. Please, will you?'

She was pouting and she knew that I couldn't resist that. I drew breath sharply and nodded my agreement.

'Great!' she shrieked, and jumped across the room to

plant a big wet kiss on my cheek, her breasts bulging against her tight top. She was so obviously excited that I hardly had time to react before she bounded up the stairs to her room.

Nicole may or may not have been intentionally flirting, but my reaction was physical and I knew that I would end up making a pass at her. I was brooding on this when I heard her coming downstairs, high heels cracking hard on the stairs.

'Well? How do I look?' she asked anxiously, walking into the centre of the room.

I could hardly believe my eyes and my astonishment must have been clear to see as she paraded and twirled around in front of me. She was wearing a short black dress that seemed to have been sprayed on; it left nothing to the imagination. It was cut low so that her pert breasts were almost fully displayed, the nipples threatening to pop out at any moment. The dress was very short too, even shorter than the skirt which she had been wearing earlier, and it barely managed to cover her backside. Added to which it was so tight that I could see the full rounded shape of her posterior and the slight bulge of her belly.

'You can't go out dressed like that,' I whispered, my eyes focusing on her breasts. The nipples had become erect little points that bulged against the tight low-slung neck of the dress.

'You don't like it?' she asked, advancing towards me, every step reflected in the bounce of her firm round breasts. She stopped in front of me, legs slightly apart, the shape of her limbs emphasised by black high heels. Was she enjoying my discomfort? I couldn't tell. All I knew was that she had never looked sexier and the bulging of my prick was a painful reminder of the effect she was having on me.

'It's so revealing,' I tried to explain, my eyes travelling over her body, only inches away from me.

'What about my scent?' she asked, suddenly leaning over me, offering me her slender throat so that I could breathe her perfume. It was an aphrodisiac, making me feel almost dizzy, my eyes only inches from her breasts offered so temptingly close.

'A lovely perfume,' I agreed, aware that her nipples were such hard points against the tight velvet of her dress.

'Jim bought it for me,' she informed me, stepping away again, almost skipping across the room like an excited schoolgirl.

'But the dress . . .' I reminded her.

Suddenly she dropped the velvet purse which she had been holding, the perfect accessory for her dress. I watched as she bent over to pick it up, keeping her legs straight as she moved over at the waist, the tight dress parting her bottom cheeks before riding up sensuously over her skin. As I had thought, she was wearing no panties and for one tantalising moment I was treated to a glimpse of her bare bottom, the dark hairs around her bulging sex visible from behind. Before I had time to react she was standing again, looking at me with pursed lips, as though unaware of what I had seen and deep in thought as to what to do next.

'Maybe you're right,' she finally decided. 'Perhaps this is a bit too showy. Let me show you the next one, then you can decide.'

I didn't have the power to object, I merely nodded my agreement and followed her with my eyes as she left the room. Damn it, I knew that she was playing some strange game, flaunting her lithe young body, parading herself and enjoying my feelings of discomfort and excitement.

I stood up and walked to the drinks cabinet, adjusting my trousers, glancing down to see my cock etched against my clothing. She had to have seen that, there was no way that even a casual glance would have missed my erection. My hands were shaking as I poured myself a neat scotch and gulped down the amber drink. I closed my eyes, trying to block out the image of her breasts, trying to forget the image of her bent over, legs parted and set straight. Trying but not succeeding.

'Paul, Paul!'

I sighed, wondering what new torture she had decided to inflict on me. She was calling from her bedroom so I went to the bottom of the stairs to find out what she wanted.

'Could you just have a look at something for me?' she called, a pleading note to her voice.

I kept calm as I climbed the stairs. Her bedroom door was open and I just went in, vowing to keep cool no matter what she wanted. She was standing by her wardrobe, dressed only in a lacy bra and a short red miniskirt, just as short as the dress had been. The wardrobe door was open, a mad jumble of clothes inside it. She smiled to me in a good natured sort of way, that naive smile that she reserved especially for me.

'Could you reach up there for me?' she asked, pointing to a sports bag lodged on top of the wardrobe. The bra was almost see-through; a frilly black lace thing which lifted and parted her breasts, barely covering her hardening nipples. It was a tease but she was acting as though nothing untoward was happening.

'What's up there?' I said, sighing, looking from her breasts to her eyes, and realising just how much she was enjoying my attentions.

'I've got a matching skirt and blouse in there, I'd just like to try them on.'

'How did you get the bag up there?' I complained.

'Ah . . . Now I remember,' she exclaimed delightedly. She reached for the vanity chair in front of the dressing table and positioned it by the wardrobe. 'Jim held the chair while I just shoved things up there,' she told me. 'I'd forgotten.'

She skipped up onto the chair and I saw how unsteady it was. I did as instructed and bent over to hold it steady while she stretched up and grabbed the bag. She hadn't been lying, the bag was stuck, and as she struggled to pull it away I was treated to another view of long thighs, and this time a flash of black where she'd put a pair of panties on. At long last the bag was free and she stepped down, though not before she'd seen me eyeing up her long legs.

'Here it is, tell me what you think,' she giggled excitedly.

I watched her unzip the bag and produce a long dark skirt, the longest skirt I'd ever seen her with. Before I could make a comment she unclipped her red mini and let it fall in a bundle around her ankles. She faced me in her underwear, lacy black bra and matching knickers, with not a trace of shame on her face.

'What the hell do you think you're doing?' I demanded angrily, driven beyond endurance by her brazen exhibitionism.

'What do you mean?' she asked innocently, her eyes widening.

'What is it, girl? Are you enjoying this silly game of yours?' I bellowed, unable to control my anger any more.

'Paul, what is it?'

'You, that's what it is. Why are you parading yourself like this? Showing off in front of me, are you enjoying embarrassing me? Is that it?'

'I'm sorry, I hadn't realised this was embarrassing,' she sniffed, pouting sulkily.

'Don't act the little innocent with me,' I warned her, 'or I'll have to teach you what happens to girls that misbehave.'

Her eyes seemed to perk up. 'What does happen to girls that misbehave?' she asked, her mocking tone contrasting to the excitement I saw in her eyes. Her nipples were hard points of flesh, and I couldn't help but notice that her backside was reflected in the mirror behind her.

'They get punished,' I replied. 'And parading around in your knickers, or parading around without any knickers on at all, is a sure way to get punished.'

'But I wasn't parading . . .' she started to complain.

'Don't push your luck madam,' I warned her coldly.

'I'm sorry,' she replied softly, averting her gaze guiltily.

'Tell me the truth, were you deliberately leading me on?'

There was a lengthy pause and then she nodded. 'I could see that you were getting turned on,' she admitted. 'And I sort of enjoyed it. And the more I did it the more I enjoyed it. I've been very silly, haven't I?'

It was my turn to pause, I knew what I wanted to do then. 'I think I've every right to punish you for that, don't you?'

'I suppose so.' she mumbled.

'How do you propose I do that, young lady?'

She shrugged her shoulders. 'I don't know, I suppose you deserve to get your own back. How do you think I should be punished?'

I took a deep breath. 'You deserve a sound spanking,' I told her, exhaling slowly. 'I think the way to ensure you keep your knickers on and hidden from view is to smack you so hard on the behind that every time you sit down you'll remember.'

There was no surprise on her part, no look of horror. Instead she nodded to herself, as though she understood the justice of it all. 'Here?' she asked nervously.

'Yes, here and now.'

I pulled the vanity chair over and sat down, positioning myself so that I was comfortable. The wardrobe door, with its inside mirror, was open, and that in turn was reflected in the mirror on the dressing table. I motioned for her to step forward and she did so, glancing at me nervously.

'Across my knee, young lady,' I explained, pulling her towards me. She made no reply but knelt across my lap, reaching out to stop herself falling. In seconds her bottom, still clad in thin black panties, was presented for my delectation. She could see herself in the mirror, and the reflection of her backside too, an infinitely receding view of herself ready for punishment.

I raised my hand high and brought it down hard, the slap of skin on skin resounding around the room. My fingers stung lightly, but that was nothing to the sting she must have felt on her pert round behind. She made no sound, instead she bit her lip and looked up at me appealingly. I raised my hand again and brought it down firmly on her other bottom cheek, gratified to feel her jump when my hand landed so firmly on her taut round buttock. Again and again, six quick strokes in succession, turning her pale and delicate flesh first pink and then a deeper shade of red. Soon Nicole was squirming and moaning, her body responding to the searing heat of punishment that rained down on her posterior.

'Stand up now,' I commanded, my breath coming hot and fast as I enjoyed my task of punishing Nicole's backside.

'Oh, it hurts,' she complained, pouting her full red lips.

'It's supposed to,' I told her gruffly, noting at the same time that her nipples had grown even more erect. I could see that the excitement was still there in her eyes, and I guessed that our little session had yet to run its course.

'But I wasn't such a bad girl,' she protested, pushing out her chest so that she was flaunting herself again.

'Right, there'll be more for that.'

'More for what?' she demanded defiantly.

I grabbed her and pushed her against the bed. She fell across it, face down and bottom out. There was a black hairbrush on the dressing table and I picked it up and weighed it in my hand.

'Please, not that, Paul,' she wailed, her eyes open wide with horror when she saw me with the brush.

'I'm going to teach you a lesson, young woman,' I told her. In moments her pretty lace panties were around her ankles and her backside, patterned red by my hand, was fully exposed. Her bottom cheeks were slightly parted, and I could see the dark bud of her rear hole and the puffy lips of her sex. She looked delightful, so exposed, so vulnerable, her punished body exuding a kind of raw animal sexuality.

The first impact of the brush on her left bottom cheek echoed around the room, accompanied by her yelp of shock and pain. I reached out and smoothed my hand over her buttock, able to enjoy the heat that flamed on her skin. She moved back, pushed her bottom towards me, enjoying being touched and caressed on the seat of her punishment. Her correction had yet to end, and soon her cries of pain were a constant refrain as I let go with half-a-dozen hard blows with the hair brush. I moved round, and smacked her again, each time landing the brush precisely on her lithe young body.

Her behaviour changed subtly, her cries were deeper, breathier, and she was lifting herself, offering me her rear side for every blow. I made sure that I tanned her body evenly, smacking her hard on the buttocks, at the top of the thighs and even between her thighs.

Her strangled cry of pleasure as she climaxed suddenly brought me to my senses. What had I done? I looked down on her reddened posterior, at her writhing body, at the look of sweet pleasure that marked her face. I had punished her for sure, but much to my surprise she had found pleasure in her pain.

'Are you all right?' I whispered, letting the brush fall on the floor.

She opened her eyes and looked at me. 'That was so

good,' she sighed. 'That felt so different, it hurt me but I enjoyed it too. I don't know why . . .'

'You'd better get dressed,' I told her. My eyes travelled down over her body. Her bra had fallen and her breasts were patterned pink, her rosy nipples so enticing. Her sex was wet and pink where the brush had touched her, as for her buttocks and thighs, they were deep red and had never looked so good.

She nodded; for once she had nothing to say, as though the pain that was smarting on her pretty little backside had robbed her of the power of speech. I watched as she covered herself up, wrapping a red robe tightly around her body, looking quite chaste compared to the way she normally flaunted herself in front of me.

I went downstairs for another drop of scotch and left her standing awkwardly in her room, her eyes lowered and her face quite pale. The drink tasted good. I savoured every drop as I waited for her to come downstairs, knowing that she would have found the experience thoroughly disorientating. I wondered whether it had been the first time she'd even been chastised, certainly there had been none of the shock and horror that I would have expected.

'Paul . . .' I turned and saw that she was standing in the doorway, her dark soulful eyes looking at me nervously.

'Back to say you're sorry?' I asked her sternly.

'Sorry? But you're the one that punished me,' she whispered softly.

'Will it be the last time?'

'It stings,' she complained, neatly avoiding a reply to my question.

'Show me,' I demanded, setting my tumbler of scotch down on the counter and advancing towards her.

'But . . . but I haven't got anything on under this robe,' she told me breathlessly, her face colouring slightly.

'It's a pity you weren't so modest earlier, isn't it? Now, show me.'

'No, I won't show you,' she told me defiantly, her lips twisting into a smile. Her eyes were burning again, with an intense glow of excitement.

I strode across the room and grabbed her by the arm, pulling her towards the armchair. She struggled but her heart wasn't in it. Her squeals and complaints were empty and passionless. I positioned her beside the armchair and lifted the back of her robe, exposing her beautiful backside which was tanned a deep pink that contrasted with the white skin of her thighs. I could still make out my handprints on her flesh, but stronger than that was the array of oval marks that the hairbrush had imprinted. I stroked her buttocks and she winced, her punished flesh was warm to my touch.

'It's a shame that one session hasn't been enough,' I told her, shaking my head sadly.

'What do you mean, Paul?' she asked, her eyes brimming with tears.

'I mean that your wilful behaviour hasn't changed.'

'You can't mean . . .'

I knelt down and slipped her dainty slipper from her left foot and then straightened up. She gave a wide-eyed look of horror when I flexed the rubber sole, testing its mettle before deciding it was a good enough paddle for her posterior.

'Ten strokes of this,' I explained, 'and any nonsense and you'll get extra.'

She bit her lip and nodded, then, without prompting, she bent over the thick padded arm of the chair. Her position was perfect, backside nice and round, pink and inviting, her thighs very straight, her breasts rubbing softly against the seat of the chair. I raised the slipper high and brought it down swiftly, retribution laid against her pert young buttocks. She bit her lip and tried hard not to cry out as the first smack burned on her behind. I touched her, feeling the heat of impact with the tips of my fingers. The second and third strokes were on the same buttock, spreading that heat evenly. For the fourth stroke I switched target and when it landed heavily on her right bottom cheek she let out a howl that goaded me on for strokes five and six.

'How many have you had?' I asked, pausing for a second, wanting to keep the suspense and raise the tension further.

'Seven, Paul,' she whispered miserably.

'You'll get extra for that lie,' I whispered.

I cut off her complaint with a hard stroke of the slipper, aimed between her thighs. She cried out, but this time I noted the sigh of pleasure mixed in with the pain. Again, another stroke that brushed the underside of her thighs and touched her sex. It was happening again, she was stealing pleasure from her punishment. She was pulling herself down and sticking her bottom out, forcing herself into the stroke, accepting it eagerly. She shuddered as I dealt the last hard stroke between her buttocks, a sharp stinging lick from her slipper.

'Stay there,' I warned her.

I waited for a while, relishing the view of her punished backside, of her twin globes blazing red and pink. I wondered whether she was getting off on being exposed, after all there was no doubt about her exhibitionist inclinations, that was what had got her into trouble in the first place.

'Did you enjoy that?' I asked casually.

There was a long pause before she answered. 'Sort of . . .' she admitted hesitantly.

'Do you want more?'

'No!' she cried at once, without hesitation at all.

I nodded to myself. She found pleasure in her chastisement alright, but it was punishment all the same: painful, humiliating and to be avoided at all costs.

'Stand up and face me,' I instructed. 'You can forget about covering yourself up too,' I added.

Her eyes were lowered, and I was pleased to see that her face was as red with shame as her bottom was red with punishment. Her breasts were ripe and attractive, her hard nipples pointing out enticingly. I noted that her skin was flushed pink, with that radiant afterglow of orgasm.

Without warning I raised the slipper and brought it down sharply on her right breast. She squealed with shock, but the red imprint on her flesh made her nipples stand out even more. The left breast got the same sharp treatment, a spanking with the slipper that made her cry out.

'You can go and get dressed now,' I told her at last, satisfied that her punishment was complete.

'First this,' she said softly. She knelt down and crawled forward and touched the outline of my cock, impressed on my trousers. In seconds she had loosened my clothes and released my aching cock.

'You are such a naughty girl,' I told her tenderly, sighing as she stroked my hardness with her slender fingers.

'You can always punish me . . .' she whispered, and then closed her luscious red lips around my cock.

It was heaven, admiring her punished backside while she mouthed and sucked my cock. She knew what she was doing and I had never felt so much pleasure. She teased and caressed until I thought I would be the one screaming. And then I felt myself explode, filling her lovely mouth with wave upon wave of thick creamy come.

'You'd better clear up,' I told her later, kissing her mouth and stroking her hair.

'Sure,' she agreed lazily, 'Jim will be home soon. Let this be our secret, our little secret.'

I nodded. That was what it was exactly, our little secret. The last thing that I wanted was for my son to find out what I had been doing with his girlfriend.

Glory, Glory

As weekends go it promised to be a tricky one for Gloria and Ricky. More so for Ricky as he knew that Gloria's parents didn't like him. No, that wasn't really strong enough to describe what they felt, it was a feeling more akin to total hatred. Ricky had no illusions about what they thought; he'd been listening in on the extension when Gloria's dad had described him as a short-haired lay-about, and then added, as a polite afterthought, that he was a piece of shite that Gloria would be better off without. At the time Ricky had almost pissed himself laughing. Being hated by your girlfriend's parents was a matter of pride, and he'd been boasting about it on campus for days afterwards.

The problem was that Mr and Mrs Topbridge had sent their delightful daughter, Gloria, to university to get herself an education. More than that, they had some quaint ideas straight out of the Stone Age; for example they imagined that a university education would prepare their daughter to live a full and worthwhile Christian life. You know: good works, daily prayer, abstinence in all things (except prayer of course), and complete chastity. It amazed Ricky no end that the nineteenth century was still extant in deepest Cumbria.

Gloria was the sweetest daughter any couple could have. She lived by all her parents' stricture bar one – thou shalt not lie. It was an easy arrangement. Every night she made a point of making a reassuring phone call home then, as soon as the phone was down, she'd clamp her lips around Ricky's eager prick. He used to say that it was to wipe away the taste of the lies. She'd just tell him to shut up and enjoy it.

Things had been going great, until they paid a surprise visit one day. Ricky had to pretend to be a visitor to Gloria's flat, the flat she shared with Lucinda, who just happened to be away on a field trip that day. And Ricky, being a bit of a smartarse, had engaged Mr Topbridge (no first names, naturally), in conversation on their favourite subject – religion. It was the nearest Ricky had come to being beaten up in a long time. He hadn't realised just how *robust* Mr Topbridge's religion was. The last straw for them was finding out that Ricky was a mature student, a 25-year old who had been out of work for two years before returning to study.

After that it had been beseeching phone calls and dark threats in an effort to get Gloria to ditch the undesirable. And Gloria, being a stubborn sort of young lady, was determined not to give in to any sort of blackmail, particularly emotional blackmail with financial penalties attached. It was then that she had conceived of the idea of attempting a reconciliation. She made Ricky buy some underwear, some shoes and a sense of compromise (not necessarily in that order). Before he had a chance to complain she bought the train tickets, packed the bags and put the cat out.

'Remember,' she cautioned him, as the train pulled into a dismal-looking station (the weather deciding to match Ricky's mood), 'be polite, and for God's sake keep off religion.'

'And you can stop fucking blaspheming,' he mumbled, stepping out onto the platform as if it were a gangplank he was going to have to walk.

'And no taking the piss,' she added, smiling brightly as she saw her mother rushing towards her, arms outstretched and a happy smile making her look almost human.

'Glory, you look wonderful,' she enthused, giving Gloria a bone-crunching hug.

'Hello, Mrs Topbridge,' Ricky said, forcing a smile.

'Hello, Richard, how are you?' she asked, shaking his hand with all the passion of a bank manager meeting a bankrupt.

'Fine thank you very much.' He smiled, picking up the cases as the two women linked arms and headed towards the exit. He followed glumly, struggling with the cases, and trying to figure out if Gloria had packed the kitchen sink or the fridge.

The dull blue estate car was waiting in the car park, and under the grey cloud it looked suspiciously like a hearse to Ricky. Mr Topbridge was there, both faces at the ready: the happy smile for his daughter and the aggressive sneer for his daughter's lover.

'And how are you, Mr Topbridge?' Ricky asked politely, stowing the cases in the back of the car.

'Can't complain,' Mr Topbridge complained, his ruddy features clamped tightly, eyes glaring with dark suspicion.

Ricky rode back to the house in silence, blocked out of the conversation completely, while Gloria gossiped non-stop, complete with detailed reports on her friend Lucinda, who had mysteriously reappeared after her parents had left the flat. He listened to her go on and on, marvelling at her inventiveness and at her skill in telling a complete pack of lies. There was never any hesitation in her voice, not even any pauses for breath. It made him nervous in a way. Somewhere deep in the back of his mind suspicions were aroused. If she could lie so well to her parents, what was to say she wasn't doing the same to him?

The house was filled with the smell of food. It was going to be a full family dinner; the entire Topbridge clan had been assembled. Gloria's little sister, Pauline, was introduced; a perfect looking seventeen-year old that set Ricky's prick twitching appreciatively. And their favourite cousin, Christine, a grim looking twenty-year old with a fantastic chest that sort of wobbled precariously when Ricky shook her hand. He shook her hand twice in fact, once when they were introduced, and then ten minutes later when he introduced himself again. Gloria thought it was funny; she giggled like a silly schoolgirl, but the rest of the family took a rather dim view of it.

'Behave,' Gloria had hissed later, forgetting that she had been the only one laughing. Ricky had been too busy studying the perturbation patterns of Christine's beautiful tits.

The only one of the family missing had been Tom, the eldest son, the future head of the family and a paragon of virtue by all accounts. 'I can't wait to meet him,' Ricky confided to Mrs Topbridge, and his smile had been so sincere that for a moment she had forgotten herself and smiled back.

'He's a good lad,' Mr Topbridge announced, reminding his wife that she was a Topbridge and that Ricky wasn't and shouldn't be treated like one. 'Not like some I can say,' he added pointedly.

'Come on, daddy,' Gloria chided softly, joining her parents and Ricky in the kitchen. 'Richard's a good lad too. He's done ever so well in his exams, haven't you Ricky.'

'What are you studying?' Mr Topbridge asked, his thick eyebrows forming a posse at the bridge of his nose.

'English Lit,' Ricky mumbled, noting that the posse looked more like a lynch mob now.

'Typical,' Mr Topbridge said, looking first at his daughter and then at the sad specimen he saw before him. 'Why aren't you studying a real subject? Civil engineering for example, now there's a man's subject for you.'

'Is Tom a civil engineer by any chance?'

'That's right, and doing bloody well at it. Pardon my language,' he remembered to add, turning to his wife who nodded her head sagely.

'But literature's important too, daddy,' Gloria continued, fighting a losing battle against her father's open hostility.

'English literature? It's all girls in miniskirts and boys smoking them reefers,' Mr Topbridge announced. And then, because the subject was obviously too highly charged for him to take any longer, he turned and marched out of the kitchen, his wife following in his wake.

'It's not all girls in miniskirts,' Ricky complained, pulling Gloria towards him.

'No, it's not is it, some of the boys have got them on too,' she giggled. He gave her a quick kiss on the mouth but she pulled away, her eyes fixed on the kitchen door in case Mr and Mrs Enlightenment returned.

Ricky reached down. She was wearing her longest, loosest skirt, the folds of material obscuring completely the shape of her deliciously long thighs and the outline of a backside he used to love kissing. His hand caught the hem and lifted it up, then he slid a palm up the smoothest skin of her thigh and then round to feel the shape of her backside.

'It's the girls with the long skirts I love the most,' he told her hotly, lifting the skirt high so that he could stare greedily at her bare arse-cheeks. It had been part of the deal, the only way she had of persuading him to stay the weekend. She had to be pure and chaste on the face of it, all long skirts and loose tops, but underneath she had to be naked. No knickers, no bra. It gave him a permanent hard-on, knowing she was naked under her skirt; that she was parading herself for him right in front of her smug hypocritical parents.

'Stop that,' she whispered, her words turning into a sigh as his fingers stroked her pussy lips from behind.

'Are you wet?' he teased her, slipping a finger into her pussy and rubbing in and out.

'Don't . . . Don't . . .' she sighed, pressing her backside up, opening herself to his probing finger while begging him to stop.

'Tom's just called,' Pauline cried, stomping into the kitchen to find her sister at the table and Ricky standing by the sink and sucking his fingers thoughtfully.

'What is it?' Gloria asked, crossing her legs tightly and looking at Ricky with an intense and faraway look in her eye.

'He won't be able to make it until late tonight,' Pauline reported, utterly crestfallen by the bad news.

'Shame,' was all Ricky could say.

The meal had been pretty much a major disaster. Gloria had warned Ricky not to talk about sex, religion or politics. So, as soon as grace was said (to which Ricky could do nothing but gawk like a tourist doing the lost tribes of the Amazon), the discussion went straight to politics, religion and sex. And, despite Gloria's well aimed kicks under the table, Ricky couldn't help but talk about religious flagellation, the antics of medieval monks and nuns, contraception and the sexual heresies of the Anabaptists. Ricky liked to impress people with the breadth of his knowledge, but somehow it didn't work with the Topbridge family. By the end of the evening it seemed that even Gloria was going to join in with the tarring and feathering.

The discussion was drawn to sudden stop by Mr Topbridge declaring it was time for bed, it was gone ten o'clock after all. If they expected any protests from Ricky then they were sadly mistaken, and for the first time ever he was found to be in perfect agreement with Mr Topbridge.

'You've got Tom's old room,' Mrs Topbridge explained, showing him into a small bedroom at the top of the stairs. The walls were still lined with posters of bridges, motorways and other feats of civil engineering.

'He was always a bright lad,' Mr Topbridge explained proudly, standing at the door to make sure that Ricky didn't wander.

'Yes, I can see that,' Ricky agreed readily. 'Look, that's a picture of the M25, he didn't work on that did he?'

The door was slammed shut and Ricky found himself alone at last, just him and the M25 to share the room with. He listened at the door and heard the growling undertone of an unhappy Mr Topbridge bitching like a good 'un. The door was locked of course, from the outside, but Ricky hadn't expected anything else. They had a fixed notion of him as a randy little git, which just went to prove that even they couldn't be wrong all the time.

He waited a few more minutes and carefully peeled away the poster of the M25. It was there, just as Gloria said it would be, a small round hole about three inches in diameter. Originally there had been one larger room, but it had been partitioned with plasterboard, and then someone had cut the hole out of that.

'Glory, you there?' he whispered into the hole, unable to see anything in the darkness of the room next door.

'Shh, not so loud,' she whispered, so close to the hole that he saw her lips in the darkness and felt her breath on his face.

'What's this, an early example of civil engineering prowess?'

'Don't be like that, Tom's alright,' she said defensively.

'Sorry, but they were getting on my tits,' he grumbled.

'Well, how about getting on my tits?' she asked, shifting about.

Ricky's eyes lit up as he saw one of Gloria's lovely breasts pushed into the hole, her white flesh and red nipple poking through it. He was on hands and knees in a second, his mouth clamping feverishly on her nipple, sucking in the hard little bud and flaying it with his tongue. In a few moments she was sighing. He could just make out the soft whisper of her breath through the wall, her nipple was red and aroused and seemed to pulse as he played with it.

'Wait,' she whispered, pulling her breast away. Again there was a moment of shuffling clothing and then he saw that she was offering him a rear view of her pussy. She was in some strange contorted position up against the wall, but he didn't care. His fingers found her wet and warm, aching for his touch. He slipped one finger and then another inside her. There was no room for the soft stroking niceties, the wall blocked her off so that she was a pussy and nothing more. It was a strange kind of turn on, and he realised she was getting off on it as much as he was. His fingers were going in deep and hard, the two digits forming a prick that fucked her relentlessly, slurping in and out of her wetness with an urgent rhythm that she was forced to accommodate.

He felt her tensing, heard her stifled cries of pleasure and then she froze for a second before falling away. When he looked through the hole he saw a vague outline of her body lying flat on the bed, arms stretched out and head thrown back.

'How was it for you darling?' he whispered sarcastically, sucking her lovely juices from his fingers.

'I told you we'd have fun,' she whispered, sitting up close to the hole again. She puckered her lips through the hole and he kissed her, his tongue finding hers.

'You sure you and your brother just used to talk through this thing?' he asked suspiciously.

'Don't be horrible,' she said, but in the darkness he couldn't see her expression. 'Quick, someone's coming . . .'

'Well it ain't me,' he complained, covering the hole

with the poster once more. His prick was aching for release, and he couldn't wait to try to fuck her through the hole, the weirdest kind of fuck he'd ever imagined. He listened intently but all he could here were muffled voices. Someone tried the handle of his door and he was in bed so quick he wondered how he'd got there in the dark.

'Glory . . . You there?' he whispered through the hole after a few minutes of welcome silence.

'Shh . . .' he heard, and felt the breath hot on his face again.

'Now, it's my turn,' he decided greedily, pressing himself flat against the wall and poking his raging prick through the hole.

He waited for a moment and then felt Gloria's lips caress the very tip of his cock. It was heaven; her soft fluttering lips explored him very slowly, very tentatively, tracing the full length of the thickly veined shaft. Her touch was soft and fleeting, her fingers tantalising. He sighed when her mouth closed around the full purple dome, her tongue swirling maddeningly around the tip and then the underside.

She sucked him perfectly, building him up to fever pitch and then slowing the pace, keeping him on the edge for ages, stringing out the pleasure so that he was begging her to let him come in her mouth. Her tongue was electric, gliding up and down his tool when she wanted to make him buckle and cry out with lust. And then, like an expert fellatrice, she pulled back the velvet skin of his cock and emptied him on her waiting tongue. He spurted out endless wads of thick cream, pumping it into her hot little mouth so that she could swallow every drop.

Ricky lay back, his head spinning and heart thumping. Boy, he'd had some good blow jobs in the past, but never that good. Never even half that good. There were noises again on the landing, and for a while he slept, but when he awoke Gloria answered his call and she suckled him to climax again, with the same feverish skill that had him begging like a slave.

The next morning he was late down for breakfast. His eyes were red rimmed and black bagged, ready for the dustmen to cart away. Gloria was packing away the breakfast dishes when he ambled into the kitchen.

'That was fantastic,' he told her, seizing the chance of being alone to give her a quick kiss and to grope her naked breasts under her sack-cloth T-shirt.

'About last night . . .' Gloria began to say apologetically.

'It was brilliant, we'll have to put a hole in the wall back home.'

'I didn't realise they were going to move me,' Gloria finished, turning to face the kitchen door.

'Move you?' Ricky asked, turning to the door at the same instant.

'Yes, have you met my brother Tom? He had my room last night.'

'Hi Ricky,' Tom smiled in greeting. 'We haven't met properly, but I feel like we're old friends already.'

Family Fortune

The window was open and the slight breeze parted the net curtains, letting the unfiltered light flood through the room. Stephie stood at the window, biting back the tears, her mood in stark contrast to the pureness of the summer day. Outside the sunlight sparkled on the silver blue of the pool, beams of light reflected back from the unbroken surface, dancing with the light ripples from the breeze. Beyond the pool were the grounds. Beautifully arranged gardens, fountains, gravel paths through the shrubbery and then, right at the end, the heavy border of trees that marked the high walls that enclosed the estate.

In every way it was the ideal country mansion, at its very best in the still afternoon light of a perfect summer's day. So fine, and yet at its heart something rotten. Stephie turned away, dazzled by the light that flashed so vividly from the pool. She turned and found that her best friend, Ariana, was standing in the doorway, watching her closely.

'Don't look so unhappy,' Ariana said softly, her own voice tinged with unhappiness. She wore a very simple white cotton dress and in the sharp light it was clear that she was naked underneath. Her nipples were dark disks against the thin cotton and the join of her thighs was marked by a dark crease.

'Why shouldn't I look unhappy?' Stephie demanded, her voice quivering with hurt. Her dark eyes flashed angrily and then she felt the tears well up, ready to cascade down her pretty face.

'Is it so bad?' Ariana asked, taking a step into the room. 'Is Timothy so repulsive?'

Stephie looked at her friend uncomprehendingly, as though seeing for the first time a new side of her character revealed; a side that was dark and nasty. The two women had grown up together, had been closer than sisters, but now Stephie felt as though they were strangers.

'He's your husband,' she cried. 'Don't you think it wrong that he wants to make love to me? Do you really see nothing wrong in that?'

Ariana turned away for a moment. 'Don't make it sound so awful,' she whispered. 'He's an excellent lover, you'll enjoy it, you both will.'

Stephie ran across the room and threw herself on the bed, sobbing her heart out. She had never wanted Ariana to marry Timothy, no matter how long his family tree or no matter how big his fortune. There was something corrupting about him, as though he were consciously trying to live up to the image of a decadent aristocrat. His latest idea, bedding wife and friend at the same time, was one of a long line of such escapades.

There had been the time when Stephie and Ariana had walked in on him and the gardener, a tall muscular Spaniard. Timothy had merely smiled and invited them to join in, though as his prick was deep between the Spaniard's backside it wasn't exactly clear what he had wanted them to do. Stephie and Ariana had backed away, red faced and embarrassed, but later that evening Timothy had regaled them with the story of his seduction. Stephie could still see the smile on his face as he explained that the Spaniard could suck cock better than any woman could, though he added that he had no objection to Stephie trying to better him.

It would not have been so bad if he were more discreet, but he seemed to get an extra kick out of flaunting his sexuality as much as possible. At one family party he had managed to bed one of his own cousins, a shy young lady who fell for his charming manner and classical good looks. He had made love to her in the master bedroom, with the window open to the balcony, so that the sighs and moans of her orgasm had floated across the lawn like an early morning mist. Poor Ariana had to pretend that nothing was happening, and the pitying looks she got from her family and friends were like an elixir for him.

'Please don't cry,' Ariana whispered helplessly, putting her hand to Stephie's shoulder. She leaned over and kissed the shoulder, her lips cool and soft against Stephie's skin.

'Go away, leave me alone,' Stephie cried, burying her head in her pillow, wanting to blank out everything. She felt horror, disgust, shame and most of all pity. She felt so sorry for Ariana, and yet there seemed to be nothing she could do. Ariana left the room, her face a picture of defeat.

Stephie's tears carried her to a dark dreamless sleep, through the humidity of the afternoon and into the coolness of the evening that settled slowly over the great house. When she awoke, hours later, it was as if the ugliness that had spoiled the perfection of the summer's day had not happened. The house was still, at rest after basking in the heat, the silence heavy and melancholy.

Stephie rose and bathed quickly, the coolness of the shower refreshing her spirit somewhat. She tried not to think of Timothy and Ariana, instead she wandered through the house alone, enjoying the building that had yet to be served up to the public. She loved the house. It was the only thing that tempted her to return time and again to visit her friend and her errant husband. She walked the corridors like a thief, lost in silent admiration of the treasures it contained. So many rooms to explore, so many surprises to discover. Timothy's family had made their money in the new world, alert to the possibilities of trade, while most of the other great families of the age had slumbered through the seventeenth century. It alone explained the fact that the family had been able to keep the house private, and to prosper when others had been forced to seek alliance with the rising class of merchants and bankers.

'You wouldn't have liked great uncle,' Timothy commented, startling Stephie who had been gazing at one of the immense family portraits that glared down from the wall of one of the many chambers in that wing of the house.

'Wouldn't I?' she asked sullenly, looking at him sharply.

'No, he didn't like wilful like girls like you. He'd have had you strapped by one of his slaves before having you for himself,' he smiled, the idea obviously appealing to him too. 'And if you were still stubborn he would have handed you over to the slave to give you a smidgen of the new-world experience.'

'That isn't even funny,' Stephie said. She turned and walked across the chamber, certain that he would follow.

'I don't think it was meant to be funny, Stephanie, darling. He was a humourless old bastard really, no sense of humour at all. It's said that once one of the tenants on the estate had complained that the master had taken the virginity of his, the servant's, daughter. In actual fact the master had taken the man's daughter, mother and grandmother, and no doubt he would have taken his daughter's daughter in turn if he'd lived long enough.'

'Is that why you want to have sex with me and Ariana, because we're more like sisters than friends?'

Timothy laughed. 'I see, you think I'm trying to emulate the old bugger. Well, that's an idea isn't it. Only thing is that the old boy didn't bother to marry the tenant's daughter to have her. They did things with greater style in the old days.'

'I suppose you think that's funny,' Stephie sniffed, leading the way down the central staircase to the main dining hall.

'Yes, I do actually,' he said with a smile. 'Now, have you and darling Ari worked anything out yet?'

'No, not at all,' Stephie replied bluntly.

'How tedious this all is,' he mumbled under his breath, loud enough for Stephie to hear although she made no comment.

The dining hall was an oak panelled delight that would have pulled in the American tourists by the coach load: high ceiling, intricate workmanship, coats of arms wherever you looked. It was the perfect setting for a medieval banquet, and Stephie had heard that recreating a bawdy medieval orgy was high on Timothy's wish list. He was a man who took his desires seriously. He liked to expound on the things he wanted to do, almost as much as he expounded on the things he had already done. Sometimes he'd pause in the middle of an episode to glance at Stephie, who always listened to his adulterous goings on in stony silence. Ariana on the other hand had long since accustomed herself, she even enjoyed adding the odd detail to the story, just so that everyone knew she wasn't the martyred wife but a willing participant in all his sexual adventures. It was an act, and everyone knew it was an act except Ariana herself.

Dinner passed peacefully. Conversation was light and inconsequential, and at the close of the meal Ariana was glowing, her face lit up by the simple happiness of it all. Timothy had been a charming host, Stephie a grateful guest and Ariana herself so happy to have the two people she loved the most acting with pleasant civility to each other. She could ask for nothing more.

Stephie was reading a book, her window open to the welcome breeze of the night, when she heard a gentle knock on the door. She froze. For a second she feared it was Timothy but then she heard Ariana's reassuring voice whispered from behind the door.

'I just wanted to talk,' Ariana said apologetically.

'Where's Timothy?' Stephie asked suspiciously.

'Preparing for a trip down to the City,' Ariana assured her, walking across the room to sit on the very edge of the bed. She was still wearing the same simple white dress that she had on earlier; cool and loose, it did nothing to conceal the gentle curves of her body, from the fullness of her breasts to the swell of her backside.

'What do you want to talk about?'

'Why can't you and Timothy always be like you were tonight? Why can't you just be friends?'

Stephie sighed. 'Because he wants to be more than friends. Come on Ariana, you were there when he asked, no he demanded, I suck his cock. Didn't that mean anything to you?'

'But there's nothing wrong with it,' Ariana insisted. 'Why have you turned into such a prude all of a sudden? You never used to be like this. Have you really forgotten what we used to do?'

'No, I haven't forgotten,' Stephie said softly, lowering her eyes. 'But that was different, that was ...' she searched for the word but couldn't find it. 'That was different,' she repeated firmly.

'That was worse,' Ariana smiled. She leaned across the bed and took the book from Stephie's hands. The friends looked at each other for a second, melting into each others' eyes. Stephie made the first move, edging forward, parting her lips for the kiss that she longed for. They kissed long and hard, mouths duelling, breath shared, tongues exploring. They parted and looked at each other again. Their faces were flushed red, their eyes sparkled with desire.

Stephie reached out and stroked Ariana's breasts over the thin covering of virginal white cotton. The nipples soon stood hard and erect, pressing against the softness

90

of the cotton, the colour dark against the whiteness. They kissed again, fingers exploring softly, flitting touches against breast and thigh and face.

'Make love with me,' Ariana breathed, an aching whisper escaping from her red lips.

In a moment Stephie was naked and wrapped in Ariana's arms, her mouth sucking furiously at Ariana's nipples, still clothed in thin white cotton. Her own nakedness was caressed by the butterfly touch of the night-time breeze. She opened her thighs and guided Ariana's fingers to the heat of her sex. She was wet, the nectar slick between her thighs. Ariana's touch was sure, a knowing caress that teased her friend's clitoris exquisitely.

Stephie responded instinctively, opening herself, letting herself go to the waves of pleasure that pulsed from her hot sex. Her nipples throbbed while they were suckled, teased with teeth and tongue until Stephie could hold back her cries no longer. She arched her back, threw her head back and felt the shuddering ecstasy of orgasm.

'Well, well, this is a nice little gathering, isn't it?'

Stephie froze, Timothy's voice draining the pleasure away from her. She opened her eyes and saw him standing before her, one hand on Ariana's shoulder, a possessive gesture that was not lost on either woman.

'I knew you two were close,' he continued, a sick smile stretching the features of his face to make him look hideous.

'How long were you watching?' Ariana asked softly.

'Long enough. My, Stephie darling, what a passionate young filly you are. And there was I thinking you were a frigid little bitch. Or is it that you're frigid with men but a real nympho with the gals?'

'You wouldn't understand,' Stephie spat angrily, sitting up on the bed but making no attempt to hide her nakedness.

'Oh but I would. You've taken my wife from me. This is adultery in the grand manner, isn't it. Do you know, I can just see the headlines now, think of the scandal.'

'You wouldn't,' Ariana whispered, thoroughly appalled by the idea.

He smiled. 'Oh but I would, dearest. It would make such a change to see your name dragged through the mud as well as mine.'

'You can't do this to us,' Stephie cried, her eyes wide with alarm.

'Don't tempt me,' he murmured darkly.

'Please, Timothy,' his wife begged, her eyes filling with tears.

'What do you want?' Stephie demanded, looking at him sharply.

'So businesslike,' he complained. 'You know what I want, you turned me down earlier today.'

'How do I know that this will be the end of it?'

'You won't, Stephie, darling. But don't worry, you have my word as a pervert and a lecher that I just want to fill that lovely little mouth of yours with come, just this once. Is that too much to ask for?'

'Please, Stephie,' Ariana pleaded, holding Stephie's hands tightly.

'I have no choice,' Stephie agreed coldly, flashing Timothy a look of pure hatred.

'Good. Before we begin, however, my darling wife has to be punished.' He smiled to her wickedly. 'Can't have you throwing yourself into bed with every close female friend that visits, can we now?'

'But . . . Please Tim . . .'

There was no deflecting him. Reluctantly Ariana lifted her skirt to reveal her naked backside, her full round buttocks displayed completely, the bulge of her pussy displayed to perfection when she bent over.

He unthreaded his belt slowly, flexed it once and then brought it down hard on her pert little bottom. She squealed, forced her mouth shut and suffered the half-dozen strokes in silence. By the end of it the top of her thighs and her arse cheeks were flaming, her skin tanned a deep red where the leather belt had touched her so forcefully. She started to get up but he pushed her down and forced two fingers into her pussy. She groaned, sighed, her body collapsing into a heap as he frigged her to climax with a few quick strokes.

'She loves the belt, though not as much as the riding crop,' he commented cruelly to Stephie, revelling in the shame on his wife's face. 'You can go now,' he ordered, and silently Ariana walked away, deliberately avoiding her friend's eyes.

'Did you have to beat her?' Stephie asked after Ariana had left.

Timothy laughed. 'You know she loves it, Steph. Why shouldn't she get some pleasure tonight as well?'

'You are just so devious,' she said, lying back on the bed, her pussy tingling with excitement. The way he beat Ariana had excited all three of them, and now she couldn't wait to get his long hard prick between her thighs.

'Years of breeding, darling,' he said, stripping off quickly. 'Did I ever tell you about my ancestor that liked to . . .'

'Enough of that,' she interrupted impatiently. 'I've been waiting for your cock all day, I can't wait any longer. Fuck me nice and dirty,' she sighed. 'Nice and dirty.'

Beauty and the Beast

Belle lived on the edge of the village, in a tumbledown house with her father and two sisters. It was a poor house in a poor village and every evening, when the sun fell behind the distant mountains, the house was shrouded in the dark cold shadow cast by the castle high on the mountain peak to the south.

Once, when Belle was a child and her mother still lived, she had asked her who inhabited the castle. The woman had looked at Belle with tired eyes and whispered, 'The Beast lives there. Alone with the base desires that no man should have. Beware my darling, always fear the Beast.' Belle had shuddered, and though her mother had long since passed away the words had remained fresh in her mind, a powerful and frightening warning.

Belle's father was a good man but weak, and the men of the village would take him for a fool. Often they would invite him to the tavern and once there make him drink ale until he was roaring drunk. And when he was drunk he forgot all about his daughters, he forgot about their poverty, about their humble existence in the shadow of the mountains. When he was drunk he was a man again, a hero, a lord, ready to prove his worth to all the world.

On such occasions the innkeeper would send a boy round to Belle's house, summoning her to retrieve her father. It always filled Belle with such shame to see him so drunk, his voice raised in imaginary triumph to the raucous and cruel laughter of the men from the village. And then they would tease her too, pulling up her skirts to expose her long shapely thighs, pinching her nipples shamelessly, rubbing themselves against her body as she struggled with her father. They teased her too because she was still a child at the age of eighteen; her body still chaste and untouched by any man. The teasing made her so ashamed, her pretty little face would flame red and her clear blue eyes would fill with tears.

One evening, when the summer had already given way to autumn, the young innkeeper's son came knocking on the door of the small cottage. Belle rushed to the door, her long blonde hair flowing like gold about her pretty shoulders.

'Belle, Belle,' the young man said breathlessly, looking at her with sadness in his sharp brown eyes.

'What is it Pierre? Is it father?' Belle asked, her heart sinking at the thought that she would have to rescue him once more from the circle of sneering men in the inn.

'Yes, Belle,' Pierre said softly, and something in his manner made Belle fear the worse.

'What's happened? What is it Pierre?' she asked urgently.

'It's the hunters from the village, they were just joking with him Belle but he took it so seriously . . .'

'Took what seriously?'

'You know what he's like when he's had his fill of ale. He's a lion, a champion. We couldn't stop him Belle . . .'

'Please, Pierre,' Belle implored him, her blue eyes open wide with mounting fear. 'Tell me what has happened.'

'He's gone to the castle, Belle, to kill the Beast.'

Belle fell backwards, fainting with fear and horror. Pierre reached forward and took her by the waist. He held her close, his hot breath on her fair skin. She opened her eyes and gazed into his, searching for the sign that Pierre would help her.

'We must stop him,' she whispered, holding onto his strong muscular arms for support.

'No, Belle,' Pierre said softly. He kissed her gently, his lips pressing hers, his hands brushing her breasts like whispers. 'Your father has taken the fastest steed in the village. All is lost, the Beast will have devoured him already. Forget him, Belle, forget him completely.'

Belle's eyes fluttered, the feel of Pierre's fingers playing softly with her nipples took her breath away. She felt a fire igniting in her belly, making her feel hot and languid. But the delicious feeling could not mask out the full horror of the situation. With an effort she pushed Pierre away, kissing him softly on the lips as she did so, as if the desire that he had awakened in her was fighting back against the urge to save her father.

'What can you do, Belle?' Pierre demanded angrily, releasing her from his manly grasp.

'I can go to him, save him. Perhaps he has fallen, perhaps he has become lost in the great forest, perhaps . . .'

'Stop it, Belle,' Pierre snapped irritably. 'Your father was a drunkard, a good-for-nothing and it is better that he's gone.'

'No!' Belle sprang forward furiously, the anger pulsing in her veins. She pushed Pierre away forcibly and ran past him to the horse tethered at the front gate. In a moment she was riding away, through the darkness and towards the forest, Pierre's angry shouts lost in the wind rushing through her hair.

Belle rode hard and fast, not wanting to stop, not wanting to think of all that Pierre had said. The galloping of hooves, the feel of the strong animal between her thighs, the exhilarating feel of the night air rushing past, soothed her anger. In a while she was riding through the forest, the darkness closing in on her; the thick trees crowding round her as she rode.

A path through the forest seemed to open up and

when she looked back it was gone. It was as if the forest were opening itself for her, sucking her into the darkness that led to the castle. The canopy of trees obscured the moon and the stars, and when at last Belle was at the castle gate she suddenly felt nervous, realising that she had no way back, no way to navigate through the darkness.

Belle dismounted. She held the reins tightly and pulled the horse towards the gate, glad to have the hot sweating animal beside her, its breath misting in the cold night air. The drawbridge fell suddenly, the rattling chains and booming wooden track frightening the horse. It reared up, knocking Belle to the ground then bolted away into the forest that swallowed it up, leaving her alone and afraid.

She walked hesitantly across the drawbridge, following the candlelight that flicked before her, floating like magic on the air. She walked through long corridors of stone, the light leading the way, cutting a path through the darkness just as the forest had opened for her. She was led into a great dining hall, the table set for two, a flickering candle throwing a soft orange light.

'Hello? Is anyone there?' Belle asked, her sweet voice carrying like music into the thick black darkness.

'You have come,' a voice boomed from the darkness. It was a deep voice, rich and powerful.

'I've come for my father, is he here?' Belle asked, spinning round slowly, searching for the source of the great voice. It had affected her strangely, making her nipples pulse as they had done under Pierre's fingers.

'Yes child,' the voice boomed, 'he is here. Locked in a dungeon where the light never shines.'

'Please sir, he meant no harm,' Belle pleaded. Her eyes filled with tears.

'Nonsense!' the mighty voice cried angrily, the echoes bouncing from wall to wall until it faded to silence.

'Please sir, let him go. He is a good man, foolish at

97

times but good at heart. Please sir, I have two sisters and without him they are lost.'

'I care nothing about your sisters! I care nothing for him. He came here to destroy me, do you wish that I allow him that pleasure?'

'No, sir, no. You are kind, I can feel it in your voice. Please spare him, great sir, take me in his place.'

There was a pause and Belle breathed hard, her heart pounding while she waited for the Beast to decide. She had not lied, there was indeed something in his voice; some undercurrent that she hardly understood but which she was certain carried with it the seed of good.

'There is a steed that awaits him at the gate. It is your choice, child. I give you the key to his cell, you may decide which of you is to stay.'

From the darkness the key floated forth, hanging in the air before Belle's disbelieving eyes. She reached out tentatively, sure the ghostly key was an image borne of her fear. She touched it and it was cold and real; a solid iron key that weighed heavy in her hand. The light floated before her again, ready to lead her to the dreaded dungeon under the castle.

'Thank you good sir,' she cried happily, her great joy filling her with optimism. She ran quickly, her bare feet padding on the stone floor of the castle. The dungeon was deep underground and Belle let herself be guided by the strange light. The dark caverns echoed with the cries of lost souls wailing in the night, evil spirits cackling and baying for blood. Belle ignored everything, carried along by her certainty that the Beast was good at heart just as her father was.

'Belle, is that you?' a tired voice asked, peering from the jet black cell at the beauty cast in gold by the flickering light.

'Yes, father,' she sighed, pushing the key into the rusty old lock and turning it with all her might.

'No, Belle, you must leave. You must leave.'

The door creaked open and the old man fell forward, clasping his beloved daughter in his tired old arms. 'No father, you must leave now. There is a mount waiting for you, to carry you through the forest back to my poor sisters.'

'But the Beast?'

'I will stay in your place father. Now, you must leave before he changes his mind.'

'But he is a Beast. You are so innocent, child, you do not understand what cruel and base desires lurk inside his soul.'

'Surely they are stories to frighten children,' Belle said bravely, managing a half-smile to hide the fear deep in her heart.

'No, Belle,' the old man whispered. 'I have already experienced the evil in his heart.'

Belle cried out, putting her hand to her mouth and staring wide-eyed at her father. He had staggered out into the light and Belle saw that his hair had turned from jet black to snow white, and his tired eyes were full of the horrors of which he spoke.

'I must stay father,' she said weakly. 'I have promised the Beast and cannot break my word. Please father, leave now and forget that you ever had me as a daughter.'

The old man kissed Belle on the forehead, his eyes filled with tears and then he followed the light that was for him. In a moment he was gone and Belle was trembling, more alone than she had ever been in her life.

'You stayed,' the Beast said simply when Belle returned to the dining room.

'As I said I would,' Belle replied, holding her head up defiantly, willing herself not to be afraid of the thing that spoke from the shadows.

'You are foolish. More foolish than I ever imagined possible. Did you not see the fear in his eyes? Did you not comprehend the terror that he has suffered?'

'But there is something noble in you, sir. I can sense it. Am I not right, sir?'

The laughter filled the great room, reverberating and resounding until it filled Belle's ears with its harsh evil sound. She fell to the ground, covering her eyes as the thing emerged from the shadows.

'Do not speak of nobility to me!' the Beast roared. 'Look at me child! Am I noble? Am I?'

Belle looked up, her face as white as a sheet. The Beast towered above her, a foot taller than any man she had ever seen, its body swathed in bands of leather and thick animal hides, great thighs like an animal, arms bulging with hard muscle. Its face was obscured by a mask, but its eyes shone through two slits. Dark eyes that burned with a radiance that could have been good, evil or something beyond that.

'Please, sir . . .' Belle whimpered, turning away from the vision before her, half-man and half-animal.

It bounded forward, and with one swipe of its hand it had torn Belle's dress to shreds. She flinched and tried to crawl away but it held her fast. Her nakedness was before the Beast, her long thighs of alabaster, her round breasts with red-tipped nipples like ripe berries, a tight triangle of hair to obscure the fleshy pink between her thighs. She was afraid, but excited too. The Beast's hot breath caressed her nipples and kissed her lips with a whisper.

'Such purity . . . such purity . . .' the Beast whispered to himself, his voice lost in wonderment. 'Such purity needs to be defiled!'

The Beast seized her in his hairy arms and turned her over, letting her fall to the ground once more, her full round bottom sticking up in the air. He touched her vilely, parting her bottom cheeks, stroking her between the legs, rubbing his hands up and down her long thighs. Belle cried out, too afraid of him to enjoy the sensual feel of his body against hers.

'To be defiled!' the Beast repeated, his voice low and guttural.

He pulled Belle closer and kissed her on the neck. His mouth was hot and sensuous, his lips skated over her soft skin. He moved down and kissed her between the bottom, his tongue snaking gently into her tightly puckered rear hole. Belle struggled, but the feel of his hot wet tongue entering her from behind made her feel faint with a sudden passion.

Belle struggled, trying to fight the strange passions bubbling inside her. She pushed and kicked, her tiny fists nothing against the Beast's great body. This futile resistance inflamed the Beast's anger and he pulled away from her, his long sinewy tongue still tingling with the forbidden taste of her rear hole. He pressed her down with one heavy hand and then began to beat her mercilessly, spanking her naked bottom with slow deliberate strokes.

Belle screamed. She could feel the soft white skin of her tight round bottom flaring red. But her cries were to no avail; the Beast knew no mercy, and the chastisement continued until Belle's cries had become soft whispering sighs. Belle ceased squirming. The stinging fire on her red bottom cheeks was transformed into a delicious sensation pulsing through her body, making her nipples tingle with pleasure.

The Beast moved round, his hands seeking Belle's breasts and then pulling at the nipples, his claws squeezing tightly so that the pain danced through her. Belle felt lost, his strong arms were everywhere, touching, teasing, hurting, soothing. His tongue was now lapping at Belle's sex, the treasure that she had so jealously guarded from the louts in the village. She sighed, opening her thighs to his tongue which was alternately soft and smooth or hard and violent, going into her far deeper than any man could with any part of his body.

'And now to take you!' the Beast roared, licking his

lips like an animal about to devour its prey. 'I'll take you just as I took your father!'

Belle screamed. The Beast drew back and pulled the hides from its body. Her eyes were fixed on the monstrous organ that jutted from between its thighs. She wanted to scream again but held back, her voice lost in amazement. The Beast's stiff organ rose violently, many inches long, many inches round, the purple tip as long as her fingers.

'Please don't hurt me,' Belle whispered. She drew back instinctively, suddenly realising that her sex was aching, pouring forth a thickness that was white and creamy.

'Do you desire me, Belle?' he asked, his voice losing the cold harsh edge.

'Yes ... yes ...' Belle cried joyously, tasting the sweetness pouring from her sex, putting her fingers between her thighs and then sucking them clean.

'Do you desire the Beast? The thing that will take a woman and use her like whore? The thing that will mark you with its scent the way an animal will mark its mate? Do you desire the animal that is man and the man that is animal?'

'Yes! Yes!' Belle cried.

The Beast rose silently, its cry of triumph shaking the very foundations of the castle. It stood over Belle and marked her as its own, a pure silver liquid gushing from its hardness, spraying over Belle's nakedness, making her body shimmer and sparkle under the candlelight. Belle lay back, letting the hot liquid bathe her body, splashing onto her reddened nipples, onto her belly, into her sex, sighing with a secret pleasure as she did so. The Beast anointed her with the silver rain that jetted from his hard animal maleness, directing it from head to toe, to cover Belle in his essence.

Then Beast fell upon her, turned her over once more and pressed his hardness deep into Belle's aching sex.

Belle cried out, mewing like an animal, letting the pleasure pierce the shell of humanity. She was part beast too now, part animal and part woman. The stiff tool filled her, pressed the damp walls of her sex, going deep to the heart of her pulsing cunt.

'Harder! Harder!' she cried, the eruption building inside her as the Beast covered her body. She screamed as her body froze, her back arched and her reddened buttocks pressed hard against the mat of hair that covered the Beast's body. She had crossed over, she was part of him now. No longer Belle but the Beauty that Beast had desired.

Exchange

Edward had expected to find Mercedes curled up in front of the TV when he returned home early from work. The world of afternoon television seemed to be endlessly fascinating to her, a world peopled by bronzed Australians facing moral dilemmas which were tackled with a cup of tea and lots of hugs. There was nothing like it on French television and it had seemed to Edward that Australian soaps were the highlight of Mercedes' visit to England.

He slipped off his coat and stashed the briefcase in the study on the ground floor. The house was silent and he savoured the peace and quiet, a haven compared to the hustle and bustle of his office, or the organised madness of the motorway. Perhaps Mercedes had gone out for the day. She had spoken a number of times of visiting central London and he had supplied her with travel details and timetables. He hoped that she had in fact gone out, it would leave him an afternoon of peace and quiet to enjoy.

Back in the sitting room he poured himself a scotch and looked around. As usual the evidence of Mercedes' presence was all around: the shoes she had kicked off casually and left in the middle of the room, a Parisian magazine left lying on the sofa, an empty coffee cup on the floor, waiting to be accidentally kicked over. It was annoying that she was so untidy because Jennifer had left strict instructions about it before she had departed. At the time Mercedes had listened gravely and assured

Jennifer that all her instructions were to be followed to the letter.

The drink felt good, the warmth oozing down Edward's throat and spreading through his body. The strains of the day were beginning to fall away and again he closed his eyes to appreciate the heavy silence of the house. The exchange visit had been Jennifer's idea and, though reluctant at first, he had finally agreed to it. His wife had decided to pick up on her French again and had enrolled for classes at the local college. It had been a good idea; Edward often travelled to France on business and though he could order a meal and make himself understood to taxi drivers he could not hold a conversation with his French associates. There was no time for him to take classes but Jennifer was a good teacher and she was soon helping him with the language too.

The exchange visit was the perfect opportunity for her to take a break in Paris and to practise the language with the natives. However they had both imagined that the student she would exchange with would be of a similar age to Jennifer, in her late twenties. Mercedes had turned out to be not yet twenty and able to speak perfect English. Still, she was keen to travel to the UK and her own family just as keen to have Jennifer visit them. Perhaps, Jennifer had joked, it was the family that wanted to learn English and not Mercedes.

It was too early for a second drink, and besides, there was probably still time for him to call Paris. He picked up the empty coffee cup from the floor and walked across to the kitchen. There again Mercedes had left her mark: a sink full of cups, saucers and plates, an open jar of coffee left on the counter, the kitchen table strewn with newspapers and breadcrumbs. Why did the girl never clean up after herself? He was certain that she was very different at home. Jennifer had described Mercedes' family as very nice, with a large house full of people that was somehow always spotlessly clean. By their own reckoning Mercedes was a bit of a tearaway, an impulsive, bright, inquisitive sort of girl who liked to do things her way.

Edward sighed. He would have to have another long talk with the girl. But he feared that it would go the way of all the talks they'd had: she would listen sombrely, nod in all the right places, call him *Monsieur* in a voice of utmost respect, and then carry on regardless. Still, it had to be done. The only consolation was that the first week had passed and that she would be gone in another.

He ascended the stairs wearily, wishing that the week would pass quickly and then things could return to normal. Next time, he promised himself, he and Jennifer would go away together. The unexpected noise from his bedroom made him stop in his tracks. He pressed himself against the wall and inched towards the door. If Mercedes was out then who was in the room? Very slowly he pushed the door open, the bright sunlight from the bedroom spilling out into the hallway.

Thankfully the door failed to creak its normal complaint and as it opened slowly he could see clearly what was going on. The wardrobe door was open, the mirror on the inside of the door catching the light. Mercedes was standing by the wardrobe door, rifling through the hangers heavy with clothes, closely examining the contents of the shelves and the rack on the door.

'What the hell are you doing in here?' Edward demanded angrily, pushing the door open completely and bounding into his room. He was furious. Mercedes was staying in the guest room and she had no business whatsoever going through his and Jennifer's bedroom.

Mercedes stepped back, her mouth open and her blue eyes wide with shock. The colour had drained from her face and for the first time since she had arrived she was completely speechless.

'This is our room,' Edward cried, his anger undiminished. 'You have no right to be in here. What were you doing? Well, girl, what were you doing?'

Mercedes gasped for air, her full red lips opening and closing and unable to form coherent speech. She was dressed casually in a loose T-shirt and a short black skirt, slit at the back. Her eyes were made-up: long fluttering lashes, eyebrows pencilled darkly to frame her pretty blue eyes. Full lips outlined in red lipstick that contrasted with the slight golden tan of her skin.

'Well? I'm waiting,' Edward continued, advancing a step towards her. His glance fell on the open wardrobe and he understood at once what it was that had drawn her attention.

'I was looking for something to wear, monsieur,' she managed to say, her voice soft and nervous.

'You have your own clothes, what did you want?'

'I wanted to travel to London, monsieur, but I did not have a summer jacket to wear with this ... I thought perhaps that madame may have had something appropriate ...'

'Is that why you were looking in my wardrobe?' Edward demanded, pointing to the rack on the open door. It was lined with belts, canes, a heavy black paddle, all reflected in the bright light of the mirror.

'I ... I ...' She struggled for an explanation but instead her eyes became fixed on the implements of punishment so neatly laid out.

'You were stealing,' Edward decided suddenly, his voice losing the harshest edge of anger but becoming lower and more devious.

'No, monsieur! You are mistaken ... This is not true ...'

'Perhaps, perhaps not,' Edward said. 'But how would it seem to your college if I rang them and explained these circumstances? Even the suspicion would look very bad for you.'

'Please, monsieur, I am very sorry for this. I did not

107

come to steal. I was here to search for a jacket . . . in the beginning.'

Edward nodded. He could see that the truth was going to come out. She was not a thief but neither was she always truthful. If Mercedes had really been looking for a jacket she would have looked on the coat rack downstairs, or else she would have looked in Jennifer's side of the wardrobe. As if to prove the point he opened the other door of the wardrobe to reveal the closely packed hangers full of Jennifer's clothes, all of them apparently undisturbed.

'The full story, girl,' he told her firmly. He closed the second door of the wardrobe but left the first one open, noting the way that the young French girl's eyes kept returning to the long leather belts and the canes hanging from the rack. How long had she been studying the various instruments of punishment in his collection, he wondered.

'I was looking for a jacket but when I opened the wardrobe I saw these things. I was fascinated by it, monsieur . . . They are not for wearing?'

Edward smiled. 'No, they are not for wearing,' he admitted. 'They are for using, for punishing bad girls who should know better.'

'Like me?' Mercedes asked, her voice barely a whisper. She looked at Edward strangely, her eyes filled with fear and excitement in equal measure.

He nodded. 'You have taken advantage of my hospitality, young lady. This has been the last straw. I have a good mind to send you packing this instant, and to inform your family about your behaviour while you have been here. Do you think they will be pleased to hear this? Will it make them proud?'

Mercedes shook her head slowly. He could see the implications filtering through her imagination, the horror of it dawning slowly. Her eyes returned to the instruments of punishment, and the fascination that she felt was self-evident. Any other woman would have ignored them, closed the door, not even noticed them, but not Mercedes. Just the look of the long bamboo cane with the curved handle seemed to attract her gaze and attention.

'I am truly sorry, monsieur,' she whispered, looking up into his eyes appealingly.

He reached out and took the cane from the rack, then swished it once through the air for effect. She swallowed hard but did not try to run away, she did not even cry out in horror.

'You know what this is for,' he told her calmly.

She nodded, and then, without bidding, she turned her back to him slowly. She began to bend over at the waist, moving as though in a trance.

'No, across my knee young lady,' he commanded. 'You've acted like a silly child and that's how I'm going to punish you.'

She did not know what to do or how to react. She walked across the room towards him, stopped in front of the mirror and waited. He sat on the bed and motioned for her to join him, pointing to a spot six inches from his feet. When she was ready he put his hands under her short skirt and pulled her knickers down. The pretty white bundle of frills slid down her smooth thighs to her knees. Her face was bright red with embarrassment and her eyes resolutely avoided his.

Her skin was soft and warm and he could easily guess how it would react to a few firm strokes. He bent her over his knees, positioning her so that she was well placed and balanced over his lap. She made not a murmur of protest, moving as though in a dream. Her skirt went up slowly and the strong afternoon sun warmed her legs as the hem was pulled over her waist. She had firm round bottom cheeks, pert and well shaped, the groove between bottom and thigh deep and attractive.

'Please, monsieur ... Please ...' she whimpered,

finding her voice at last. It was too late, she was spread across his knees, her delicious derrière displayed completely in the clear orange light. She tried to kick out but her panties held her feet together.

'This is no time for tantrums,' he told her gruffly.

The first heavy smack of hand to bottom silenced her completely. He looked down and saw her softly tanned skin marked red with the imprint of his fingers and palm. His guess had been correct. She had the sort of soft, mellow skin that would colour intensely at the softest spanking. His fingers rubbed the redness, tracing the slightly raised shape of his own hand on her hot skin.

The second hard spank matched the first on the other bottom cheek, marking her symmetrically so that the terrible smarting pain would be balanced. It was her first time, he was certain of that, and he intended to make sure it would not be an experience she would easily forget. He began to spank her rhythmically, smacking fully with the flat of his hand, first on one cheek and then on the other. Her golden orbs clenched and unclenched as he beat her soundly, tanning her skin until it glowed red all over. He dealt swift blows at the top of the thighs also, and then aimed several between her bottom cheeks so that she shook all over with the impact.

'Well?' he demanded, forcing her to her feet.

When she did not speak he grabbed her by the shoulder and took her to stand by the mirror. She looked over her shoulder at the punished globes of her backside, patterned a deep even red all over. Her eyes widened, as she was displayed, her backside still quivering with pain.

Her nipples were hard, dark points pressed suggestively against her white cotton shirt. Her lips were slightly parted and her eyes misted over slightly. She had enjoyed her punishment, though he did not think she had ever expected to receive such chastisement.

110

'I'm sorry, monsieur . . .' she whispered, her voice hot and breathless. She parted her legs slightly and bent over, sticking her bottom out more to get a better view of it in the mirror. Her eyes had been filled with tears but now she seemed more interested in how she looked.

'So you should be, my girl,' he said softly, almost indulgently. 'Now, what are you going to do next?'

'Next?'

The house downstairs was still a mess and there was no way that Edward planned to clean up after her. The cane was on the bed; the object of her fascination had yet to be applied to her pert and punished behind. 'I want you to clear up the mess you've made in this house,' he told her simply. 'The kitchen, bathroom and sitting room look like they've been hit by a bomb. Clear it all up.'

'Yes, I will clear it all up, monsieur,' she promised eagerly. She looked up and caught Edward's eyes in the mirror. They looked at each for a moment and then she turned away, her face blazing red with embarrassment again.

'Good. I'll inspect it all when you've finished and if it's not up to scratch you know what to expect,' he warned her.

'The bamboo?' she guessed hesitantly.

'That's right,' he smiled, walking across the room to pick up the thin cane. He could see that it held some symbolic power for her; that she feared it as much as she was fascinated by it.

'Shall I begin now?' she asked.

'Yes, but remove your skirt and knickers completely. I want you to remember why you've been punished.'

Mercedes smiled. 'But I do, monsieur,' she sighed, rubbing her bottom with her hands. For a second she sounded grateful, there was none of the belligerence or defiance he had expected from her.

She posed herself in the mirror, examining the marks

on her body, pressing her fingers hard against the reddest parts of her bottom cheeks. She unclipped her skirt and it fell to her ankles, leaving her naked apart from the flimsy covering of her T-shirt. As she walked out of the room Edward watched her go, her punished flanks rippling sexily as she walked. She was showing off, and a quick cut of the cane made her yelp with pain. The red stripe cut a distinct track across the curves of her derrière. She almost jumped out of the room, clutching her painful bottom tightly, her first taste of the cane making her move like lightning.

The call to Paris got through at once, and in moments he heard Jennifer's cheery voice. 'How's Mercedes coming along?' she asked brightly.

'I've finally had to take her in hand,' Edward admitted, smiling to himself.

'I see,' Jennifer said, pausing for a moment. 'How did she take it?'

'She's downstairs cleaning up after herself, with her bare backside smarting from a good spanking.'

'I see,' Jennifer repeated. 'Do you think she'll be good from now on?'

Edward laughed. 'Not if the way she's been studying the cane and the belts is anything to go by. I expect that the next week's going to get very interesting.'

'I'm just sorry I'm not there to see it,' Jennifer sighed dreamily.

'Don't worry,' Edward promised her. 'This exchange trip was your idea, and it's not entirely Mercedes' fault things have turned out this way.'

There was a long pause at the other end of the phone. 'Will I get the cane or the belt?' Jennifer asked.

'Both,' he promised her.

Later, as he walked downstairs with the cane in his hand, he imagined the anticipation and excitement that Jennifer would enjoy for the next week, thinking of the punishment to come as soon as she was home. Her backside would be tingling before the first touch of the belt or the cane.

In the sitting room Mercedes was sprawled out on the couch, belly down. Her pert backside was a bright pink and sticking up in the air as she watched the opening credits of yet another Australian soap opera. Her long limbs were spread nonchalantly across the sofa and he could see the tinge of dark hair between her thighs just visible from behind. Young and wilful, impetuous and individual, the bare handed spanking had not been enough. Her pretty backside would have to take a lot more correction if things were to change. The cane almost twitched in Edward's hand, readying itself for action, it was going to be a *very* interesting week ahead.

Party On

I waited in the shadows, a lone figure hidden in the darkness, my breath misting in the cold night air. I was watching and waiting, eyes fixed on the brightly lit entrance to the night club where two big bouncers, in black jackets a size too small, were screening everyone going in. I had been waiting for an hour, during which time I had been getting colder and hungrier, before I saw Ali arrive.

My heart sank when I laid eyes on her. She was gorgeous: tight black zip-down top, short skirt, bare legs and high heels that would have had any other woman tottering about like a drunk. Her long blonde hair had been swept back, and her lips were prominent pink petals even from my distance. She beamed at the doormen, who were falling all over themselves to chat her up, alternately talking to her and making veiled comments to each other.

She was alone, which was a relief I suppose. When she managed to extricate herself from the attentions of the doormen she went in, and I saw the way the two ugly giants followed her wistfully with their eyes. I stubbed out my cigarette and emerged from the darkness, certain that I had not been seen. It was no surprise that I got a surly sneer from the doormen. For a moment I was sure they were going to bar me but the bundle of notes in my pocket was too good to turn away.

Inside, the music was deafening, the harsh rhythm pulsating and mutating all the time. I was disoriented for a few minutes as the flashing lights and the loud music conspired together. I bought an overpriced drink and settled into a corner from which to search for Ali. I wished she'd chosen something else to wear, something which would make her stand out from the crush of bodies and the darkness of the corners. It was early still but the club was already filling up. If it had not been for the card left in her bag I would have had no idea where to look for her. The story about visiting her friend Louise hadn't fooled me for a moment.

I spotted him first, a tall good-looking youth with bulging biceps displayed by a leather waistcoat which he wore open. He was just her type. Young, fit, handsome and predatory. He was with friends, a loud group of guys holding court in one of the larger alcoves closer to the bar. From there they could leer at the pretty young women dancing to the music, or on their way to the bar. They were in fine spirits, laughing and joking, eyeing up the local talent with obvious relish. When I saw him I knew that it was inevitable that Ali would see him too.

I spotted her a few minutes later; she was giving someone the brush off. I could see the disappointment in his eyes, lip-read her big flat 'No!' to whatever he had suggested. She attracted men like flies, and delighted in swatting them off like flies too. She didn't even turn to watch her would-be suitor amble away disappointedly, her eyes were already trained on the large group by the dance floor. I was in a good position to see it all. She looked at him, he looked at her, she waited then looked away, he waited until she looked back. I felt like David Attenborough witnessing a courtship ritual, though I guess David Attenborough had never felt the way I did about what was on display.

Lover boy slipped away from the group with pats on the back and loud cheers of encouragement from his beery mates. Ali was pointedly looking away, staring at nothing while secretly preening herself, making sure her

115

lips were wet and glossy, that her skirt was straight, that her top was open enough to give him a good view of her full round breasts. I got a hard-on just watching her, knowing that she was probably wearing nothing but the top and the skirt, and that in her excitement her pussy was going to get very hot and very wet.

Her first reaction to his approach was an emphatic shake of the head, accompanied by an equally emphatic laugh. This wasn't a brush off, this was a come-on in a big way. I could see her through his eyes: she was thrilling and sexy, a delicious looking woman in her middle-thirties who promised all the sexual experience that no girl his own age could possibly match. Her eyes scanned him in the same way that he was eyeing her; they were eating each other up within seconds. The heat they were generating must have been intense, I'd never seen anything so blatantly sexual. He reached out and touched her, stroked her face and neck with the palm of his hand. There was no hesitation, no doubt, just pure sexual confidence.

I watched them helplessly. They were kissing passionately within minutes of meeting, their mouths locked together tightly. I could see his hands smoothing down her back to take hold of her firm round backside. My guess must have been right. From the excited whispers and her delighted laughter I guessed that she had confirmed to him that she was knickerless under her short skirt. Then it was her turn. I saw her hand rubbing up and down his crotch slowly. She turned towards his friends and nodded her approval, eliciting a cheer from the crowd.

She walked across towards the group, the zip of her top lower than it had been, her ample cleavage expertly exhibited. She and lover boy were kissing again, eating each other intensely, silencing the crowd around them by the pure animal frenzy. They separated for a moment and I caught a glimpse of her face, eyes wide with ex-

116

citement, her lips puffy, face flushed. I had never seen her look so beautiful, and the pain I felt was so exquisitely intense I almost lost control.

Lover boy took her by the hand and led her into a corner. For a few moments she was hidden from me completely. I panicked until I found a new place to sulk. I was closer, I could see them clearly, and in the quieter sections of the music I could even make out snatches of conversation, not that there was much talking going on. Almost the first thing I saw was Ali wrapped in his arms, her mouth glued to his while his hand explored the inside of her top. He had zipped it open and was pawing at her breasts, pinching her nipples so that she would cry and gasp into his mouth. I wasn't the only voyeur though, a number of his friends had gathered round and were watching, enjoying the spectacle.

She became aware of the audience, but it only served to turn her on more. Sure, she complained, but lover boy knew what to do. He turned her towards his friends and pulled her top away completely, exposing her chest. He cupped her breasts, squeezing them, displaying them, playing with her nipples while biting her neck from behind. She threw her head back, her sighs lost in the music but I could hear them perfectly in my mind. She was loving every second of the exposure, her wildest exhibitionist fantasies come true.

Soon she was back in his arms, snuggled up to him, running her hands through his bronzed and hairless chest, or else teasing his cock over his tight leather jeans. Her top had fallen away completely, and she was shamelessly flaunting herself. He pulled her closer towards him and then lifted her skirt. I could almost feel the excitement in the air as a dozen male eyes homed in on her gloriously naked backside. He was stroking her thighs, pulling her buttocks apart, really getting off on displaying her to his mates like that.

The excitement was too much for her. I recognised

117

the signs, saw her head fall loose for a moment, her mouth quivering. She climaxed joyously with his fingers stroking her pussy softly, teasing her the way she liked, only this time it was in public. That was too much for one of the audience. I heard the angry exchange of words between lover boy and one of his mates, and for a moment I hoped that there would be a fight to break up the party. But Ali pacified her man by unzipping his jeans and kissing his prick lovingly. All the while moving herself into position so that his mate could begin to fuck her from behind.

I felt sick, standing there in the shadows and watching my wife being fucked in public by a complete stranger, while she was giving head and showing every sign of enjoying it. Her skirt was high around her waist, and in the muted light of the disco her body was a pale delight. I could see that two hands held her firmly by the waist and pulled her back and forth onto a thick hard cock. She was writhing, pushing her arse up to meet his cock, her breasts jigging back and forth with the rhythm, her nipples scraping against the smooth leather of lover boy's jeans. Her mouth was rotating and sliding up and down lover boy's cock, and he was jerking up and down to fill her mouth with all he had.

Ali is good with her mouth. I could see lover boy trying to hold back, but she was hungry for his come and she always gets what she wants. He crowed when he climaxed, spraying his seed deep into her mouth, making her swallow it for all his friends to see. He was the sort of bloke that had no shortage of women, you could see it in his arrogance, but I felt a perverse sense of pride in knowing that he'd never met anyone like Ali before.

Once he had finished it was natural that he would be bundled out of the way by some of his more eager friends. Again I hoped that a fight would break out and end the whole exhibition, but the alcove was reasonably shielded and I'm certain that apart from the little coterie around Ali no one else knew what was happening. My heart sank when the fight failed to materialise, and instead a second prick was thrust in my wife's willing mouth. A tough looking black guy was feeding her his cock, and the sight of his dark rod disappearing into her mouth was almost too much to take, the erotic contrast of dark skin on light adding an element that I knew was not lost on the rest of the audience.

The guy at the back finally finished, almost falling over her as he spunked into her sopping pussy. There was a queue to take her. Looking carefully I counted at least six other men waiting to have their turn. There was a shuffling of bodies, and before I knew what was going on Ali had been lifted and carried onto the low table that was in the centre of the alcove. She was put onto her back and the black guy straddled her, now able to fuck her in the mouth as though it were a second pussy. Someone else was between her thighs, really giving it to her with all his strength. She wrapped her legs around him, her body moving wildly as he repeatedly thrust into her. I could imagine how wet and sticky her cunt would be, awash with her juices and the spunk from the first man.

The black guy pulled away sharply and a sudden burst of strobe light caught the shower of come pouring from his cock into her open mouth. The flicker of the lights caught it so that it seemed as if a stream of thick semen were being pissed onto her tongue. She swallowed it all, enjoying every drop that rained down onto her. The sight made the man fucking her also shoot his load, the look of pure pleasure caught on his face by the same burst of strong white strobe.

That scene, caught forever in my memory, of streams of come pouring into her open mouth while a second man pumped his into her cunt, acted as a catalyst. She was surrounded by men, six or seven of them, all caught up in the same hypersexual frenzy. She was sucking on one man's prick again, I was certain that her lips were smeared with semen. Another man had turned her over and was screwing her from behind, her pussy already soaked with come. In her hand she was wanking another man, while another two were either wanking themselves or were rubbing themselves on her body. I had never seen anything like it, and I knew that I would live with the picture imprinted on my mind.

I remember seeing her drenched in come. It was spurting onto her breasts, pouring from her mouth, sliding wetly between her thighs. She climaxed repeatedly, her body a blur between the strong young men worshipping her. I lost count of the number she took in her sex, or in which position she took them. I could not keep track of the ones that filled her mouth with their salty juices. Nor of the ones that sprayed come onto her nipples, over her thighs, over her taut round arse-cheeks.

At last my prayers were answered. There was a commotion, loud shouts, threats of violence. People were being pushed back and I sighed with relief. The two burly doormen, gorillas in evening wear, shouldered everyone aside. Ali was hurriedly dressed before the assembled masses. Every person in the club had to be watching, and the doormen pulled her away. The crowd was angry. They had missed most of what had happened but the story was passing from ear to ear over the throbbing music. I saw the incredulous looks she got, the disappointment in the men's eyes, the spite in others, and excitement in most.

I knew what was going to happen next. She was taken into the office, and though the doormen took it in turns to keep people away, it was plain that they were having their fair share of what had been on offer.

I walked out of the club gasping for air, sucking it in as though it would clear my head. It was impossible to understand what had happened, how it had gone so far.

My darling wife had taken more cock than she had ever dared imagine: none of her fantasies would have prepared her for the sheer number of men that had fucked her. Always outrageous, she had outdone herself completely.

She looked dazed when she emerged from the club. Her hair was a mess and her clothes were skewed. I pulled up in the car but it took a moment before her eyes cleared and she recognised me. I opened the door and she climbed into the seat next to me. Before she had time to say anything I accelerated away, fearing that the rush of people emerging from the club would disturb us.

I drove for miles, aimlessly, in silence, breathing in the strong smell of spunk and perfume that came from my wife's body. Finally I pulled up in a lay-by and turned to her. We had nothing to say. Our mouths met and I tasted the essence of cock on her breath. Her breasts were clammy, sticky with spunk that I would have to suck away. She opened her thighs when I touched her and I felt the spunk seeping out, flowing freely from her pussy.

'Did you like it?' she asked me huskily, taking my fingers and pressing them into the flowing river of spunk that coated her inner thighs.

'Of course I did, darling, but it was agony, the way it always is' I sighed.

She smiled and took my fingers and put them to her mouth, sucking the cream into her mouth so as to feed it back onto my tongue.

Assignment

Felicity arrived promptly at three that afternoon, just as had been agreed previously. She was good like that, Clive could not fault her there. In many ways she had been the perfect secretary: attentive, hard working, punctual, very good at her job in every conceivable way. Damn it, she'd even had the right degree of sexiness, and she knew how to charm clients, that too could not be denied. Perhaps that should have been a clue, the fact that she was so perfect in every respect.

'I hope I'm not late,' she remarked with a smile when he opened the door to her. She knew she wasn't late and was making a point of it, but he could forgive her the small conceits.

'No, you're right on time, as usual,' he said, making way for her. She was wearing a smart business suit of short skirt, white blouse and matching jacket. The eye was drawn naturally towards her, to her long silky smooth legs, the pale tan of her flesh contrasting with the darkness of her clothes. She liked to look good, that was obvious, and as always she had done a perfect job.

He showed her the way through the house and up the stairs to his office, aware of the way she was looking round with unconcealed interest. It was the first time she'd been to the house, and of course she was curious to see her employer's home. The office was the largest room in the house, on the first floor overlooking the garden, and beyond that the woods. Though functional it was a bit more relaxed than his other office, though it

122

was still a working room and not a den for him to hide away in.

'There's lots of space,' she said, going straight over to the window to look out across the way.

'I get a lot done here,' he explained, trying to carry on a conversation he hadn't planned on.

'There are less distractions here, I suppose,' she said, turning from the window and flashing him a smile. Her long blonde hair caught the light, her golden curls cascading over her shoulders, lighting up her eyes and face.

'Yes, very few interruptions,' he agreed woodenly. 'Would you like a coffee before we start?'

'Love one, thanks,' she agreed.

'Make yourself comfortable then,' he suggested, pointing to the computer at his desk.

'Do you want me to make it?' she offered helpfully. 'If you let me know where the kitchen is I can do it.'

'No, it's OK. Why don't you get ready, I'll only be a few minutes.'

He left her at the desk, leaning over to switch the computer on. Her short skirt revealed much of her long thighs, and the way she moved, slow and sinuous, only accentuated the fact. She had never looked so beautiful. The streaming sunlight heightened it, and the severe cut of her suit added to it too.

There was no point rushing the coffee, and he settled back against the counter as the aroma of fresh coffee wafted around him. It gave him to time to think, to ponder on what to do next. He was attracted to her of course, what man wouldn't be? And her choice of outfit was designed to allure, she was sending all the right signals. Not that he needed such signals, he'd long understood what the message was. In the past she had worn skirts inches shorter than the one she was wearing now, and worn blouses that exposed the firm bulge of her breasts. Her eyes sparkled when they spoke and she liked to lean across his desk in a manner that was painfully arousing sometimes. It was even Felicity who had suggested working together during the one weekend when his wife was away.

Carefully carrying two mugs of coffee on a tray he made his way back up the stairs, the heavy foot falls and heavenly smell of fresh coffee signalling his arrival. She was at the desk, busy tapping at the keyboard. She turned and smiled at him. Her jacket was draped neatly over the back of the chair, and she was perched on the very edge of the seat. Her legs were crossed over, her sharp high heels glossy black in the sunlight, skirt pulled back an inch more to reveal long, lithe thighs that were all the more attractive because they were bare. Her white blouse was unbuttoned and the lacy whiteness of her bra almost visible.

'That smells good,' she exclaimed, reaching out to take the cup that was offered.

'Started already?' he asked, gesturing at the computer screen.

'Yes, I was just reviewing what you'd already done,' she explained quickly.

'How did you know the password?' he asked casually.

'I guessed. I just tried Cleo and it let me in,' she said, with a slightly apologetic shrug.

'Too obvious really,' he mumbled to himself. Having his wife's name as his password had been painfully obvious, and now that he thought about it he could have kicked himself.

'Oh damn!' she shrieked suddenly, pushing herself back from the desk as the coffee splashed down all over her.

'Are you OK?'

'Oh, I'm so sorry!' she wailed, standing up and trying to brush the wetness from her clothes. Somehow she had spilt waves of coffee all down her blouse and over her skirt, making a real mess of things. The desk was splashed with coffee too, as was the screen and keyboard.

'It's not your fault,' he said, though his voice indicated otherwise. While she was more concerned with her clothes his first concern was the computer, and the few tissues to hand were used to wipe the coffee from that.

'What do I do now?' she complained, looking down at herself pityingly. Her clothes were ruined, the snow white blouse would never be the same again, and the skirt sported a sharp jag of darker colour where the drink had soaked through.

'You'll have to change,' he told her, realising that there was no alternative.

'But Mr Sheppard, I haven't got anything else . . .' she said, looking at him with widening eyes. Was she really that shocked? Or was it a game she was playing?

'I'm sure that Cleo's got something that fits,' he suggested, smiling for the first time.

'Won't she mind?' Felicity asked, also breaking into a complicitous smile.

Clive shrugged. 'She's not here to mind,' he said. 'And besides, this is quite innocent, isn't it?'

'That's right,' she agreed, happily, 'it was an accident.'

The master bedroom was on the other side of the landing, just a few steps from the office. 'This is a lovely room,' she commented admiringly, taking in the bedroom which had been designed by Cleo herself.

'My wife's an interior designer,' he explained proudly. 'She's very good.'

'Now,' he said, crossing over to the wardrobe, 'let's find something for you to wear.'

'You choose,' she suggested. 'Dress me the way you'd like me.'

'Flirting again,' he laughed, then turned to look at the neatly arranged outfits hanging in the wardrobe. Cleo liked to dress up, and her range of outfits was more than a match for anything that Felicity had worn

125

to the office. He flicked through quickly and selected a loose fitting dress, long enough to cover everything and so remove temptation completely.

'Well?' Felicity asked, her voice a low whisper. She had slipped off her top and her skirt and was now standing in the centre of the room clad only in bra and knickers. Her hands were crossed coyly over her chest in a gesture of modesty that did nothing to dispel her seductive smile. Her legs were slightly crossed over, one in front of the other. Her skimpy white panties barely concealed the bulge of her sex. As he stared she shook her head, letting the long golden tresses fall over her shoulders.

'You look stunning,' he said finally.

'Do you really think so?' she asked, turning to one side, adopting a pose.

'You know you do,' he told her.

She turned her back to him, showing him her behind, the skimpy pants pulled tight against her bottom cheeks. The supple curve of her back was unblemished, the tone of her skin perfect. 'Do you really want me to wear that?' she asked, pointing to the long straight dress he was holding. 'I could work like this if you like. Until my clothes dry.'

'And we'd work, would we?'

She smiled coyly. 'We could do lots of things . . .'

'It was a happy accident then, the coffee?'

'What do you think?' she asked, lowering her eyes coquettishly.

'I think you have a great deal of explaining to do.'

'Oh my God . . .' Felicity gasped, stepping back, her face a picture of dismay as she looked up to see Cleo standing in the doorway.

'You look surprised to see me,' Cleo said, a smile forming. She raised her eyebrows expectantly, waiting for Felicity to get over the initial shock and to try to explain what she was doing.

'But ... but you were supposed to be away ...' Felicity mumbled, looking beseechingly at Clive for support.

'And that gave you free reign,' he remarked, walking across the room to join his wife. 'That's why you were so keen to join me this weekend.'

Felicity grabbed her wet clothes and held them tightly against her chest, trying to cover herself only moments after flaunting her desirable body. Her face blazed red with embarrassment and her eyes were filled with nothing but confusion.

'Perhaps you'd like to explain this?' Cleo suggested, holding up Felicity's black handbag and taking a blue diskette from it.

Felicity looked dumb, her eyes fixing on the small square of plastic that Cleo held up, the silver cover catching the light from the bedroom window. 'I just wanted to make a safe copy of our work,' she whispered feebly.

'Is everything on there?' Clive asked.

Cleo nodded. 'All the files that you'd been working on at home, including the tenders for jobs that we'd only just started working on,' she explained.

'I'm sorry ... I didn't want to do this,' Felicity admitted, bowing her head contritely.

'You've been breaking the law,' he explained coldly, 'you do realise that. Why did you do it, Felicity? You've been treated well, your salary's more than fair. Why did you betray us like this?'

'I didn't want to ...' she wailed, collapsing onto the bed, throwing herself face down and burying her head in the pillows. 'Nick made me do it, he said that it wouldn't do any harm ... He said that it would help us ...'

'Enough of that, girl!' Cleo snapped angrily.

'It wasn't my fault ... I didn't want to do it ... Nick forced me ...' Felicity sobbed.

'You won't get any sympathy from us,' Cleo told her. She unclipped the handle from the patent leather handbag and strode decisively over to the bed. Without hesitating she swung the looped strand of shiny black leather down onto Felicity's pert backside.

There was a sudden silence and Clive could not help but stare at the thin red stripe that his wife had smacked down onto Felicity's curved backside. A moment later Felicity dared to look up, lifting her head from the furrowed pillows to meet Cleo's steel grey eyes.

'I've been so stupid,' she mumbled, 'that's probably the most I deserve.'

'What you deserve,' Cleo decided, 'is a sound spanking, young woman. If I were in your position that's what I would hope for, unless you'd prefer to tell your story to the police.'

'This Nick, is he your boyfriend?' Clive asked soberly.

'No, not exactly. He's a friend of a friend, but I owed him some money and he said I could pay it off by getting a few files from your computer,' Felicity confessed. Her bottom was prominently displayed, and across it the red stripe was like a beacon that attracted the eye.

'We'll deal with him later,' Cleo said. 'Now, young woman, I think it's time you accepted your punishment.'

There seemed no hesitation in Felicity's eyes, only a sparkle of excitement that she could not quite hide. There was relief also, as if a great weight had been removed from her shoulders. 'Which one of you is it going to be?' she asked softly.

'I want you across my lap,' Clive said, pointing to the end of the bed.

'I am ever so sorry, Mr Sheppard,' she apologised, crawling across the bed to where he had pointed. She moved sinuously, her graceful body toned and tanned, a sleek creature captivatingly attractive.

He exchanged a sly smile with his wife and then proceeded to the bed. He sat comfortably and then made way for Felicity to crawl over his lap. She moved into position without question, as though it were something she was used to.

'You've been punished before?' Cleo asked, voicing the question for both herself and her husband.

Felicity's face coloured red as she nodded. 'Yes,' she admitted, her voice barely audible. 'I've been smacked before . . .'

Clive raised his hand and brought it down, silencing Felicity and Cleo at once. Felicity winced, held her cry and dug her long painted nails into the bed. Her body was warm and sensual across his lap, and when he breathed, her scent filled his lungs. Her lacy white panties could not hide the blush of her flesh, reddening quickly where his heavy slap had landed. A second smack, focused on her other bottom cheek, was followed by a third and a fourth. He smacked her hard and rhythmically, the flat of his hand tingling as he beat out her punishment. She was moving against him, unable to stop herself as the chastisement proceeded.

Five, six, seven. Each slap sounded through the room, and her body responded as she accepted the pain. At last she could hold back no longer, she squealed and buried her face in her hands, her long legs kicking as the strokes became harder and more deliberate.

'Stop that, girl,' Cleo commanded, annoyed by the kicking and struggling. She moved forward decisively and grabbed hold of Felicity's knickers and pulled them down sharply, exposing the punished curves tanned a deep red by the volley of hard smacks.

'Please . . . I'm sorry . . .' Felicity whimpered miserably.

'You need to be taught a lesson,' Clive hissed.

Again he began to smack her, his hand moulding to the globes of her behind, each stinging impact making her gasp audibly. At the top of the thighs her skin had reddened and her strength was going. She could no longer hold her composure. As her flesh burned he could see the moisture pour from her sex, the redness of her bottom spreading through to arouse her sexually.

At last the spanking stopped and Felicity almost fell to the floor. She stood up shakily, her hands moving naturally to her behind. Her face was still red, but now the flush was of excitement and not shame. All thoughts of modesty had disappeared, she no longer tried to coyly conceal her sex, all she wanted to do was to rub away the smarting pain from her behind.

'Stop that,' Clive snapped, grabbing Felicity's wrists and pulling her hands away from her behind.

'I'm sorry, Mr Sheppard, but it does sting so terribly,' she complained with a pout. Her panties slipped down from between her thighs and down to her ankles, a frilly white bundle between her feet.

'How often have you been spanked before?' Cleo demanded, exchanging a significant glance with Clive.

'Not often,' Felicity mumbled, looking away from Cleo's piercing stare.

'Obviously,' Clive remarked. He could see the finger marks on her backside reflected in the mirror by the bed, the outline of his hand over her bottom cheeks and upper thighs.

'Why were you here today?' Cleo asked, taking a step behind Felicity. She reached down and ran her hand over the reddest parts of Felicity's behind, her fingers lightly stroking the heat away.

'To get the files,' Felicity confessed sullenly.

'Then why did you try to seduce me?' Clive asked, tightening his grip on her wrists.

'I . . . I didn't . . .' Felicity whispered, swallowing hard as she realised that she was caught in his iron grip.

'But you did, my dear,' Cleo whispered softly, her voice filled with menace.

'No, the coffee was just an unfortunate accident.'

'You'll be punished again for the lies,' Clive warned. 'Now, the truth if you don't mind.'

'It was Nick,' Felicity wailed. 'He said that if we had sex you'd want to keep quiet if you discovered that the files had been copied.'

'He sounds like an excellent character,' Cleo sighed. 'Is he the one that punished you before?'

Felicity seemed to lose the power of speech. She shook her head slowly. Her cascading golden tresses caught the sun and her mouth formed words that did not come out.

'Did he threaten you with punishment if you didn't co-operate?' Clive suggested. He did not relax his grip on her wrists, instead her pulled her arms lower, forcing her to bend at the waist, giving Cleo a better rear view.

'Or did he spank you as a reward?' Cleo suggested, smiling broadly.

'How did you guess?' Felicity asked, her voice filled with surprise, her eyes wide with shock.

'I understand,' Cleo assured her sympathetically. 'You did wrong though, and you've been punished for it. Now it's my turn to punish you, for trying to seduce my husband.'

Felicity cried out as the leather strap landed suddenly on her already punished bottom cheeks. She tried to escape but Clive held her fast, pulling her arms lower and forcing her to bend over to receive her second dose of correction. The strap swished through the air and landed with a crack of sound, each stroke succeeded by a gasp of breath from her pretty lips.

Cleo showed no mercy. She was as ruthless as Clive had been, marking Felicity's behind with line after line of redness. She understood the feelings running through the punished girl's mind; she understood also the way the pain had become pleasure through some mysterious process.

'We'll deal with Nick ourselves,' Clive was saying.

'You'll deliver the diskettes but the data will be meaningless and it'll ruin whatever scheme he's cooking up.'

'In the meantime,' Cleo added, wielding the strap with just that extra bit of severity, 'we will have to continue to look after you in case you get into more trouble.'

'If you're to remain as my employee then you have to accept your punishment regularly, both from myself and from Cleo,' Clive added.

'Yes . . . Sir . . .' Felicity sighed, lifting her pert backside higher as the strap came down hard against her naked flesh.

Christmas Wrap

Even the Christmas tree looked limp, sad branches raining needles onto the carpet, the decorations looking tatty and tawdry where they had once seemed lively and fun. Paul looked at it sadly, the pattern of pine needles on the floor showed the outline of where the presents had been, the brightly wrapped packets that he had secretly been buying up for months, and had then taken great pains to keep hidden from Bev's prying eyes. Christ, that had been difficult. In the weeks leading up to Christmas she had been like a little kid, searching in every corner of the flat for the presents that she knew must be there.

Paul turned back to the telly. The tired old comedian was annoying him so he flicked to the big film, but that was even worse so he switched it to the next channel and then the next. Nothing doing, it seemed like there was a conspiracy to remind him of Bev. The comedian reminded him that you need company to enjoy a joke, and the smoochy film on the other side was even more painfully obvious.

Snapping off the television plunged the room into a silence which emphasised Bev's absence completely. How could she do this to him? The question had been going round and round in his head, like a vulture circling overhead, and still he couldn't understand it. Sure, they had their troubles, everybody did, but to walk out three days before Christmas was a blow that he had never expected.

He stood up unsteadily, waited until the world stopped spinning and opened his eyes. What he saw was not a pretty sight: the remains of a badly cooked Christmas breakfast, lunch and dinner spread over the table and carpet, a pyramid of empty lager cans which was topped precariously by a plate full of dead pud and brandy custard that had set with the consistency of concrete. It was horrible, and he felt horrible and he wished desperately that Bev was with him still.

The clock on the wall was crawling. Every minute seemed to take an hour, the second hand taking a breather after every tick. It was only nine o'clock but Christmas Day was over as far as he was concerned. He turned the light out in the empty room and dragged one foot in front of the other up the stairs. His head felt heavy, but after the dizzy spell on standing up, the drink had failed to have any effect. That was bloody typical of course. On every other day of the year he only had to sniff alcohol and he'd keel over drunk, and on the one day of his life when the oblivion of drunken stupor was the best place in the world he couldn't get there.

The arguments had been getting worse, and more general, and more frequent and more bitter and . . . There were lots of things wrong, he couldn't deny that. He liked to go out with the lads a bit too much, he liked a drink even though he couldn't handle it. That's where the arguments had started, and they had finished when she came out and told him that he was a lousy lover. That hurt. It hurt so much that he responded with a stream of abuse that had finally sent her running for her bags. His apology came too late, when she was already getting in the cab and he was bellowing from the bedroom window.

He wasn't a lousy lover, that was crap. Crap. Absolutely. The problem was that she had a libido in overdrive and it was matched stroke for stroke by an imagination that would have done the Marquis de Sade proud. You name it she was into it, any perversion you cared to mention, whereas his idea of wild sex was to do it doggy position while the football was on. He'd never had any complaints before, so why did Bev have to be different?

She was different, he thought gloomily, sitting heavily on the end of a bed that suddenly seemed to have the same proportions as the Sahara Desert. Bev was funny, clever, attractive, and just too bloody sexy for her own good. Paul missed her more than he would ever have admitted to her. He'd been chucked before but it had never left a great big gaping hole in his life before. He would do anything to get her back, he decided, though he knew it was too late for that.

He slumped back on the bed and stared emptily at the ceiling. What a Christmas it had turned out to be. It should have been the best ever but it was the worst. He had so much planned, the presents were going to be a surprise and he knew that she would have loved them. He turned his head and looked down at the untidy bundle of presents that he had thrown into the corner. His were mixed with hers, all of them unopened, the shiny paper and pretty ribbons a symbol of the good times that might have been.

He exhaled heavily and told himself to snap out of the self-pity that he had settled into. Self-pity was in some ways the most comfortable mental state to be in, it meant that he didn't have to do anything, and besides it wasn't his fault in the first place. Damn, there he was again, slipping into that same awful way of thinking. If Bev were with him she'd soon put him right. Self-pity was not something she enjoyed, either in herself or in others. Except that Bev wasn't with him . . .

'Stop it!' he cried, and his voice rang through the room. Sometimes there was nothing else to do but get off your arse and do something. This, he told himself firmly, was one of those times. He got up and ignored the dizzy spell, forcing it out of his mind purely by effort of will. That was better, he was going to get himself into shape and then get Bev back. It was early for New Year's resolutions, but not that early.

The first present he opened was from Bev: a very expensive bottle of aftershave that she would have forced him to wear. He put that down, grimly deciding that he was going open every single present in the house. Next was one of his presents for her: a pair of expensive black stockings, very fine and very silky which would have looked brilliant on her long shapely legs. Naturally the stockings had to have matching suspenders and a very lacy G-string, and a silk top to tantalisingly clothe her adorable breasts (the memory of her hard nipples in his mouth made him go hard somewhere else).

In no time he was surrounded by the sexy lingerie he'd succeeded in keeping hidden from her. In retrospect he wondered whether it wouldn't have been better to let her find it all. Strangely he no longer felt so depressed. Being surrounded by all the lingerie somehow made her seem less far away. The stockings felt so smooth and sensual, and the thought of the G-string pulled tight between her backside was immensely arousing. His cock was stiff and painful in the tight confines of his jeans, so when he undid his trousers and pulled his boxer shorts down he breathed a sigh of relief. Perhaps the drink was having an effect after all; he was feeling incredibly horny all of a sudden, and the lingerie around him was becoming a real turn-on.

He was now down to the last of the presents, one from her and one to her from him. He opened the present he'd bought her, a compact electric shaver, one that she'd been angling for for some time. That left the last present. He recognised the wrapping paper, it was the special thing she'd bought him. He could still see the wicked grin on her face when he'd picked it up and given it a shake to try and work out what it was. His guesses started out being cold and ended up being colder. He really had no idea what it was. With a surge of excitement he ripped the paper off to find a long slim velvet covered case – a watch case he guessed immediately.

Wrong. He opened the case gingerly and then almost dropped it. There, nestling on a bed of silk, was a seven inch dildo; a smooth black surface that tapered off at the end. A dildo. Christ, what the hell was she doing buying him a plastic cock? Wasn't his own good enough? Is that what she was telling him? His anger fizzed up suddenly then died away as he caught himself thinking the way she said he thought – like an unimaginative dickhead.

He edged the dildo out of its case and held it loosely in his hand, as though afraid to close his hand around the thick hardness of it. It felt heavy, very smooth, sensual almost. If Bev were with him ... But Bev wasn't with him, her things were. The stockings were draped across his lap, and when he moved his prick was caught up in the thin filmy material; a silk touch that sent shivers of pleasure through him. He picked up the G-string and brought it to his face. It felt soft and satiny, and if it had been perfumed with her pussy he would have breathed her bouquet as though it were perfume.

Unimaginative? The shock of her departure and the array of her sexy underwear were combining to loosen the imagination that had atrophied. He closed his eyes and saw Bev in front of him, her long legs clad in stockings, the dark band in contrast to her creamy skin, the G-string pulled tight into her pussy, a pussy that was freshly shaven for his delight. He opened his eyes. The stockings were murder against his skin, and the G-string in his hand was driving him crazy too.

Perhaps it was the drink, but he didn't care. He put the dildo on the floor and then stripped off quickly, throwing every item that he shed into a corner. Nervously he picked up the stockings and started to slip them on but stopped. It didn't feel right, his legs were too hairy and the stockings were snagging on the tight curls. Without stopping to analyse the situation he grabbed the electric shaver and walked into the bathroom. The jet of steaming water from the shower head did nothing to dampen his mood. A quick lather up and his wet razor had taken off most of the hair on his legs. The petite electric razor cleaned him up properly. When he finished he looked in the full-length mirror and admired his legs; long, slim and now very smooth. He didn't forget to shave his face too before returning to the bedroom.

The stockings fit like a dream, slipping onto his smooth legs and emphasising the contours of them. Of course the suspender belt was required. A bit fiddly to put on but soon that was in place too. His cock was hard, a raging erection that throbbed like crazy, a thick tear of fluid coursing slowly down the veined length of it. It was an effort but he didn't give himself a quick shuffle. Being that excited was a pleasure in itself and he didn't want that pleasure to end too soon.

A quick glance in the mirror brought a smile to his face, the first smile of Christmas. Putting on make-up was not as easy as he had imagined. The lipstick looked like it had been applied with a Dulux roller. Luckily Bev always kept a supply of wet wipes on the dressing table. Three attempts later his lips were a deep shade of scarlet, and his pouting and posing in the mirror were making him feel even more horny.

Unimaginative? He hadn't had so much fun in ages, and the tension in his balls was fantastic. His cock was now glistening as it dribbled and drooled silvery fluid. A quick dash of mascara and eye-pencil finished the job. As a first attempt the effect wasn't too bad. A bit amateurish but more than acceptable. He'd never been the most macho character around, and his boyish looks had certainly been softened by the make up into a very girlish look.

Finally he remembered the last of the lingerie. The silk top was fairly loose around his chest, it covered his nipples and upper chest, though he realised that the effect would only be complete if he shaved under the armpits. That would do for next time, he promised himself, not even realising that he had decided there was going to be a next time.

And then the G-string. He slipped it on very slowly, studying himself in the mirror excitedly. The stockings did look good. His legs looked long and elegant, all that was missing was a pair of stiletto heels, like the ones that Bev liked to pose in. The G-string fitted very tightly over his cock, and the pleasure as the silky material rubbed against the glistening skin was indescribable. He tensed up and managed to avoid spilling his load, but the excitement was getting too much. Christ, it was probably better than doing it doggy position when there was a London derby on the box.

He turned round and looked over his shoulder into the mirror. The white G-string was pulled tight into his backside; a tiny white sliver of material up into his arse-cleft. When he bent over a little he could see the suspenders pulling tight across his buttocks, edging the arse-cheeks slightly apart so that he could see the thin white material cupping his balls.

'Well, Paul, I don't know what to say,' Bev said softly.

'Oh shit . . .' Paul groaned, looking up to see her framed in the doorway. She had her arms crossed over her chest, her lips pursed angrily, eyes staring at him in all his feminine glory.

'I came back for my pressies,' she explained, 'but I never expected this.' She looked down at the torn packages, at the carpet of Christmas wrapping paper, at the empty cellophane wrappers. 'Are you wearing my pressies?'

Paul closed his eyes and nodded. 'Do you like them?'

he asked weakly, trying to force a smile from her lips. She was wearing a short black skirt, stockings, high heels and a white top. She looked delicious.

'What about my present?'

'Your present?'

She smiled and walked into the room. First she went to the dressing table. She had her back to him so he couldn't see what she was looking for. He stood awkwardly in the middle of the room, his cock now only semi-erect in the tightness of her G-string. He closed his eyes again and wished the world would open and swallow him up.

'You look lovely darling,' she whispered, and kissed him unexpectedly on the mouth.

It was like an electric shock, that and the feel of her fingers sliding up his thigh. He opened his eyes and looked into hers. She was smiling and her breath was hot against his lips. They kissed again, more hotly this time, his passion growing as her fingers slid under the thin band of the g-string. She stroked his balls softly and then moved up towards his rear hole. Her fingers were wet, she had oiled them with something.

'Oh God . . .' he whispered, tensing suddenly as her finger pressed smoothly into his rear hole.

'Why did we have to fight for this to happen? Why couldn't we have been like this before?' she asked, her eyes clouding with tears.

He moved back, lifting his foot and twisting round slowly as the dildo moved into his oiled backside. The pleasure was explosive; he felt as though he'd been split in half with ecstasy. He collapsed onto her shoulder, kissing and biting her neck and throat, while the dildo was pushed deep inside him. The penetration was an avalanche of pleasure that lasted forever.

'We'll always be like this now,' he gasped, 'if you want to.'

'I do want to,' she cried, kissing him on the mouth

again. 'Now, be a good girl and fill your knickers,' she ordered, and he gasped loudly as he felt the jism spilling from the G-string and dripping down the soft flesh at the top of the stockings.

Bev knelt down in front of him and began to lap at the hot semen, her lipstick leaving red smudges on his skin, like pleasure trails that echoed the pleasure vibrating in his anal hole.

Mysterious Ways

Mama and Papa were both engrossed in their novels when I came down from my chamber. They looked so happy: Papa puffing away at his pipe, Mama ensconced in the old leather armchair, both of them silently lost in the dream worlds of their books. How happy they looked, so content and at peace with the world. My heart was filled with a strange kind of joy, and I wished that they would stay so happy and content forever.

'Emily, my dear,' Mama sighed, looking up from the thick volume she was lost in. 'Is the coach here already?'

'Why, yes, Mama,' I assured her, bustling into the warmth of the sitting room. 'It is past seven o'clock.'

She beamed me a smile, her pale blue eyes flecked with such an innocent love. 'You must hurry, my dear, Aunt Constance will be waiting.'

'Yes,' I agreed, 'I don't want to make her cross. I do so hope that we will be studying one of her more uplifting devotional tracts this evening.'

Papa coughed throatily. 'Not too uplifting, one hopes,' he mumbled grumpily. 'A bit of fire and brimstone's required to keep the more flighty members of her group in line. Eh, my dear?'

Mother nodded, in complete agreement with Papa as always. 'A bit of fire and brimstone to keep the devil at bay,' she added softly.

'I'm sure you're right, Papa,' I said, rushing over to give him a quick kiss on the cheek. He covered up his book rather quickly, slapping the pages together with a loud thump. He smelt of stale tobacco and brandy, the way he always did. The smell of father. Grand patriarch and provider for our little house.

'Of course I'm right, girl,' he said gruffly. But there was no fooling me: underneath his stern and authoritarian exterior he had a heart of gold. I knew that he loved being told he was right; there was nothing in the world that he liked more, except perhaps for the gentlemen's library that he kept hidden from feminine eyes.

'Do say a prayer for me too,' Mama said. 'I do so wish I could join the younger ladies in your good works,' she added wistfully.

'No, Mama,' I told her, keeping the panic from my voice. 'It's best that Aunt Constance school us in the ways of the Lord, after all, she has so much experience.'

'How right you are, dear,' Mama agreed pleasantly. She motioned me over, gave me a quick kiss and sent me on my way.

I stopped at the door and took one look at them again, so happy in the warmth of their little world. I was on my way at last, checking my reflection in the ornate mirror by the door. Hat straight and secured with a large pin, a silk shawl to cover my tight fitting, full-collared dress and dainty black ankle boots. Father might complain about the fripperies and frivolities of fashion, but I had a duty to myself to dress well.

The cab was waiting, and as I stepped out into the murky darkness my heels snapped hard on the ground, the sound echoing down the avenue. The smog was thicker than usual and the flickering gaslights could only manage a diffuse orange glow. The cab driver was waiting – a dark figure hunched over. He gave a nod of the head to acknowledge my presence and then once I was comfortable, a cry to set the horse going.

I sat back, my heart beating and pounding in my breast. Our fortnightly meetings at Aunt Constance's chamber were always so very interesting, especially for

143

young ladies of a certain social standing. Constance was not my real aunt, but it was what we all called her, those of us that attended her evenings of devotional study. She had the same austere manners as my father, the same strictness of speech and thought, the familiar harshness of belief. Ah, what belief. In Aunt Constance we girls had the perfect vision of what a good Christian woman had to be. That's not to say she was one of the wizened old hags that the lower classes looked up to, nor did she breathe fire like the Methodist preachers that frightened the children in Sunday School. Aunt Constance was altogether more sophisticated and more refined in her bearing.

I was so wrapped up in my thoughts that I barely looked at the dark streets through which the cab rattled and rocked towards the river. The narrow cobbled streets were filled with the hoarse shouts of newspaper boys, of ragamuffins playing in the streets, of tired old beggars making their dreary rounds. It was only when we crossed the river at London Bridge, old Father Thames alive with the bright lights of the barges wending their way up-river, that I paid more attention. The mist had descended even more thickly, turning the grey streets of Borough into threatening caverns where the dangers lurked in every shadow. I felt a surge of excitement as we passed close to the taverns frequented by the rough and ready dock workers, singing and fighting in the narrow streets, watched by the sullen faces of their children and urged on by the screeching of their sluttish women.

We passed the rough houses and the warren of slums close by the river and then towards the more pleasant avenues and drives that were more familiar to me. I noted the presence of a bobby as the cab pulled outside the grand house of dear Aunt Constance. He nodded his respectful greeting as I climbed down from the cab, wrapping the shawl around my shoulders, and I smiled back politely. I paid the cabby and gave precise instructions for him to return at 10 o'clock, for father would have been most cross if I were one minute late.

This had been my first trip alone. Normally my cousin Faith, recently wed, accompanied me on my visits to Aunt Constance, though she had been taken poorly and it was only with the fullest entreaties that father had allowed me to travel by myself. I was seventeen, and soon to be wed if a suitable boy could be found, and so Papa was always most careful to ensure that I retained my good name.

The door was opened by Annie, Constance's delightful young maid, who greeted me most profusely. She was such a pretty thing, my own age exactly, that I was often sorely tempted to kiss her deliciously red lips, if only to see the look in her bright blue eyes.

'Are they all here?' I asked her nervously, glancing at the imposing grandfather clock that ticked away the seconds in a majestic sweep of its hands.

'Yes, Miss Emily, all here,' Annie confirmed, showing me into the parlour.

'Ah, Emily my dear, here at last,' Constance said, her voice carrying that stern note of admonition that we all secretly feared.

'I'm sorry, Aunt Constance,' I whispered, my face growing red with embarrassment, 'but cousin Faith has been taken poorly . . .'

'Poor dear, we will all say a prayer for her,' Constance announced, signalling for me to take my place. A row of straight-backed chairs had been arranged for us, ringing the room completely, all facing the centre where Constance held court. She was an impressive woman, very tall, with a fashionably petite waist, a full bosom and a face that was at once so very pretty and yet so very stern.

'You've missed the first part of our evening, Emily, dear,' she continued, her hands pressed together under her chin. 'We were studying one of the holy texts, which

I am sure you will want to take home to read this evening.' I nodded furiously, aware that many of the other young women were still looking at me. 'Now, ladies, I think that we have meditated enough on the sins of the flesh. Remember ladies, that there is no recourse from the sins of lasciviousness: "There is a dreadful Hell, and everlasting pains, Where sinners must with devils dwell, In darkness, fire and chains". Amen.'

'Amen,' we murmured in unison, all of us secretly in thrall to the stern-faced woman before us, the centre of our attention and devotion. Never had we seen a woman so powerful, her personality more forceful and compelling than many of the men in our lives. I for one knew that for all his harsh words, father could not match the authority of this godly woman.

I sat and listened, transfixed and in awe, as Aunt Constance outlined the terrors of Satan and his fearful kingdom. I listened and trembled as she described, in detail, the horrors and the tortures of hell, painting a picture with such verisimilitude that it was possible to believe that she had only just returned from a visit to the bowels of the earth. We heard her describe the multitude destined for hell; the painted whores that walked the streets, the adulteress in her chamber, the hussies that danced and drank and fornicated.

Suddenly she stopped and a hush fell over the assembled young ladies; a hush of expectation, a pregnant pause while we waited with bated breath for her to paint the final scene in her horrid picture of the decay of the soul.

'What is the root of all evil?' she asked, her voice suddenly lowered. 'What is the source of the sin of fornication? The spring from which the most vile and obscene desires arise? The male of the species,' she hissed in answer. 'It is the male of the species who is fired by hungers that are against nature. It is the male of the species who is debased and depraved, the male of the species that is corrupt in body and soul. This, ladies, is the essence of our godly message. Let us not be defiled by their wicked desires, let us not fall under the sway of their grand words and deeds, for under the cloak of goodness there lurks the serpent of desire.'

There was a murmur of assent, the young women present in agreement with Aunt Constance and her sermon of goodness and hope. We vowed, all of us, never to allow our bodies, that temple of the spirit, to be defiled by the base motives of man. We were a sisterhood, united in our devotion to the Lord, and united also in our devotion to Constance, His vessel and disciple.

The murmur of voices died down and Constance raised her hands to silence us and to draw our attention once more. 'The Lord has sent us another repentant sinner,' she informed us, raising her eyes to the heavens with thanks. 'A sinner ready to repent lustful sins, a sinner ready to take the first step on the stony path to righteousness.'

A young woman beside me cried, 'Praised be to the Lord,' but I gave her a sharp look that silenced her at once. We were all filled with righteousness and the desire to do the Lord's bidding, but we had standards to uphold, and such Methodist practices were simply not acceptable in present company. I caught Constance's eye and saw that she approved of my stance. We were ladies after all, not the wives of navvies or miners. Suitably chastened, the young woman turned back to Constance who was ready to continue.

'Sisters of the Lord,' she cried, 'we have among us one that has seen the error of libidinous and carnal desire, and is ready now to pay penance and to seek His forgiveness.'

A curtain was drawn back and there was a sharp intake of breath as we all set eyes on the sinner arraigned before us. He was a handsome lad. In age not more than twenty; tall, fair of hair and skin. Around his neck he wore a black sign that announced, in bold white letters, SINNER AND FORNICATOR. His eyes were averted and his face was washed red with a shame that coloured his ears and cheeks. Constance snapped her fingers imperiously and he walked forward, joining her in the centre of the room. The large sign covered him up, but I could see that he was not properly dressed for a gentleman, and that added to the surge of excitement that made me feel quite giddy.

'Confess your sins,' Constance commanded, and we all craned forward to hear him.

'I have sinned mightily against the Lord,' he began, his voice quivering sensitively. 'I have twice visited houses of ill-repute and enjoyed the bestial pleasures of the flesh with the painted whores therein. I confess that I took pleasure in my abasement, and that I would have continued on my path to the gates of Hades had I not . . . Had I not been fortunate enough to be introduced to Aunt Constance, who has convinced me of the error of my ways. "Praise the Lord, for he is Good, and all who seek Him shall find Eternal peace". Amen.'

There were several murmured amens, but mine was not one of them. I confess that the young man had fired my imagination. Despite the shame that blemished his fair skin I found him to be quite handsome, with eyes that were sensitive and intelligent and a mouth that was firm and manly.

'What do you wish now, young man?' Constance asked, her voice almost a whisper.

'I wish to do penance,' he whispered in reply, the words almost forced from his lips.

I was trembling with excitement. Strange thoughts filled my head and I confess that I felt a delirium pass through my body. My bosom heaved in the tightness of my corsets and I felt a fire ignited deep in my belly. I fidgeted on my seat, unintentionally rubbing my thighs together, and the friction seemed to produce spasms of pleasure that made me sigh inaudibly.

'Step forward, young man,' Constance commanded loudly, 'and let the lines of scripture be written in flesh.'

The young man obeyed, and there were squeals of

astonishment, not to say delight, when he turned around and bent over at the waist. He was wearing britches, but so very like an undergarment that the muscles of his thighs were clearly discernible. My eyes were fixed on this poor individual. I traced the contours of his masculine body and, though it shames me to admit it, I could not help but stare at the roundness of his flanks and the dark pouch between them.

With a characteristic flourish Aunt Constance produced a thin rattan cane, of the sort that was used to chastise naughty children during Sunday School. We all shivered. There were few young ladies present that did not harbour unpleasant memories of correction at the hands of strict parents or teachers. I for one had only been caned the once but I vividly recall the feeling of shame as it was administered and the sharp pain and the rush of tears it provoked.

I watched, wide eyed and open-mouthed as Aunt Constance raised the cane and then swung it down hard on the young man's posterior. How it whistled through the air, and the sharp snap of sound as it fell on its victim was echoed by our cries and exclamations. The young man winced sharply but he held his prone position, bent over at the waist, fingertips touching his toes. Down it came again, and then again and again, hard smacks on the behind, each one as hard as the last. The young man twisted and turned, his face screwed up in an expression of exquisite pain, but not once did he complain, not once did he utter a cry of pain.

'Thank you, Aunt Constance, for punishing me most soundly,' he managed to say, his voice a hoarse whisper. 'And thank you, ladies, for bearing witness.'

'Now, young man, you will stand in the corner while we ladies say our prayers,' Constance informed him sharply, as though his penance had not been enough punishment. He obeyed meekly. He stood in the corner, facing the wall, hands on head, while Constance led us in prayers.

Nervously I looked at the clock, it was almost ten and I could feel the minutes ticking by. It seemed to be taking an age for the ladies to thank Aunt Constance, and from the flushed expressions and bright eyes I guessed that many of them had enjoyed the experience a great deal. It was one of the delights of Constance's evenings, and arguably it was why her ladies were such devotees of her inspirational evenings.

At last Constance and I were alone, apart from the young man who remained in the corner, his punished backside surely aching him still.

'It was a most inspiring evening,' I said, thanking Constance as best I could.

'I haven't forgotten the text for you to take home and study,' Constance said, smiling indulgently as she saw me sneaking a look at the young man across the room.

'Thank you for that, Aunt Constance.'

'There is more, I can tell,' she surmised. 'Perhaps you will assist me in the final act of the evening?'

'But Mama and Papa are waiting,' I sighed wistfully.

'Would you wish me to inform them that you were derelict in your duties, my child?'

I shook my head vigorously. 'I would do anything to help you in your good works, Auntie,' I assured her.

'Good. I shall of course pen a note to your parents, thanking them for raising such a fine Christian young woman. Now, to work,' she added crisply.

We walked to the other side of the room, where the young man was as still as a statue. At close quarters he was even more handsome than I had imagined, with a fine nose and chin that bespoke good breeding. His face was still blotched with areas of red and I guessed that the shame was ready to flare up again.

'Well, young man,' Constance barked. 'Was your punishment sufficient for your sins?'

He swallowed hard, his Adam's apple bobbing up and down. 'No, Aunt Constance, I fear not,' he confessed, averting his gaze shamefully.

'Then I fear that more pronounced measures may be necessary,' Constance declared sorrowfully. 'Emily, my dear, please fetch two of the canes from my drawer. Be quick child, for this sinner must face his harshest test.'

I flew across the room, hardly daring to think about what was to happen next. There was a bundle of canes in the drawer and I snatched two and skipped back to Constance. I squealed like a child, I could not help myself when I saw how she had prepared her young man. His britches were round his ankles and his buttocks fully exposed to view.

'Silence, child,' Constance snapped at me, taking one of the swishy canes from my hand. 'It is obvious that we have not written our scriptures deep enough,' she explained, and illustrated this by tracing the fine red lines that were drawn from buttock to buttock on the young man's flesh.

My face was ablaze and I felt as though my heart would burst from my body. Never had I seen such a thing, his muscular thighs were bristled with fine blonde hairs, and the valley between his bare buttocks was similarly patterned. I took a step back, faint perhaps, and set eyes on the dark pouch between his thighs.

'Enough of that, girl,' Constance barked impatiently. 'We have the Lord's work to do. Do not let your sense of modesty prevail over that, my child.'

'Yes, Aunt Constance,' I whispered, aware of the wet heat that stirred between my thighs.

'Now, young man, you have been an extremely naughty boy, for which you are to be punished most severely,' she told him, her voice stentorian and imposing.

'Yes, Aunt Constance, I have been very naughty,' he admitted, daring to look at me for a moment.

I felt rapture; the look of supplication in his eyes was most enticing and, in a way I could not understand, it triggered tremors of sensation that radiate from the wetness between my thighs.

'Let us begin,' Constance said. And indeed she began, snapping the cane sharply on the left buttock. I watched it land, heard the swish, the snap and then saw the thick red stripe imprinted on his flesh.

It was my turn. I felt pity for him but I also felt a sense of duty. I raised the cane high and brought it down swiftly on his right buttock. Constance examined him carefully and then nodded her approval; the line across his flesh was just right. We were indeed writing lines of scripture on his flesh, thick red stripes across his bare skin, tightly packed lattices of pain that we rained on him in turn.

His pain had to be intense, but he kept his tongue, releasing only a serious of sighs and moans as the intensity of our punishment increased. At last he shuddered and fell forward slightly and at that time Constance signalled for me to stop. We looked at him for a moment, feasting our eyes on this fine young man who had so willingly submitted to our divine punishment. I was certain that it had done him some good and I felt a glow of satisfaction as I had never felt before.

Annie was summoned and her eyes lit up with excitement when she laid eyes on our prone young man, his manly body patterned red by our supple canes. She was sent off to call a cab for me. Time had flown by so quickly and it was now almost eleven o'clock, not a time for a young lady to be out alone.

'You may wait outside in the hallway until the cab arrives. I will of course pen a note of thanks to your dear parents, God bless them.'

'Thank you, Auntie,' I sighed. One last departing look at our young man and then I tore myself away.

I caught sight of myself in the mirror and was surprised by the pinkness of tone and the light in my eyes. I looked radiant, and that was exactly how I felt. Radiant and righteous, certain in the virtue of my good work that evening.

Constance emerged from her parlour a minute later, a strange look on her face. I rushed to her, suddenly fearful. Never had I seen her look so uncertain.

'Tell me, dear child,' she said, choosing her words ever so carefully. 'Does your father have in mind a suitable young man for your betrothal?'

The question was unexpected and my surprise expressed itself in the look on my face. I shook my head, then remembered that Father had spoken highly of Albert Linklater, a distant cousin of mine who was seeking a wife. 'There may be someone . . .'

'This may be an odd request, my child, but surely the Lord works in the most mysterious of ways. Our young penitent is no other than George FitzWilliam, an eminently respectable and fine young man, with all the good breeding and family connections that any father would look for in a prospective son.'

'Constance, what are you saying?' I asked, forgetting myself completely.

'I am saying that the young man we have so recently punished has indeed found the road to salvation. He now seeks a good wife, and none could be better than the wife willing to administer strict punishment in the name of good and decency.'

Annie caught me as I fell faint, my head spinning with excitement and confusion. I remember nothing after that. I came to much later to find myself back at home, in the warmth of the family domicile, and Aunt Constance and Father discussing the arrangements for my marriage to George FitzWilliam.

The unfamiliar fire in my belly suddenly flared excitedly and I could not wait to wield the cane once more for my beloved.

Staying Over

I looked at Jan and smiled shyly, my face turning red when she returned my smile with one of her own. The more I blushed the more she seemed to enjoy my discomfort, until I turned away from her, certain that my face was a red blaze of colour. Jan always did that to me. She could reduce me to a mumbling, shy, adolescent embarrassment whenever she liked. She was a few years older than myself, I put her at around thirty, very attractive, funny, intelligent and more sophisticated than I could ever be. Added to which she was my husband's boss's wife and a near neighbour of ours, though her massive house was a mansion compared to our little place a few streets away.

The memory of our first visit to Jan and Peter's house was still very fresh. It was the first time I had met them and I was terrified that I'd do or say the wrong thing and land my husband, Chris, in trouble. In the event Jan was wonderful. She put me at ease at once, made me feel very welcome and by the end of the evening we were firm friends. Except that she could turn me into a silly schoolgirl at will. All it took was a certain look, a comment or turn of phrase and I'd be blushing furiously, much to her obvious enjoyment.

We were at her house, just the two of us, because our husbands were away, out on Territorial Army manoeuvres somewhere in Germany. Usually when Chris was away I'd stay on my own, but this time Peter had suggested that I stay the weekend at their house. It was only Jan's phone call that had persuaded me to stay with her, she seemed so bubbly and eager that I hadn't the heart to say no. Besides which both of us liked a good natter and she had a lot more gossip to tell me, especially about business and I was keen to hear from the horse's mouth how my Chris was really doing at his job.

'Come on, Susan, there's no need to look so embarrassed,' she laughed, waving her glass of white wine at me. 'I was only asking.'

'I know, but it's just that . . .' I let my voice trail to silence. She had been talking about sex again, teasing me because she knew how embarrassed I got talking about it. She was sitting on the sofa opposite, shoes off, feet up, cradling a glass of wine while we talked. Even at home she looked fabulous: very long shapely legs, lithe body, looking relaxed and comfortable. I was sitting in the armchair, dressed in a long, floppy skirt and loose top, and not looking half as good as she did, despite the fact that I was just out of my teens and a lot younger than her.

'I'm only teasing,' she smiled, swinging her long legs over the side of the sofa. Her skirt rode up and I was treated to a glimpse of bare thigh and a flash of black lacy panties. For some reason my heart was racing and I suddenly feared that she had seen where my eyes had been, and that she'd know I had been eyeing her long smooth thighs.

'I thought we were going to be talking about the office,' I said, changing the subject rather sharply.

'Oh that,' she sighed, walking barefoot across the room to get the bottle of wine. 'Who wants to talk about that boring old thing?'

'Is it true that Peter's got a new secretary?' I asked innocently.

She laughed as she poured herself another glass of white wine. 'You mean the delectable Miss Fairfax?'

'Is that her name?' I asked, in my best butter wouldn't melt in my mouth voice. I had heard all about Miss Fairfax from Chris, who described her as a hot young thing with less skirt than brain, and who was lusted after by every man in the company. Her speciality seemed to be low-cut blouses and dresses which allowed her to show off her ample cleavage, for which most men were eternally grateful and were willing to forget her nasal twang and terminal stupidity.

'Naughty, naughty,' Jan cautioned, wagging a finger at me. She offered me the bottle but I shook my head, afraid that a second glass of wine would go straight to my head and loosen my tongue even more.

'I don't know what you mean,' I laughed. For the first time that evening I began to feel comfortable. We were about to have a real cat-eat-cat session, with Delia Fairfax as our mutual victim.

'I know all about Miss Fairfax,' she assured me, returning to her seat. 'All breasts and no brains, or at least that's what all the guys are saying. Though I don't hear them complaining when she has to bend over to pick up her work and they get an eyeful. Does your Chris complain?'

That stung, sort of. 'Well, she's not Chris's secretary, is she?' I sniffed.

For a moment I was certain that I'd overstepped the mark. Jan's face seemed to darken, her eyes narrowed menacingly and I was sure that a storm of invective was on the way. I held my breath but the moment passed, her smile returned and I could breathe again.

'There's one good thing that you can say about Delia,' Jan said, 'and that's that she responds well to a firm hand.'

'What do you mean?' I asked, confused by the unexpected remark.

Jan sipped from her glass, looking at me with her pretty blue eyes which scanned my face looking for

meaning in my blank expression. 'Just that she under-
stands the need for discipline sometimes, not like a lot
of young girls these days.'

I wasn't sure whether there was a barb in there directed at me. 'You mean you've met her?' I asked,
deciding not to take the bait.

'Of course, Susan,' she replied blithely. 'You don't
think I'd let a pretty little thing like her near Peter without first seeing what she's like.'

'No, of course,' I agreed. I wished that I had as much
say in things as she did, but then being the boss's wife
certainly had its advantages. 'So,' I asked, 'what's she
really like?'

Jan laughed again, her blues eyes sparkling, her red
lips parting over even white teeth. When she laughed
like that, so natural and attractive, I felt a sudden stab
of emotion deep inside me, something that I was only
vaguely aware of. 'She's as busty as the men say, and as
flighty too, but she's harmless really. I'd say that she's
just a bit younger than you, though perhaps not as
pretty, and certainly not as intelligent.'

I blushed, I couldn't help it. 'Thanks,' I mumbled.
'Chris never says those sort of things to me.'

'Do men ever?'

'No, I suppose not. Though I wish he'd stop drooling
so much whenever he talks about Delia Fairfax . . .'

'Back to Delia again,' Jan sighed, shaking her head
sadly. She lay back on the sofa again, crossing her legs
over and letting me look at her smooth, tanned skin.

'Well, I'm sure she doesn't have to dress in those
skimpy outfits,' I complained, suddenly angry. I realised
that my glass was empty and just then I desperately
fancied another drink. I stood up and saw that Jan was
glaring at me again, obviously annoyed with me.

'It seems to me,' she said slowly, 'that you're jealous
of her, and it does you no good at all.'

'Why should I be jealous? Because I don't flash my

whatsits every chance I get?' I was getting angrier and angrier, and forgetting that Jan's husband had the power to fire and hire Chris. I ignored the icy look and crossed the room to pour myself some more wine.

'That's not a very nice attitude,' Jan said coldly, dropping the temperature in the room by half-a-dozen degrees. She still looked beautiful though, her diamond earrings adding sparkle to her face, her prominent lips pursed and pouting. It confused me, the fact that she could look so attractive when she was angry, and the fact that I was noticing how good she looked.

I picked up the bottle shakily and began to refill my glass. The neck of the bottle was dappled with droplets of condensation and I watched it slip from my hand, falling in slow motion with a sickening finality. The bottle smashed hard on the polished mahogany of the coffee table, not smashing but bouncing on the table top and then falling to the floor. The deep scratch, almost a dent, in the table top was a crescent that stood out a mile away. If that were not enough I stood, completely dumb, and watched the cool white wine pour into the thick pile of the carpet, waves of yellowy liquid glugging out and soaking into dark patches.

'For God's sake pick it up!' Jan cried, racing across the room.

I couldn't say a word. I was transfixed by the sight of the bottle emptying on the floor. My horror was absolute; the scar on the coffee table was leaping out at me and grabbing me by the throat. It wasn't wine spilling out on the floor, it was my future seeping away.

Jan grabbed the bottle from the floor but it was almost empty. She glared at me angrily and if looks could kill then I was a dead woman for sure. She pushed me out of the way but there was nothing she could do, the damage had been done, and done by me.

'I'm sorry,' I whispered, amazed to find that the power of speech had returned at last.

'Sorry? Sorry? Is that all you have to say?' she screamed, absolutely livid.

'I'm sorry, I'll pay for the damage of course . . .' I said quietly, backing away from her slowly.

'Of course you'll pay! Look at it! Look what you've done!'

'I'm sorry . . .'

'And you had the gall to complain about Delia?' she continued, raising her eyes in disbelief.

'I said I'm sorry,' I said in a voice so small it was hardly there.

'At least Delia knows when she's been a bad girl.'

That did it, my sense disappeared there and then, finished off by the mere mention of Delia Fairfax again. 'What do you mean?' I whispered.

'Delia Fairfax would not only have cleared this mess up, and offered to pay for the repairs, but she would have accepted her punishment too.'

'I will pay . . .' I repeated, aware that I hadn't even tried to clear the mess up.

'And the rest?'

'If I need to be punished . . .' I began then stopped. It occurred to me that I had no idea what I was talking about and rather than make an even bigger fool of myself I shut up.

'You do need to be punished, young lady,' Jan warned me. Her temper seemed to be going and I was grateful for that and eager to seize on the chance to make things up.

'What sort of punishment?' I asked innocently. I imagined that I'd have to spend the weekend doing all the washing up, and the hoovering, and any other task deemed appropriate.

Jan went back to the sofa and sat down, placing her knees close together and sitting on the edge of the seat. 'Come here,' she ordered, pointing to a spot a few inches to her right.

I walked across the room, trying not to look at the damaged coffee table. The sheen of polished mahogany was spoiled by the deep crater I had accidentally created. I stopped in front of her, ready to be lectured and strangely excited by it.

'I think that a firm spanking is in order,' she explained, in a voice so clear and commanding that it went straight to the heart of me. 'You've been a bad girl, not just by making the mess but also what you were saying about Delia, and what you were inferring about her and Peter.'

My mind had stopped at the word spanking. I looked down at her, my heart racing and my face flushing red with shame. 'A spanking?' I repeated nervously.

'Yes. I think you'll remember it well, and it'll teach you to behave yourself in future,' she explained calmly.

I could think of nothing else to say, my mind had gone completely blank. My only thought was that I shouldn't cry; that I would hold back the tears of confusion and horror that welled in my eyes. Jan patted her knees primly and I understood that she wanted me to lie across her knees.

'Skirt up, girl,' she said briskly, in the no nonsense voice which turned me into jelly. Very slowly I hiked up my long, loose skirt, lifting it higher, above the knee, over my bare thighs until it barely covered my knickers. My face had never been redder and I hardly dared to look at her, knowing that her eyes were eating me all up.

When I hesitated she grabbed my wrists and pulled me over her knee, balancing me on the end so that I had to reach out to hold myself in place. She pulled my skirt up all the way, revealing my lacy white panties pulled tightly between by firm round bottom cheeks.

'Is this going to hurt?' I asked, stupidly. I had never been spanked before, not even as a child.

'It wouldn't be a punishment otherwise,' Jan told me. If I had anything else to say it was silenced by the sudden stinging on my behind. I squealed, shocked by the hard smack which fell on my right bottom cheek. It hurt terribly, a sharp stinging on my flesh. I looked back and saw Jan's hand raised high again. She brought it down hard on my backside again. I bit my lip to hold back my cries. Again and again she raised her hand and brought it down hard, smacking down with a sharp slapping noise that filled the room with its heavy rhythm.

Before very long my behind was alive with a red, smarting pain that seemed to ooze through my body. The burning sensation was worsened by the feeling of abject shame and humiliation that I felt. I buried my face in the pillows on the sofa as Jan proceeded to give me twenty hard strokes with the flat of her hand.

'I hope that in future you'll behave yourself properly,' Jan told me. Her voice had lost none of its venom and I knew she was still angry with me and that made me feel worse, much worse.

'I will, Jan, honestly I will,' I promised tearfully.

She allowed me to stand up, and unzipped my skirt so that it fell in a bundle around my ankles. I knew that the redness of my behind was matched by the redness of my face as I stood in front of her, my backside quivering and stinging with the residual pain of so many bare hand smacks.

'Turn round then, let me look at you,' she ordered.

I turned round and she touched me, stroking her hand to my punished skin, over the lacy panties which had been pulled tighter into my body as I had been bent across her knees. She hooked her finger under the panties and began to inch them down. Instinctively I grabbed my knickers and tried to pull them up and as I did so I nicked her skin with the sharpness of my long painted fingernails.

She slapped my hand sharply and pulled my panties down to my knees, exposing the roundness of my bottom to her view. She touched me firmly, pressing her fingers into the heat of my flesh. It felt good, the raw heat cooled down by the pressure of her fingertips, sending spasms of pleasure that pierced my body.

'Look.'

She showed me her hand, a red mark across her first finger, where I had scratched her with my fingernail. 'I'm ever so sorry,' I whimpered.

'Not sorry enough obviously,' she said. 'Stay there.'

I didn't have the heart to disobey. I felt miserable. The pain in my flanks had lost the sharpness and was now an ebbing warmth that was affecting me strangely. I was miserable but excited also and that made me feel nervous. Jan had walked across the room and was now returning. The slipper she held in her hand made my heart sink even lower for I knew that I was to be punished again.

'I said I'm sorry,' I whispered, rooted to the spot and unable to move.

'That's all you've been saying all night.'

She sat back down, this time her skirt was raised high and I couldn't help but stare at her lithe thighs, her skin smooth as silk and tanned a pure gold. I went across her knees again, this time with my knickers around my ankles and my pink derrière completely on display. I clenched my backside, embarrassed by my nakedness, and certain that she was enjoying my shame in some way.

I turned in time to see her lift the heavy leather slipper, one of Peter's I guessed. Her hand was poised for a moment and then came down swiftly, in a graceful arc that finished with a wicked smack on my bottom. This time I did not scream. I clenched myself again as the leather slipper was applied slowly and methodically by Jan. She beat me on both bottom cheeks, at the top of my thighs, between my thighs. The pain was incandescent as each blow was stroked onto my bared backside, first on one side and then the next; a pause between each stinging stroke.

Jan's thighs beneath me were a torment. She felt warm and soft, and the rubbing of her skin on mine was driving me insane with pleasure at the same time as the pain on my sore round cheeks. The heat on my behind slowly merged with the heat in my belly until I didn't know what was what. All the sensations merged into one powerful feeling of excitement. My strength ebbed away, my thighs had parted and I was lifting my bottom up to meet the downward stroke of the slipper.

'Well, well,' Jan remarked, dropping the slipper beside me on the sofa. I winced when her fingertip made contact with my raw backside.

'Don't ... please don't ...' I begged as she stroked her hand over the curves of my backside, and then over the groove between my buttocks and thighs. I was still over her knees and vulnerable and she was exploring my body completely. I didn't have the strength to stop her, no matter how much I tried to squeeze my thighs together.

Her fingers stroked between my thighs, teasing me deliciously. I caught my breath, held it and then sighed, unable to hide the fact of my pleasure. Her fingers teased into my body and touched me there, sending a million spirals of pleasure through my soul. I lifted myself, opening myself to her explorations.

'Look,' she said, offering me her fingers, coated with moisture from my sex.

I was overcome with shame. That which I had struggled to keep hidden was now apparent. She had spanked me and I had found pleasure in it, excited by my punishment and by the beauty of her body.

'Please, don't tell Peter or Chris ...' I begged her, sighing once more as she rubbed her fingers between my thighs, caressing my tight rear hole before entering my wetness again.

'You *have* been a bad girl,' Jan said, smiling, 'and I'm sure that the men are going to want to know all about it.'

'Please, I'll do anything,' I wailed. I tried to lift myself but she used her hand to spank me hard, three swift strokes at the top of the thighs. I could do nothing, except take my spanking and listen to her.

'You've always been a good girl,' Jan told me, her voice becoming tender once more. 'Today I saw a side of you that I didn't like, and I think that it's going to take a few more sessions before you've really understood what it is to be good. Like Delia I think you need a firm, female hand to keep you in place.'

'Yes, Jan,' I submitted softly.

'Good. It's still only Friday night, we've got two days before the boys get back, that's two days for me to straighten you out. Agreed?'

I nodded vigorously. My face was red again but secretly I was thrilled. I didn't know why, but I understood then and there that Jan wanted to help me. Besides which I was starting to enjoy the discipline which she had so adroitly administered.

'Good. Now, up you get. I think it's time for us to go to bed, you can clean up tomorrow.'

'Yes, I will, I promise,' I said. I stood up and bent over to pick up my skirt and clothes and she touched me again, running her hand over the length of my thigh and stroking my sore bottom cheeks. I accepted her touch with a smile, wincing only when she touched the sorest marks left by the slipper.

'Right, I suggest that you have a quick shower and then I'd like a word with you in my room before you retire. Oh, and leave your clothes here, I think that you should perhaps spend some time walking around like that, it'll remind you of why you've been spanked.'

I accepted that also, without question. A shower sounded so inviting and I skipped up the stairs feeling elated, happier than I had been for a long time. The hot water soothed my body and as I soaped myself my body responded naturally. My nipples puckered as the water trailed down between my breasts. My backside was a haze of feeling, very warm and exciting, and I couldn't help but touch myself where Jan had touched me. I felt deliciously sensual and the pleasure I gave myself was complete bliss. I emerged from the shower feeling more refreshed than I had done for a long time.

Putting on a robe I went directly from the shower to Jan's room, across the hall from the spare room that I was staying in. I was naked under the robe and my body was tingling all over. I knocked hesitantly and waited for Jan's answer before going in.

'I just wanted to check your bottom before you go off to sleep,' she explained, apparently oblivious to my shy looks at her half-naked body. She had undressed and was wearing only a lacy half-cup bra and black panties. There was no doubt that she looked after herself, her body was firm and well-proportioned with large nippled breasts, a firm stomach and incredibly long legs.

'The pain's not so bad, now,' I told her.

She motioned for me to go over to where she was standing, in front of the mirrored doors of her wardrobe. She made me turn my back to them and then let the robe fall from my body. I turned and saw my nakedness reflected back to me, and my pink skin became a glowing red on my well-marked backside. The image excited me, my nipples hardening visibly as Jan watched.

'Bend over,' she ordered.

When I looked round I could see my nether regions exposed in the mirror, the tautness of my bottom pulling the bottom cheeks slightly apart, the dark crease between my thighs displayed fully. She touched me again, intimately caressing my body, her fingers teasing the labia apart to seek the juices of my body.

165

'Tomorrow morning I shall expect breakfast from you,' she informed me. 'I'll expect you to clean up the house and to arrange the repair of the coffee table. Understood?'

'I will, I promise,' I replied contritely.

'Any infractions will be severely punished,' she added.

'I'll do my best to be a good girl,' I assured her, in deadly earnest.

'Good. I want to leave you with something to think about,' she said.

The belt whistled through the air and striped my backside forcefully. I had been lulled into a false sense of security and I couldn't help but cry out. She looked intent and neither my cries nor my appeals for mercy were going to deflect her. Six hard strokes of the belt were applied, each biting cruelly into my already punished behind. I could see my reflection. My bottom displayed to perfection while she chastised me expertly.

'Now you can go to your room,' she said, running a fingernail along one of the tracks raised on my skin.

I stood up shakily, my eyes filled with tears and yet unable to hide my hardened nipples or the flush of red across my breasts. I was aroused and excited beyond endurance by this beautiful and powerful woman. She kissed me once, touching her lips to mine, sucking the breath from my body and igniting fires of desire deep in my heart. We parted though I didn't want to, but she pointed to the door and I limped out of the room, disconsolate and confused, my bottom marked with thick red stripes cut by the belt. It was going to be a long night, but already I longed for the new day to begin.

Staying Over 2

The long dark hours of the night had been a torment for me and, much as I had wished for a long dreamless sleep, the moment I had drifted off I was sucked into a strange fantasy that had disturbed me all the more. Waking up to the brittle light of dawn I could remember nothing of that strange dream but that Jan's lips had been fire on my body, the same fire that she had inflicted earlier than evening on my backside – first with her hand, then the slipper and finally the belt.

What was I to do? Not only had I made a fool of myself in front of Jan, whose husband Peter was my husband's boss, I had also been punished by her. My mind still reeled at the thought – that I, a grown woman, should be put over another woman's knee and soundly spanked. What was worse, much much worse, was that she had touched her fingers to the moistness of my sex and discovered that I had been aroused by it all. It was something I did not understand, but the more she had beaten me, the more she spanked and punished, the more excited I seemed to become.

I dressed quickly after my shower, loose skirt down to my ankles and floppy sweat shirt that hid the contours of my pert breasts. Deliberately shapeless, I was dressing to cover myself up, too afraid to think of what the new day might bring. I skipped down the stairs quietly after getting dressed, hoping that I'd be able to concentrate on breakfast and not have to think too hard about what had happened. My only desire was to please

Jan, hoping that she'd forgive me for drenching the carpet with white wine and scarring the coffee table with the bottle that I'd dropped.

Thankfully she was still asleep when I came down, and I had the luxury of silence as I cooked up breakfast. I was with Jan for the whole weekend. The last thing I wanted was to end the weekend in Jan's bad books, especially as I knew that her husband Peter always took her views seriously. My husband, Chris, would have been furious if he'd seen the mess I had made on the carpet and the damage I'd done to their furniture.

'Ah, fresh coffee,' Jan exclaimed, walking into the kitchen suddenly, startling me.

'Sorry . . .' I whispered apologetically, 'I hope I didn't wake you. I was doing my best to be quiet.'

She smiled at me, her lovely blue eyes filled with amusement. 'No, it's OK, you didn't wake me. Now, I'd love a cup of that coffee.'

I jumped to it, hands almost shaking as I poured her a cup of piping hot coffee. She had taken a seat at the breakfast bar, perched high on one of the stools, her legs crossed over casually. Her pretty red robe scarcely covered her long bare thighs and my eyes were drawn to them. She had such lovely, tanned skin; smooth and flawless. It was impossible not to feel a temptation to reach out and touch her. I looked up and her eyes were on me, sinking deep into my own. I blushed and turned away from her piercing gaze.

'I'll ring up and find someone to repair the coffee table,' I told her, placing the coffee on the bar beside her.

She turned towards me, her robe slipping open at the chest to reveal the deep cleavage of her breasts, tanned the same golden colour as her thighs. 'It's a Saturday,' she pointed out coolly. 'I just hope you're lucky enough to find someone.'

'I am ever so sorry,' I repeated, my voice trembling.

Her nipples were pressing against the thin silky robe, two points that were bulging against the scarlet material. Why was I looking at her? I felt the fear and confusion deep inside me, and yet I could hardly keep my eyes from her body.

'Well,' she purred wickedly, 'I can always put you across my knees again, young lady. Don't think that I've forgotten, or that I'll let your bad behaviour pass.'

I swallowed hard. 'No, of course not,' I agreed, as though it were entirely natural to be hauled across the lap of another woman and to have my naked bottom tanned red. The thought meant that the red flush of shame did not leave my face. I stood awkwardly in front of her, feeling like a silly schoolgirl about to be punished. The memory of her hand coming down so hard on my quivering bottom cheeks was imprinted on my consciousness. I could see it and feel it even as I stood there.

Breakfast was an awful, tense period. I was on tenterhooks, afraid that I'd make some stupid mistake and have to pay for it. In contrast Jan was completely relaxed and in fact seemed to take some pleasure from my squirming, fearful condition. I noticed the way her robe kept falling open, how she crossed and uncrossed her legs and enjoyed the way I watched her.

'I'm going to take a quick shower,' she told me. 'There's a towel in the airing cupboard, be a darling and bring it up to me in a moment.'

I nodded and watched her go. The silk robe was cinched tight around her waist, her long thighs barely covered, her tight round behind wrapped in red silk. My hands were shaking when I turned back to the breakfast things. Quickly I cleared everything away, anxious not to displease her.

I could hear the spray of the shower as I nervously approached the bathroom. My heart was pounding as I clutched the heavy pink towel, still warm from the airing cupboard. I knocked gently on the door, waiting for her order to enter. The water was turned off and then she called for me. I pushed open the door and entered the humid atmosphere of the bathroom.

Jan was naked, her body glistening with a thousand jewels of water, rivulets of it running down her golden flesh, over her shoulders and between her thighs. She looked gorgeous and my eyes drank in every inch of her nakedness. She was standing in the shower, arm outstretched with a wry smile on her face. Her eyes sparkled with that faint good humour, as though she enjoyed my discomfort. Shakily I reached out to give her the towel, mesmerised by her sensual smile. How I could let it happen I don't know, but all of a sudden her smile was gone and I was looking at the towel around her ankles, soaking in every drop of water that fell from her body.

'I see you haven't completely lost your touch,' she snapped coldly.

'I . . . I . . .' I whimpered, my face draining of colour. I knelt down quickly and picked up the towel. It was completely soaked through and now utterly useless.

'Is there another one downstairs?' she demanded impatiently.

'I've got one in my case,' I reported, remembering that I'd packed extra in my overnight case.

'Get it quickly then,' she snapped, 'or would you rather I froze to death?'

I hated the sarcasm in her voice and knew that the biting anger would inevitably lead to something else. I sprang across the house to my room and returned, holding the towel close to my chest, my heart pounding loudly. I could hardly believe what had happened, especially after the effort I'd put in to preparing breakfast.

She snatched the towel from me and began to dry herself, stepping out of the shower at the same time. I watched her patting herself dry, her skin suffused with excitement, her nipples puckering so that they were hard

brown peaks on her full, round breasts. Her eyes were
ice cold, regarding me with nothing but anger.

'Will I be punished for that?' I asked, my voice a
whisper that hardly came out.

'Oh yes,' she told me, without a shadow of doubt.
'You'll be punished, and punished well.'

'But, Jan,' I said, looking at her earnestly, 'it was an
accident . . .'

'It was carelessness,' she replied, pulling her scarlet
robe tightly around her waist. 'Don't think you can talk
your way out of this, young lady. Delia knows enough
not even to attempt that now and I'm sure that eventually you'll learn the lesson too.'

I had completely forgotten about Delia, the flighty
young secretary whom I had been jealous of. She too
had been punished by Jan. Had she taken her punishment more calmly than myself? I had never even set eyes
on her, but knew that she was a lively young thing, and
very attractive according to all the men. I had a sudden
vision of her bent over Jan's knees, her pretty little rump
being soundly spanked. I was a strange idea, but for
some reason it excited me immensely.

'Step into the shower,' Jan ordered, snapping me back
to the real world.

I complied, stepping out of my slip-on shoes and into
the shower. The tiles were wet and slippery with water.
She reached down and lifted my long skirt, pulling it up
and over my waist, exposing the black panties I was
wearing.

'Hold this,' she told me, giving me the tight bundle
she'd formed of the hem of my skirt.

I held my skirt high, knowing that I had no choice.
I could feel her eyes assessing my body, travelling up
over my calves, over my thighs to rest finally on my
rounded posterior. Was I still red from the previous
day's punishment? I didn't know, but in any case my
tight black panties would have kept that well hidden.

171

The first stirrings of desire were making me wet between the thighs, making my pussy tingle deliciously.

Without warning my panties were pulled down, pulled roughly from my body and forced down between my knees. Now I was exposed completely, my bottom cheeks displayed to Jan's obvious satisfaction. She touched me, rubbing her fingers inside my thigh with the kind of firm, sensual caress that caused an instant tremor of pleasure to pass through me.

'Bend over,' she continued, barking her order.

When I obeyed she pressed a finger into my wetness, as though checking to confirm that I was aroused. I could feel the moisture coating her fingers and my face burned with embarrassment. My sighs of pleasure were silenced by an angry slap on the thigh.

'I do think,' she explained, 'that by the end of the day you'll not even be able to sit down. I can see that I'm going to have to be very stern with you. Do you understand?'

'Yes, I think so,' I murmured, too afraid of her to disagree. Lovely Jan, whom I had always admired and liked, was turning out to be a disciplinarian far more strict than I had ever imagined possible.

'Count out the strokes,' she added.

I tensed, hoping that I could keep down the pain. She raised her hand and brought it down swiftly, the crack of flesh on flesh resounding around the room like an explosion. It pained, white-hot and intense, the first stroke touching me on my exposed behind. My thighs quivered as I let out a great cry of horror and complaint.

'Silence!' she demanded. 'You failed to count out the stroke, I'll start again, just as I will every time you forget.'

Stupid me! I clenched my muscles again but to no avail. She hit home with a firm handed slap at the top of my right thigh. It felt as though the world were on fire, the sudden intense sensation giving way to a terrible smarting pain. My skin was glowing. I didn't need to look to know that. This time I didn't make the same mistake, I exhaled the count of one as though it were the only thing that mattered.

Bent over at the waist, skirt in hand, backside blazing, I counted out each stroke in turn. She was cool and efficient, spanking me on each bottom cheek, making sure she turned every inch of my derrière red with pain. I howled and wriggled, the heat oozing into me, tunnelling into the desire that I could not deny. At last I was crying, wet tears rolling down my face as the pain turned to pleasure and I teetered on the edge of climax. She stopped suddenly, reached down and stroked her fingers between my thighs.

'You *bad* girl,' she scolded. My bottom was ablaze with red heat and I raised myself, waiting with delicious expectation for the blow to land.

I screamed and wailed as the jet of cold water blasted down onto me. She had turned the shower on and the ice-cold water rained down on me, soaking through my clothes. The cold water cascaded down my skin, over my spanked backside and down my thighs. It was not what I had been waiting for, and my desire seemed to expand, so that my body hungered for release, longed to feel her fingers inside me.

'I want you dressed and downstairs in five minutes flat,' Jan warned me, turning off the cold water.

I stood up, my body weak with desire, my backside smarting horribly. The cold water did nothing for the heat inside me, which blazed like an underground fire deep in my soul.

Jan was waiting for me, sitting in the front room, her arms crossed impatiently across her chest. The stern look in her eye had not softened and it filled me with trepidation. I had dried myself quickly and changed clothes. I was now wearing a summer dress a good few inches above the knee, and so thin that she could see that I was without a bra.

'There's still the repair to the coffee table to arrange,' she reminded me. 'And there are lots of things to do around the house.'

'I'll get onto someone about the coffee table immediately,' I offered. My backside was burning, sending conflicting signals through my body, but I knew that I had to fight the strange feelings bubbling up inside me.

'Will I have to punish you again today?' she asked, her eyes gazing directly into mine.

'I hope not,' I answered, my voice small and vulnerable.

'Turn around, let me see your bottom.'

I turned and lifted the back of my dress, letting her see the skimpy white briefs I was wearing.

'Take your knickers off,' she ordered. 'I want to see how well you've been chastised.'

I obeyed and slipped off the white panties. The cool air touched my burning backside, which was red with her finger marks, a fact I had verified with a quick look in the mirror.

'Good,' she said, smiling. 'You look like you've had a thorough spanking, Delia is going to like that.'

'Delia?' I repeated.

'She's on her way,' Jan reported, a malicious grin on her face. She was enjoying herself. Her blue eyes were wide with delight and her smile was pure, wicked pleasure.

My world was falling apart. Not only was I being punished and somehow finding a perverse pleasure in it, now my punishment was going to become common knowledge. My mind raced with all the possibilities: Delia telling everyone at the office about it, the story spreading like wildfire until Chris heard about it.

'Please, Jan, anything but that,' I whispered, my vision blurred by the tears swelling in my eyes. How could she be so cruel, I wondered?

'It's for your own good,' Jan told me, her voice suddenly losing its harsh tone, and sounding almost tender.

'Please, can you just spank me and forget about anything else?'

'No, this is for your own good, young lady,' Jan told me.

I looked at her. Her breasts were almost completely exposed by her thin robe, and her bare thighs did strange things to my imagination. She stood up and walked towards me, her robe falling completely open.

Her kiss was electric and I felt as though she were passion itself. I let her kiss me on the lips, let her stroke my stinging bottom cheeks, let her caress my nipples through the thin cotton of my dress. I would have done anything for her, anything at all. I longed to touch her back, to feel her thighs and breasts, to taste her flesh but I resisted the temptation and held back.

'Be a good girl now,' she whispered.

In a daze I set to work, only vaguely aware that I was naked under the thin dress I wore. She touched and caressed me every time she passed, keeping me hot and excited. I called and arranged for someone to repair the coffee table, then I did the household chores. I followed her around like a puppy. Each time I saw myself in the mirror I saw the same confusion mixed in with sexual arousal, what was Jan doing to me?

The carpet was slightly stained after my accident with the wine the previous evening and so I got down on my hands and knees with the carpet cleaner and began to scrub it into the stained patch. I must have been working hard, really putting all my energy and attention into it, because I didn't hear the door bell. The first inkling I had that someone else had arrived was when I heard voices at the door of the front room. With a sickening feeling in my stomach I slowly turned and looked up.

175

My short dress had ridden up at the back, exposing the full length of my thighs and my naked backside, the buttocks nice and round as I was on all fours.

'I see that she's been a bad girl already,' the new arrival remarked, an amused smile on her face. Her eyes were focused on my behind and her pretty blue eyes looked as though they too could become stern and cruel if required. She was tall and blonde, her hair much fairer than Jan's, and she was dressed in a very tight, very short skirt and a tight blouse that was low cut enough to reveal the slope of her firm breasts.

'Delia, this is Susan, Chris's wife,' Jan explained, not batting an eyelid at my obvious embarrassment. 'And Susan this is Delia, whom you've heard all about.'

I stood up quickly, brushing down my short dress and wishing that the world would open and swallow me whole. Her smile grew broader. She was enjoying my distress in much the same way that Jan did.

'Hi, I never expected to meet you in this sort of situation,' Delia giggled.

'No, neither did I,' I managed to say, mumbling like a naughty child caught in the act. Would she tell everyone about what she had seen? The thought was uppermost in my mind. I was terrified that Chris would find out.

'Some coffee, please, Susan,' Jan ordered, taking a seat. She had dressed for the day, a long skirt with a split at the side that fell open when she sat down.

I hesitated. Why was I the one to make the coffee? It should have been Delia, but there was no time for me to complain. I nodded mutely and made for the kitchen, feeling at once glad to be away from Delia and at the same time annoyed that I was being spoken to like a minion. I slammed a couple of coffee cups on a tray, milk and sugar and then water for the fresh coffee to filter through the machine. The laughter I heard from the other room pierced me, like a stab wound in the belly.

They were chatting quietly when I came into the room, conspirators that fell silent when I entered. The tension was electric and I was certain that they had been talking about me. Delia was sitting on one of the armchairs and I walked towards her first, offering her the tray. She smiled and took one of the cups full of coffee, and then added the milk and sugar. As I turned away her hand stroked up along my thigh and towards my pussy, still moist with barely suppressed excitement. I had been taken by surprise, shocked that Delia should touch me in that way. I yelped my shock and turned quickly, spilling the coffee from the second cup into the tray.

'Why did you do that!' I demanded angrily, spinning round to face Delia. The coffee lake on the tray swirled around but thankfully did not leak onto the carpet. I was livid. At that moment all I could think about was my injured pride.

'Do what exactly?' Delia retorted, looking innocently at Jan as though she had no idea what I was talking about.

'She touched me!' I explained to Jan, my voice rising with frustration. 'She put her hand up my dress and touched me!'

'You're lying! I did no such thing!' Delia insisted, adopting an injured tone of voice.

'Enough of this, both of you!' Jan cried, her shrill voice bringing us both to silence.

I looked sulkily at Delia and my eyes narrowed accusingly. She had touched me, the bitch, and now she was trying to get me into trouble. I had imagined her to be a silly little flirt but never such an out and out schemer. She was trying to make me look bad so that she could worm her way further into Jan's good books.

'I had brought the two of you together in the hope that you'd be friends,' Jan explained. 'But it seems to me that both of you would rather be at each other's throat than be friends.'

'That's not true,' Delia interjected, pouting her rouged lips so that they were prominent and glossy. Her skin was milky white and the red lipstick she wore made her mouth look rosy and kissable; I could understand why the men were all in love with her.

'It's your fault,' I said quietly, looking first at her and then at Jan.

'I won't have this bickering in my house,' Jan declared. 'Do I really have to punish you both before you learn to behave?'

'But *I didn't do anything*!' I repeated, exasperated.

'Neither did I,' Delia chimed in on cue.

'That does it!' Jan decreed. She stood up, her blue eyes blazing fire. 'I think that both of you need to be taught a lesson.'

'In front of *her*?' Delia asked, her smile disappearing at last. The horror in her eyes matched my own, her sense of superiority evaporating instantly.

'Yes, in front of her,' Jan told her. 'Now, both of you, to my room.'

I could have refused. I could have simply turned around and walked out of the door, but I didn't. With pounding heart and excitement in my veins, I turned, put down the coffee tray and walked to the door. Delia had fallen silent too. She was biting her lower lip nervously. She followed me up the stairs and I was aware that she could see right up my short flared dress, which flapped gently as I walked.

Jan followed the two of us into her bedroom, her silence making us both feel even more nervous. I couldn't help wondering what she had planned for us. Whatever it was it had to be painful – I knew that much. She walked to her wardrobe and opened the door slowly, put her hand in for a second and the closed the door again. I inhaled sharply, frightened by what she had retrieved.

'Please, Jan,' Delia whispered, voicing my own feelings. 'Not the cane. We'll be good, we promise.'

'You should have thought of that earlier,' was all Jan could say, flexing the long yellow bamboo cane in her hands. Her eyes were cold. Her anger had gone and was now replaced with a cool determination to extract punishment.

'But it wasn't my fault . . .' I whispered.

'Both of you, I want you on the bed, hands and knees. Quickly now!'

We scrambled onto the bed, on all fours side by side, ankles hanging over the edge of the bed, bottoms raised high. My short dress did nothing to cover my behind but Delia's was well hidden by her tight skirt.

'Skirts up, both of you, I want to see your pretty little backsides good and proper,' Jan told us.

I flipped the hem of my skirt over my waist and as I did so I turned and watched Delia struggling with her skirt. A curt nod from Jan and I understood. I reached round and helped lift Delia's tight black skirt over her waist. Underneath she was wearing pretty lace knickers that were pulled tightly between her round bottom cheeks. I needed no bidding, I hooked my fingers under her panties and pulled them down quickly. Her skin was hot to the touch, as though her body was responding to the anticipation of the cane.

'Good, I should think that six strokes each should be enough for now,' Jan informed us.

'Please . . .' Delia whimpered, one last entreaty on her lips as Jan raised the cane high.

I screamed, my voice filling the room and drowning out the whack of the cane which landed so forcefully on my behind. I hadn't been expecting the first stroke and the agony was unbearable. I sucked air into my lungs, hoping to breathe away the intense white heat of pain. The red stripe felt like fire across my bottom cheeks, I could feel it raised against the whiteness of my flesh.

Delia cried out too, wincing and shaking as the cane swished down onto her beautifully naked behind. She ached and cried, gritting her teeth. I sneaked a look back and saw the redness flared across her firm bottom cheeks. Side by side, the two of us ached. Our naked posteriors striped red with one stroke each. I winced when Jan touched me, her long fingers exploring the single track across my behind.

The second stroke was no better then the first. I burned in agony, my bottom quivering as the redness spread across my skin. The white flash of impact turned into the intense redness that somehow seeped into the rest of my body. I cringed instinctively when the cane came down on poor Delia's backside.

A third and then a fourth stroke, me and Delia in turn. It hurt so much, more than a hand spanking, more than the slipper, even more than the belt. Yet still the fire seemed to become one with the sexual heat that ignited in my pussy. I felt excited; the pleasure incomprehensible to me but real all the same.

'Now, girls,' Jan directed, pausing to admire our punished backsides. 'I want you to kiss and make up.'

I turned. My face was next to Delia's, our eyes gazing into each other's. My mouth trembled open as the cane whistled down to strike my poor bottom cheeks. My cry was sucked into Delia's mouth, her lips crushing mine in a long, slow kiss. Her tongue pushed into my mouth, searching, exploring, exciting. She cried as the cane fell on her too, and I felt the exhalation of her breath as I kissed the agony away.

Like lovers we kissed with passion, as the cane stroked and burned, slicing into our chastised derrières. The excitement was unbelievable, I felt myself on the edge, enjoying the pain as it broke across my skin and was expressed in Delia's sexy, welcoming lips. I climaxed suddenly, the cane striking me for the last time as Delia kissed me lovingly. A moment later Delia shivered her orgasm as I kissed her, just as she suffered the last stroke of the cane too.

'Now,' Jan informed us coolly, 'I'll expect better behaviour from the two of you for the rest of the day.'

'Yes, Jan,' the two of us mumbled, still dazed by the mutual orgasm we had enjoyed as we were being punished.

'Good. Now, I think it's time you girls showed your appreciation,' Jan said, smiling excitedly. 'I think you ought to kiss me your thanks.'

'Mmm, yes please,' Delia murmured. She sat up and turned to face Jan. From where I lay I was treated to a gorgeous view of her bottom, latticed with thin red stripes that marked her skin so deeply. As she kissed her, Jan began to fondle the cane marks, making Delia squirm excitedly. I lay back, breathing hard. My bottom ached and stung, and yet I still felt excitement and desire. Lazily I reached out and touched my fingers under Delia's sex, she was wet, her body oozing the essence of her desire.

What would the rest of the day be like, I wondered? And the next day, my last day with Jan before our husbands returned home? I sighed, my mind filled with images I would not even have dared to imagine only a day earlier.

Staying Over 3

How could any of it make sense to me? Not only had I been spanked and seduced by the stern and beautiful wife of my husband's employer, my punishments had been witnessed by the young and pretty secretary of whom I had been so jealous. My mind was in turmoil as I lay in bed and thought of all that had passed in the last two days.

It had begun so innocently. Our husbands were away for the weekend and I admired Jan so much even though I had secretly been slightly afraid of her. She was always so elegant, so clever and so beautiful and yet not once did I suspect what lay beneath her stylish good manners and calm reassurance. Things had been going so well and then, in a moment I still could not comprehend, I had found myself across Jan's lap with my knickers around my ankles while she smacked me like a spoilt child.

The memory of that first spanking caused butterflies of excitement and desire in the pit of my belly. Why did I feel so excited by what was surely the most humiliating moment of my life? I could not explain it, but nor could I deny the fires that burned deep inside me and which caused my nipples to harden and the moisture to ooze between my thighs. As I lay in bed listening to the soft ticking of the clock I couldn't help but stroke the tips of my breasts, causing pulses of pleasure to ripple through my body.

What was happening to me? I longed for Jan to walk

into the room and for her to bark an order before turning me over to punish me yet again. The memory of her lips on mine was divine; her perfumed lips sucking the breath from my body and with it the will to resist. She had spanked me with her hand and then, later, with a slipper which made my bottom cheeks glow red with pain. How good it had been. The memories added to my excitement and I felt my body responding.

The slipper had not been the worst however. When Delia arrived, much to my shame, things had become even more difficult. I was burning red with shame that silly young Delia should find me on all fours, my backside exposed as I cleaned up after the mess I had made the previous evening. I was annoyed as well as embarrassed. It was bad enough being punished by Jan without having someone else along to enjoy it. My distress was obviously amusing to Delia, which only made me madder.

The end result, the cane, was far worse than the slipper or Jan's firm hand. It had cut deep into our flesh, making us yelp and cry as Jan taught us the strictest lesson yet. But from that pain, that constant stroking of deep red lines across our firm-cheeked backsides, there had come pleasure. Delia's mouth had found mine and we shared hot, passionate kisses as we were soundly thrashed with the bamboo cane.

I turned over, unable to sleep, distracted by the constant going over of all that had happened. My body ached with excitement, my nipples pressing hard against the thin cotton T-shirt I was wearing in bed. The clock beside the bed blinked back at me, the luminous dial telling me that it was only just gone two in the morning. It was no good, I knew that I wouldn't be able to sleep no matter what. Sitting up in bed the thin cotton panties I was wearing were pressed deep into the moistness of my sex, making me squirm with a momentary spasm of pleasure.

What should I do next? Jan was asleep in her own room, I was in the spare bedroom and Delia had been consigned to sleeping on the fold-out bed in Peter's study. I had been secretly disappointed with the sleeping arrangements. After the punishments and seduction I had half-hoped that Jan would let me spend the night in her room, in her arms, her naked body against my own. Making love to another woman had never even been a fantasy of mine, I was happy with my husband Chris, but now my feelings were haywire and I longed for Jan to kiss me on the lips again.

A midnight snack was not something I normally went for, but suddenly it seemed like an excellent idea. Perhaps it was the thought of getting out of my room and of having something else to think about apart from my confusing memories and desires. A glass of warm milk might even help me get to sleep I reasoned, tiptoeing downstairs quietly. The house was shrouded in darkness, the silence a blanket of serenity that I did not want to disturb. I made it down the stairs with hardly a creak of the floorboards and then went straight into the kitchen, careful not to make any noise lest I wake up Delia, asleep in the room across the hall from the kitchen.

The light from the fridge cast a diagonal of pale white across the room. Carefully I set to work, deciding that a sandwich would go well with a glass of milk. The bluish light from the cooker added a warm glow to the room as I set a small pan of cold milk to warm up. After a while I was so caught up in what I was doing that I completely forgot about the worries that had been keeping me awake.

'Have you got enough there for two?' Delia asked, startling me suddenly.

I turned quickly and clutched at my chest. 'You've frightened the life out of me,' I complained.

She giggled. 'Don't worry, Susan,' she said, 'I won't tell Jan if that's what you're worried about.'

184

I studied her for a moment and realised she was genuinely trying to be friendly. She was wearing bra and panties only, pretty black lace that contrasted with the whiteness of her soft skin and the crystal blue of her eyes. 'It's only hot milk I'm afraid,' I explained, pointing to the cooker. 'Do you want some too?'

'OK,' she nodded. 'You couldn't sleep then?'

'No,' I sighed, 'I just couldn't.'

'This is your first time, isn't it?'

I knew what she was talking about, there was no need for her to say more. 'You won't tell anyone, will you?' I whispered, averting my eyes from hers. With what she had seen, and experienced at my side, she was in a position to make my life a misery and we both knew it. Chris would be shocked if he found out about what had happened, of that I was absolutely certain.

'But you do like it though, don't you?' Delia asked, her eyes blazing wickedly.

I said nothing but my silence was testament enough to my confusion. She was so young and yet it was obvious that it was not her first time. I wondered how long it had been going on, how long she had been going over Jan's knee to receive her punishments?

'Why don't you leave that,' Delia suggested, taking the milk bottle from my hands as I hurried to make her a drink too.

'What are you doing?' I asked, allowing myself to be pushed against the kitchen wall. Her face was close to mine, her eyes sparkling with delight as I struggled with my feelings. I was aware of her scent, her near-naked body scented with perfume, her breasts pressed against my body as she held my hands at my side.

'Isn't it obvious what I'm doing?' she whispered, her breath warm against my face. Her lips touched mine, tentative, soft, inviting.

'No! I don't want to do this!' I cried, rebelling against the desire surging through my body. I pushed her away, frightened that I would succumb to her embrace and meet her kiss with an open hunger that I could not deny.

'Stop it! You know you want this!' she snapped, slapping me across the face, the sound echoing to silence as I clutched my cheek in shock. I could feel the red blush across my skin, the imprint of her fingers across my face. Tears welled in my eyes as the force of confusion and shame came over me like a tidal wave of emotion.

Delia kissed me and this time I could not resist. My face ran with bitter tears but my mouth was open to her tongue. The ache between my thighs was unbearable, my panties were wet with honey from my pussy and my nipples were hard points of flesh that longed for Delia's touch. I moaned softly as she slipped her hand under my long T-shirt and began to stroke the inside of my thigh, her fingers pressing forcefully against the softly sensitive flesh.

The darkness was banished and the kitchen was flooded with the harsh electric glare of the lights. I looked up, through the tears, and saw Jan standing by the door, her hand still on the light switch. I pushed Delia away and ran across the room, sobbing like a child towards Jan. The resounding slap across the face was the last thing I expected and only caused another burst of tears and more sobs from me. Why were they being so nasty to me? Why?

'So, this is where you've decided to play your squalid little game,' Jan stated coldly, her voice filled with anger and disgust. I shrank away from her, frightened by the hard slap across the face and the threat in her voice. She was glaring at us. She was dressed in a pretty pink robe that barely covered her long thighs and which was thin enough so that the dark discs of her nipples were discernible. With both hands on her hips and on austere look on her face she looked every inch the disciplinarian she had shown herself to be.

'It wasn't like that . . .' Delia started to explain, but I

could tell that she too was afraid of Jan's temper. The self-confidence with which she had attempted to seduce me had all but evaporated. Now she slunk against the wall, her eyes averted while she waited for Jan's reaction.

'I only came down for a glass of milk . . .' I said, pointing to the pan full of milk on the kitchen table.

'Is that why I found you in Delia's arms? Does that explain why Delia is half-naked? Does it?' Jan demanded, advancing menacingly into the room. I cringed, my stomach turning as I realised where things were going.

'It was her idea!' Delia blurted, pointing an accusing finger in my direction. She was smirking, her pouting lips parted sexily and her eyes sparkling with anticipation.

'That's not true! You've got to believe me, Jan, that isn't true,' I cried, trying desperately to defend myself even though I was shocked by the accusation. I remembered how Delia had touched me the first time we met and how she had taken great delight in getting me into trouble. Now she was doing it again.

'Quiet, both of you,' Jan hissed, cutting off my protestations instantly. Her heeled slippers clicked coldly on the tiles of the kitchen floor as she came towards me. My eyes were fixed on her body, focused on the tightly bound robe that showed the fullness of her breasts and the bulge of her nipples against the satin material. 'Now,' she continued, stopping in front of me. 'Who was it that came down here first?'

'I did,' I admitted, not daring to try to explain why or what for. My eyes were full of tears again but now there was also a feeling of desire inside me, a feeling of desire mixed in with a real fear of what Jan was going to do.

'I'm glad that you admit it,' Jan told me. She turned on her heels and marched across the room to Delia, still leaning against the wall, her arms crossed insolently across her chest. The smile disappeared from her face and I sensed that she too feared Jan, despite the bravado with which she had flung her accusations.

'It was her idea, she said she wanted to play games ...' Delia insisted, though her voice quivered as she spoke.

'I find that difficult to believe,' Jan told her, 'but I suspect that she was not an unwilling victim of whatever it was that you had planned for her.'

'She tried to force herself on me,' I complained, my heart filled with relief that Delia's plans had been found out. The prospect of an unjust spanking suddenly receded and I felt nothing but relief and pleasure that Delia was going to be punished for her sins.

'Susan, do you know where I keep the cooking things?' Jan asked, fixing Delia with a look that could melt an iceberg.

'In the drawer?' I guessed.

'Then you know what to get me,' Jan said. I watched her grab Delia by the arm and pull her roughly across the room to the heavy mahogany table which dominated the kitchen.

Jan was right, I had guessed what it was that she wanted. Without hesitation I went to the drawer where she kept the cutlery and cooking utensils. There was quite a choice but I selected the two items which I hoped might make the most impression: a flat wooden spatula and an old-fashioned wooden spoon. When I turned round Delia was bent across the edge of the table, her breasts squashed flat against the cool polished surface and her bottom offered high. Her black skimpy panties were pressed deep between her thighs, the thin black band of lace parting her bottom cheeks temptingly.

'Is this what you want?' I asked, handing Jan the spatula and the wooden spoon. She smiled slightly, her lips looking glossy and enticing, a tempting reminder of the pleasure I had experienced with her the previous day.

I stepped back a bit, anxious to enjoy every second of Delia's punishment. Her ankles were pressed together, her long legs in parallel so that her backside was nice and round and displayed perfectly; the thin wisps of lace barely covering her bottom cheeks and turning into a thin triangle of material against the bulge of her sex. Her face was pressed flat against the table and she was biting her lower lips. Her eyes looked at me appealingly. I smiled back, feeling an unfamiliar thrill of excitement at the prospect of watching another woman being spanked.

'Why is that I always have to discipline you whenever you visit?' Jan demanded coldly. 'It's not enough that you were caned earlier, now I have to punish you again, Delia. You've gone too far this time.'

'I'm sorry, it won't happen again ...' Delia whimpered pathetically, 'I promise.'

I watched, wide-eyed and excited, as Jan raised the wooden spoon high and then brought it down swiftly. A resounding smack filled the room, followed by a sharp yelp of pain from Delia. The red imprint of the spoon was clearly marked on her right buttock, the redness in stark contrast to the pale tones of her flesh. Such a small mark, an oval redness that probably stung unbearably. Before Delia had a chance to complain the spoon came down again, adding a second mark to her right bottom cheek.

I tried to resist the rush of pleasure that I felt, watching Delia's behind being so soundly smacked, but I couldn't. My breath was short and I could feel the desire in the pit of my belly, so strong and so uncontrollable. I longed to grab the spoon from Jan's hand and to continue the punishment myself, to get my revenge for the tricks Delia had been playing on me.

Four, five, six strokes of the spoon all landed on

Delia's right bottom cheek until she was squirming and groaning, rubbing her thighs together as though she could rub away the pain burning on her backside. Each stroke was hard and precise, forming a row of red ovals on her flesh, the skin raised where the stroke was hardest.

'Oh, it hurts, it hurts,' Delia wailed, her eyes filling with tears.

Each time she squirmed, each time she moved, her panties went deeper into her pussy, exposing more of her soft flesh to the bite of punishment.

'Enough of that! You know I can't stand weakness!' Jan cried, her voice making me quiver with fear and silencing Delia's pathetic sobs instantly.

The arm went high again and Jan brought it down hard, switching target to the left side, the first stroke marking Delia's other buttock. The twin globes of her bottom were ill-matched in colour; where her right side blazed pink and red, her left was still white apart from the first blush of the first stroke. I watched avidly, listening to the hiss as the spoon came down, the hard smack of impact and the whispers of pain that escaped from Delia's quivering lips.

Two strokes and then three. A pause while Jan stroked her hand across Delia's backside and then four and five. I marvelled at how precise each stroke was, at how Jan seemed to measure every ounce of pain and punishment that she so expertly inflicted. I had been lucky to escape, I knew that such a punishment would have made me scream with horror.

There was no let up. When both of Delia's perfect bottom cheeks were tanned a deep and painful red, Jan switched target again, this time aiming her strokes at the top of the thighs. Delia cried out and tried to push herself up but I stepped forward and held her down, pressing my breasts against her back as I made sure she could not move. The more that Delia squirmed the more my nipples rubbed against her through the thin material of my top, making me sigh with pleasure at the tremors of ecstasy that were triggered inside me.

'I can see what you're doing,' Jan said quietly.

I looked up at her guiltily, realising that I had been caught out. I let go of Delia and stepped back, noting that my nipples were hard points poking against my top. My pleasure had been plain to see, only I had not realised it. Delia was still lying across the table, her bottom and her thighs patterned with ovals of pink and scarlet. I could almost feel the heat from her flesh, and could only dimly imagine the torment that was pulsing through her.

'Well?' Jan demanded, placing the wooden spoon on the table, only inches from Delia's face.

'I . . . I couldn't help it . . .' I whispered hesitantly. A sharp stab of fear tore through me and with a sinking feeling I saw that I too was going to suffer the ordeal of chastisement that night.

'I expected more from you,' Jan told me, her voice emotionless. 'After the punishments you've suffered in the last two days I had hoped that you had learned your lesson.'

'But I have,' I told her emphatically, hoping that my obvious sincerity would win some mercy.

'But you haven't, my dear,' Jan said. 'It's time you had another lesson and perhaps this time you'll not forget it so easily. I've finished with you for now,' she added, turning to look down upon Delia.

Delia pushed herself up slowly. I could see her wincing with pain as she straightened out, her long lovely legs and backside smarting horribly. When she turned to me I saw the wetness between her thighs, oozing through the thin black lace that was pressed deep into her crotch.

'Please, Jan . . .' I started to beg but one look from her told me that I was only making things worse for myself. When Jan was angry there was no stopping her, she could be as strict and as ruthless as anybody.

'Take your top off and face me,' she commanded. I pulled my top off slowly, wondering why it was that I was to be spanked like this when Delia had been allowed to keep her bra on. My face was crimson with shame as I dropped my top to the floor, my chest was already flushed pink with the pleasure I had gained by rubbing myself against Delia.

'Delia, stand behind her and cup her breasts for me,' Jan ordered.

My mind was in turmoil as Delia stood behind me and passed her hands under my arms and cupped my breasts. She teased my erect nipples with her thumbs, making me sigh with pleasure much as I hated to.

'Perhaps this is the most apt lesson you'll ever learn,' Jan told me, her clear blue eyes gazing at me steadfastly.

I swallowed hard and watched in horror as she picked up the flat wooden spatula I had selected and raised it high into the air. 'No!' I cried but it was too late. The blast of impact was unbearable as the flat wooden surface made contact with my breasts, slapping down hard against my flesh and beating hard against my erect nipples. I squirmed and tried to turn away but Delia held me in place.

The searing pain burst over me again as Jan brought the spatula down hard against my breasts again, spanking me with all the power and pleasure she had when punishing my posterior. I cried as it came down again, marking my skin red and biting hard at my nipples. The pain was intense but with it there was something else, something I had not been waiting for. Each stroke brought a surge of feeling, a powerful blast of sensation that seemed to connect with the pleasure deep between my thighs.

Like a dream I watched myself being punished, Delia's hands squeezing and moulding my breasts while they were spanked so painfully. And then, before I knew

192

it, I was pressed across the table and the spanking was resumed on my bottom cheeks. As my burning nipples, bright red points that pulsed with fire, brushed the cool mahogany surface of the table I shuddered and cried out my orgasm. Never had I felt such bitter ecstasy, so painful where the pleasure was so pure.

Jan beat me beautifully, using the hard flat surface of the spatula across the tight roundness of my behind. My white panties were pulled down around my knees, exposing the heat and the wetness of my quim, swimming in the juices of my pleasure. Each stroke across my reddened bottom cheeks sent spasms of sensuality throughout my body so that it felt as if my entire being were aflame.

All the time I was aware of Delia standing beside me, her greedy eyes drinking in the vision of my punishment just as I had watched her being punished. There was lust in her eyes also. I could see her fingers caressing her body as she watched, driven beyond endurance both by her own quivering backside and by the sight of mine.

At last it was over, the painful rhythm of chastisement had ended. Painfully, almost light-headed, I pushed myself from the table. I felt strange as I stood beside Delia, both of us in a state of undress and with our bodies marked by the force of our correction.

'I want the both of you upstairs in two minutes,' Jan told us, the excitement of her eyes reflected at last in her voice. 'It seems to me that both of you are in need of longer term treatment,' she added.

'But . . . Chris gets back tonight,' I whispered, remembering that my husband was due to return. Would it mean a return to normality for me, I wondered?

'You wouldn't want Chris to find out about this, would you?' Jan warned.

'No, of course not,' I told her hurriedly. My backside was stinging horribly, the heat merging with the lava flow between my thighs.

'Good, in that case I think we can continue as we are,' Jan decided. 'From now on I shall expect both of you to report to me regularly and if for any reason I am unhappy with your behaviour then I'll have no compunction in punishing you. Is that clear?'

I looked at Delia and then at Jan. 'Yes, we understand,' Delia and I said, sighing together.

My heart was racing with excitement. I had so much to learn and now I knew that Jan would continue to be my teacher.

'Good,' Jan smiled. 'Now, both of you upstairs, you've yet to thank me in the special way that I like . . .'

My heart jumped. Secretly I was filled with a strange fear of what the future held but that fear was part of an excitement that filled me completely. I turned towards the door, certain that my life would never ever be the same again.

Coincidence

It had begun innocuously enough I suppose. Alan and his wife moved down from Doncaster to London when he was transferred to my office. Although technically I was his superior we were close enough in age and outlook that we functioned better as a team than as competitors. He was a good worker, not afraid to get involved, and not afraid of putting in any extra effort either. I liked that about him and I suppose that matched my own temperament and way of working. Moving down from Yorkshire to London was a big step for him and Madelaine to take, especially as she had already made one move from Scotland to Yorkshire to be with him.

Neither of them had friends or family down south, so it was natural that I felt a bit protective towards them both. He was a good friend, and I didn't want to lose him as a colleague either. So, once they had moved in I took them under my wing a bit and made sure that they met my friends, made friends of their own and generally settled down quite comfortably. It hadn't been difficult, especially as they were such a nice couple. He was friendly, quiet, intelligent; she a bit bubblier, very attractive and with a warm personality.

As I said, I liked them both, and when Alan told me the date of Madelaine's birthday the coincidence seemed quite fitting. We shared the same birth date it seemed, and once the two of them found out they insisted that they take me out for a special birthday treat. I wouldn't hear of it, but of course they twisted my arm, and when she gave me that special coy smile of hers I gave in graciously. As the day approached I can remember the two of them sounding me out as to what I wanted as a present. I was adamant that a night out was more than enough but they wouldn't listen. Here I did not relent and I was scrupulous about not giving them any clues as to what I might want.

The restaurant they had chosen was perfect. Excellent food, waiters that didn't patronise, service that was exemplary and an atmosphere that could not have been bettered. As the wine flowed, as well as the conversation, I thought to myself just how lucky Alan was to have a pretty young wife like Madelaine. The two of them were so obviously in love that it hurt just to look at them. It wasn't lovey-dovey and sickly sweet, which always makes me immediately suspicious, no; theirs was more relaxed, more genuine and spontaneous.

She looked good too. There was something a little bit vain about Maddy, but given that she was so pretty anyway we could all forgive her that. Dressed in a little black dress, high heels and black stockings she looked the sexiest creature on earth, and drew more admiring glances from the waiters in the restaurant than all the other women put together. Alan noticed of course and we both took great pleasure in teasing her about it, which made her blush and us laugh.

'That was, without a doubt, one of the best meals I've ever had,' I sighed, waving over the waiter.

'We should do this again,' Madelaine laughed, leaning back into Alan's arms. They were seated opposite me and she was nestling up under his arms, which were wrapped around her in a loose, protective hug.

'It's on us . . .' Alan began to say, but before he could complain the waiter was marching off with my credit card.

'Hey! That's not fair!' Maddy complained, sitting up, a look of consternation in her dark brown eyes.

'Fair or not, I've had a great time and I don't want to spoil it with any arguments,' I told her, smiling. She smiled back and then looked away shyly, as though embarrassed by the way I was looking at her.

'In that case,' Alan decided suddenly, 'I think you ought to come back to our place for a nightcap.'

'If you think I'm going to argue, then you're mistaken,' I laughed.

Maddy smiled again, glancing up into her husband's eyes quizzically. Something was going on between them, though I had no idea then what it might be.

The blast of cold air as we emerged from the restaurant into the street was bracing; a sharp jolt of sensation that cleared the mind instantly. Alan had parked his car a few streets away and now, in the sharp cold, I could see that Maddy was in no mood to walk all that way.

'I thought you Scottish girls were used to the cold,' I joked, winking to Alan, who laughed.

'No,' he replied quickly, 'she can't stand the chill, which is why I have to warm her up every so often.'

'Alan! Please!' she exclaimed, stamping her heel on the ground angrily. Her face was bright red and she hardly dared look me in the eye.

'Tell you what then,' Alan said, his voice still full of good humour, 'you two wait here while I go and fetch the car.'

'Sure, we'll wait,' I agreed. We watched him march off, bracing himself against a sharp gust that cut through the street.

'Does he warm you up often?' I teased, enjoying the flush of embarrassment on her cheeks. Her dark eyes were intense, and I knew that I was intruding on some private joke between the two of them.

'You should have let us pay,' she said softly, deftly trying to change the subject. 'You've been good to us, this was our way of saying thank you.'

'There's no need,' I assured her, touched by the

earnest tone. She was changing the subject though, and I was more than a little intrigued to find out what the two of them were going on about. 'It was worth every penny just to see the way he teases you,' I added.

'I knew you would,' she whispered. 'You two have so much in common . . .'

'We're common now are we? I'll tell him that when he gets back!'

'Oh, you! You know what I mean,' she said, giggling.

The car washed thick beams of light over us as it came to a slow halt at the kerb. 'What are you two laughing about?' Alan asked, pushing the passenger door open.

'Your wife's just accused us of being common,' I reported, sliding into the rear passenger seat.

'I did not,' Maddy protested, getting in beside her husband. Her dress rode up and I was treated to a glimpse of black stocking top against smooth white thigh. She looked gorgeous. Alan was watching me watching his lovely young wife.

'Lovely legs, don't you think?' he asked me, lowering his voice a fraction.

'Alan! Stop that!' she cried, wriggling in her seat as she smoothed her dress down. It was no good, a dress like that was designed to flatter, designed to show off not to hide.

'Lovely legs,' I agreed, delighting in the look of shame that made her face redden even more.

'Sorry, Maddy, it's just that we're so common,' he explained, straight faced so that we didn't know if he was joking or being serious.

'That's not what I said,' she insisted, obviously believing that Alan was being serious.

'Is that or is that not what she said?' he asked me.

I hesitated and tried to measure the look in his eyes. 'Yes, exactly what she said,' I agreed finally.

He nodded, as though it were the answer he wanted

to hear. Without warning he put his foot down and we sped off. The unexpected jolt of acceleration threw us back against the seats and temporarily silenced any further conversation. That atmosphere had changed, and where I had been comfortable before, I now felt more than a little confused.

Their flat was not too far from the restaurant and, at the speed that Alan was driving, we were there in a matter of a few minutes. He parked quickly and efficiently and cut off the engine before we'd even realised we were home.

'That's not what I said,' Maddy repeated, her voice low and indistinct. She was pouting; her lips pursed and kissable, red lipstick making her mouth look glossy and seductive.

'Well, I'm a common sort of guy, perhaps I misunderstood,' I said, wondering how to get the atmosphere back to the way it had been in the restaurant.

Alan ignored her and turned to me. 'A drink?' he offered, as though nothing unusual were going on. There was a look in his eye that I couldn't decipher, but I nodded.

'A drink sounds like an excellent idea,' I agreed.

We walked from the car to the flat in total silence, though I caught the worried expression on Maddy's face. Her heels smacked hard on the pavement, drawing attention to her long, stockinged legs, covered imperfectly by her short black dress.

'I hope Maddy's not ruined your evening too much,' Alan remarked apologetically, showing me into the living room.

'Listen, that was just a gag,' I whispered, glad that she'd not followed us straight into the room.

'You're a good mate,' he responded instantly, 'and you deserve better.'

'No, you don't . . .' I began but stopped as Madelaine wandered into the room, looking thoroughly downcast.

'I'm sorry,' she mumbled to me. 'I shouldn't have said what I did. I'll understand if you never want to see us again . . .'

'She's right,' Alan added. 'I'd understand if you felt insulted.'

'A drink?' I suggested, feeling thoroughly out of my depth.

'Get the man a drink, girl!' Alan snapped angrily.

Maddy jumped. She crossed the room and began to shakily pour two beakers of Scotch, only she was pouring more of it onto the floor than into the tumblers.

'Look what you're doing!' Alan scolded her.

'Sorry, sorry,' was all she could think of saying. She put the whisky tumblers down and then looked at the pool of Scotch on the floor. Taking her hanky from her bag she knelt down to mop it up. As she did so Alan and I were treated to another display of her elegant thighs, stocking tops and soft pale skin. The shape of her backside was impressed against the tight black material, leaving little to my feverish imagination.

'Enough of that,' Alan told her promptly.

'I'm so sorry,' she whispered, sounding on the verge of tears.

'You've been sorry all evening,' he said coldly. 'I think that it's time you really had something to feel sorry about.'

If I was tempted to intervene, the threat in his voice and the responsive look on her face made me bite my tongue. For a moment it seemed that I had been forgotten about, that I was an intruder on some private domestic argument. Then Alan looked at me, the harsh look on his face not matched by the excitement I detected.

'Please, not now . . .' Maddy said, her voice barely a whisper.

Alan sat down on the very edge of the sofa and motioned for her to step towards him. I watched, fascinated by what was unfolding between them. She stopped in front of him, her head was bowed and her hands were at her sides. She looked like a recalcitrant child, bowed with guilt for all her misdemeanours, meekly waiting to be scolded.

'Across my knees,' he barked. 'I shouldn't have to tell you that.'

She glanced towards me, her face red with shame, her dark eyes unable to meet my own. My heart was pounding and the excitement in the room was electric. Very slowly she complied, moving gracefully into place across his lap. Of course her short dress revealed all, and I enjoyed everything I saw. Her tight black panties were but a sliver of darkness between her bottom cheeks, the tight material parting the round globes of flesh as Alan pulled the dress higher.

In moments I was treated to the gorgeous sight of her posterior, the dress completely pulled up to her waist by her husband. The stockings were pulled tight by lacy black suspenders, which were pressed firmly across her bottom cheeks, and which served to part them slightly. Her panties were a thin satiny thread, contrasting with the whiteness of her skin.

Alan smiled. He was showing his young wife off to me and enjoying every second of it. She muffled her complaints, and stilled for a second, realising perhaps that the time for resistance was over. Her long legs had never looked better, I was certain of that.

'Next time,' Alan warned her, 'perhaps you'll think twice about making stupid remarks to our guests.'

He raised his hand high above his head and then brought it down swiftly. The slap of flesh on flesh filled the room. A sharp sound that brought a wail of horror to her pretty lips. He waited a moment, giving me time to admire the red imprint of his hand against her right bottom cheek, before marking her again. His hand made a graceful curve, then slapped down hard against

201

her bottom cheek. Again and again. I'd never seen such hard strokes of the hand. She struggled and wriggled, but to no avail, he was intent on punishing his pretty wife completely.

Her struggles succeeded only in arousing me further; each twist of her waist, each curve of her bottom revealing more of her flesh. The panties were pulling tighter between her rear cheeks, exposing more of her reddening punishment. I noted the way her cries of horror had softened, and that she seemed to be moving into each stroke. Yes, I was certain of that. I watched her lift her posterior towards the stroke, offering her pert backside for her husband to spank.

'I see what you mean about having to warm her up,' I ventured to say at last. I was smiling, not even attempting to hide my pleasure. Her backside was tanned an even pink glow, contrasting to the darkness of her stockings and the whiteness of her upper thighs. She looked delicious and, with her punished bottom displayed so prominently, I could hardly control my own feelings.

'She does need a firm hand, sometimes,' Alan admitted, slowly rubbing his palm across the reddest part of her bottom cheeks. He was savouring every second of it, and she in turn was reacting to it fully. Her breath was sharp, her eyes half-closed with pain and pleasure.

'I can see that,' I agreed.

'But we're not finished yet, are we my dear?' Alan continued, a cruel, taunting twist to his voice.

'Please ... Don't ...' she whimpered, covering her face with her hands.

'You've been very bad these last few days. A few slaps on the backside aren't enough to pay for that,' he said, then added, 'even if it does hurt.'

He pushed her off his lap very roughly and she fell heavily to the floor, her finger-marked backside making contact with the coldness of the floor. She winced, looked at me with nothing but shame in her eyes and then turned back to her husband. Her lips were trembling and I feared she might cry. She bit her lip, trying to hold back everything that she felt.

'Get that off,' he told her gruffly, pointing to the little black dress, which no longer looked as elegant as it had earlier.

'But . . . but . . .'

'Now!' he ordered, in a voice that brooked no disagreement.

She stood up shakily, keeping her back to me, and pulled the dress off over her head. For a second no one said anything as she stood balanced on her stiletto heels, an image to enjoy. She had been topless under the dress, and from the rear I could see only the gentle curve of her breasts. Now she was clad only in stockings, panties and suspenders.

'Get those off too,' Alan decided, slapping her hard on the bottom and making her squeal.

This time there were no complaints, as if she had finally realised that resistance was pointless. She unclipped her suspender belt and pulled her panties down to her ankles. Now I could see the full roundness of her derrière; the firm globes of her shapely backside flushed pink from her spanking. She crossed her hands across her chest, covering herself while keeping her back to me.

'Well?' Alan asked, turning to me with a smile. He was justly proud of his wife's body, I could see that in his eyes.

'I'm just glad you've got her under control,' I commented, unable to keep my eyes from her backside. 'Only I wonder if she's really been taught enough of a lesson tonight.'

For a moment he seemed thrown by my remark. I don't know what he'd been expecting me to say but it wasn't that. 'You don't think she's been spanked hard enough?' he asked.

I saw her swallow hard, gulping with anticipation.

'A few slaps with the hand aren't really enough,' I explained. 'It's not exactly discipline, is it? I mean you've tickled her, but that's hardly what I call punishment.'

Alan nodded, intrigued by what I was saying. I saw her flick her eyes towards me and then look away, still too afraid to look me in the eyes. I was no longer worried. I liked the look of her and was staring openly, enjoying the sight of her reddened posterior, and of the way she was standing there between Alan and myself, vulnerable and exposed.

'And what do you call a proper punishment?' he asked inevitably. I smiled at the note of challenge in his voice, my remarks had irked him in a way that he'd not counted on.

'I'll be back in a second,' I told them both, and turned to leave the room.

'Where are you going?' she asked softly, hardly daring to speak.

'Never you mind where he's going,' Alan scolded.

I was in the kitchen in an instant, knowing exactly what to look for and where. I'd been their guest many times before and knew their house as well as I did my own. In seconds I had what I wanted and marched straight back into the front room.

'May I?' I asked, pointing to the sofa.

Alan stood up to make way for me. Maddy was panicking, trying to cover her breasts and her sex with her hands, which only made Alan and myself smile.

'Across your lap, or on the floor?' Alan asked.

'My lap I think.'

She took one long, beseeching look at Alan but there was no mercy for her. I made way for her and she slipped over across my lap, the warmth of her body and the scent of her enveloping me immediately. My hardness pressed against her side, but I made no move to hide that. Her bottom was pink and soft, her buttocks slightly parted so that I could glimpse the swell of her pussy lips.

I raised my hand high and then brought it down hard. She squealed and her cry filled the room, a few decibels louder than anything Alan had elicited from her. I looked down and saw the fresh, red imprint of the wooden spoon across her right buttock. I touched it with my fingers, pressing hard against the redness, feeling the contours of the raised flesh. Alan peered across and nodded appreciatively.

Maddy seemed to be having hysterics but I didn't let that interfere at all. The spoon smashed down hard again and again – the sharp slap of wood on her firm flesh a delightful sound to my ears. I patterned her body with red marks, each as sharp and well defined as the last, across her buttocks, at the top of her legs, between her thighs. She squirmed and struggled and I was in torment as my hardness pressed her soft body.

She cried out once, louder and more intense, and I realised that the pain had become pleasure for her. Her sex was moist, and I noted the sinuous way she moved and offered herself to the strict punishment I was giving her.

'Well?' I asked, a note of triumph in my voice.

'I see what you mean,' Alan replied thoughtfully.

'Stand in the corner,' I told her dismissively. Meekly she did as she was told, easing herself off my lap and limping to the corner. She understood what I was after and she turned her back to us so that we could admire her punished backside from a distance.

Alan passed me my drink and we stood in silence contemplating his wife's chastised body.

'Do you use a strap?' I asked, enjoying the warmth of the drink.

He nodded. 'Occasionally, though I prefer to use my hand. I've thought about getting a cane sometimes, like those old-fashioned ones you see in documentaries about Victorian times. What do you think?'

'You have to be careful with a cane,' I explained, 'but if used properly they're an excellent instrument of correction.'

He laughed. 'You know,' he said, 'if I'd known you were such an expert I'd have called you in sooner.'

'She's slacking over there,' I pointed out. Maddy was no longer standing as straight as she had been, and she was touching herself surreptitiously, tracing the marks on her backside with her fingers.

'You'll stay the night?' Alan asked me quietly.

I gestured with my empty glass. 'I can hardly drive after what we've had in the restaurant and this.'

'Good, the spare room's all made up for you. Now to put things right.'

I gave him the wooden spoon and watched him cross the room. Maddy was taken by surprise when he grabbed her by the arm and pulled her to the armchair.

'Sometimes you just don't learn,' he snapped. He pushed her over the padded arm of the armchair, pushing her legs apart with his foot. She was bent over, her beautiful breasts hanging free, the ripe nipples exposed completely. There was a dazed look in her eye, as though she had no idea what was going on.

'How many?' he asked.

'Six, and make them count,' I told him.

She cried out before the first stroke had even touched her. It snapped hard on her thigh, and then again but higher up. He had taken my example to heart, and each stroke counted; each touch of the rough wooden spoon left its mark on her quivering body. She sobbed and moaned, and I couldn't tell what was pain and what was pleasure for her.

She climaxed again, clawing at the armchair as her body spasmed from the intense sensation of being punished. When he released her I knew that she had enjoyed an experience more intense than anything she had ever felt before. Not only had she been cruelly chastised by her husband, but her punishment had been witnessed by me, and I had punished her as well.

'Now it's time for you to get to bed,' Alan told her, his voice a whisper of excitement.

Hesitantly, as if afraid that she'd collapse, Maddy pushed herself from the armchair. She turned and kissed Alan on the mouth, a hot, passionate kiss that had her melting. I saw his hands reach down to explore the smarting cheeks of her behind.

At last he released her and she turned to me. Her chest was patterned red too, as though her pleasure had exploded all over her. She walked towards me and I took her in my arms. We kissed, our mouths joining, her body pressed onto mine. I could not stop myself and my arms traced the curve of her back and found the firm roundness of her bottom, her flesh giving over a raw heat that was completely sexual.

'Thank you,' she whispered, her eyes ablaze with gratitude and excitement. 'This has been the best birthday present I've ever had. I'm so happy, so very happy.'

'It's OK,' I told her. 'I'll be here tomorrow morning too. If things aren't right I'm sure Alan won't mind if I put you across my knee.'

She turned to him excitedly and he nodded his assent. 'It seems to me that I've got a lot to learn too,' he admitted. 'Anytime you think Maddy needs warming up then be my guest.'

'And this,' I said quietly, 'is the best birthday present I've ever had.'

Character Building

My hiking boots were gaining weight. Each step was more painful than the last until it took every ounce of energy just to keep going. Although I was out of breath and my body was aching in places that hadn't ached in years, Nancy was still going strong. I didn't know whether to envy her or hate her guts, but I tramped along behind her doing my best to keep up. She had that determined look on her face, eyes fixed straight ahead, lips pursed tight. It was the look she always wore in the office and which earned her more nicknames than the rest of us put together.

This weekend had been her idea and, like the idiot that I am, I had allowed myself to be talked into it. I hate the countryside. I hate the great outdoors, mother nature and all that is green and pleasant. If we'd been intended to spend time outside London, God would have put tube stations there. Nancy glanced over her shoulder at me, looking pityingly at the stupid bedraggled woman doing her best to keep up. I tried a smile but my mouth wouldn't cooperate, instead I gave her the kind of look a two year old gives to its mother.

'Just a bit further,' Nancy urged, smiling back encouragingly. Her hair was plaited French style, a long braid swinging down between her shoulders. I felt drenched in sweat where hardly a bead of perspiration touched her healthy pink skin.

'This isn't for me,' I muttered, feeling sorry for myself. I had worn shorts that were too short and my legs and thighs were prey to the bracken, twigs, branches and triffids that lay in wait for me. Somehow all the vegetation in the woods seemed to part for her only to spring back at me, perhaps sensing which of us was easy meat. And who said that plants don't have a mean streak?

'Soon be there,' Nancy told me briskly, in her best head girl voice. She'd been head girl of course, and best in class at uni and young go-getter at work. She had more balls than any of the men there, which was why they hated her guts so much. I'd asked her once whether she was getting a regular supply of testosterone but she'd merely looked at me like I'd stepped off another planet.

'I could do with some fresh testosterone right now,' I whimpered, imagining a nice hard cock slipping into my pussy to fill me up.

She stopped and turned. 'Male hormones?' she repeated, sounding disgusted by the idea. 'You'd only get lazy and untidy,' she added, smiling.

I smiled too. That was the first real smile I'd got out of her all day. 'I know,' I sighed. 'Next thing you know I'd stop lifting the toilet seat when I go for a pee. And I'd start expecting other people to make me cups of tea all the time.'

'Just a bit longer now,' Nancy assured me, taking my hot, sweaty hand in her long cool fingers.

'I can make it,' I promised, summoning up the last reserves of energy. We had been walking for miles, through woods that had to be of Amazonian proportions. The trees had seemed friendly enough in the beginning, well-behaved and evenly spaced, but as we proceeded they seemed to lose all decorum. The forest around us was chaos, an orgy of nature with the trees trying to shag each other from every angle and with the undergrowth struggling to become overgrowth.

It had been sunny but the canopy above us filtered

out the light except for a few sharp beams which seemed to slice through space to get to us. I had expected a pleasant walk through the trees not an expedition through the untamed wilds. We hadn't passed a single soul for ages, though for a while I had been certain that we were being tracked, though Nancy was oblivious to it all, putting it down to my paranoid, urban imagination.

Suddenly the trees shuffled out of the way and Nancy pointed to a clearing in the middle of nowhere. Several trees had fallen, one on top of the other, forming a quadrangle of clear space where dead leaves collected to form a thick mushy carpet of brown. It looked like heaven. Space at last to sit down and have a nice long rest, possibly for the next few days.

'I found this place last year,' Nancy told me, leading the way round the border of dead tree trunks. 'It's a good little resting place, and perfect for hiding supplies and reconnoitring the rest of the forest.'

'What are you on about?' I complained, collapsing onto the nearest available tree trunk at bottom height. My feet were throbbing and had swollen so much I thought they were at war with my boots.

She laughed, her grey green eyes sparkling with merriment. Her khaki uniform of army surplus trousers and thin cotton T-shirt contrasted with my cut-down jeans and denim waistcoat. She was dressed for world war three and I was dressed for the party afterwards. 'We've only just started,' she explained. 'We've got the whole weekend to play with.'

'I must be mad,' I sighed, pulling off each of my boots in turn. My white cotton socks had been transformed into something the Swamp Thing might keep in the bottom of his laundry basket – which was just how I felt.

Nancy parked herself beside me, dropping her rucksack onto the springy carpet of vegetation on the ground. 'I'm sorry if you're not having a good time,' she said softly.

'Well I'm not,' I sulked. All along I had told her that I wasn't the country type, but still I had let her talk me into this weekend away. What had I been thinking of?

She took my hand in hers, her cool skin in contrast to the heat that seemed to radiate from my body. For a while she just held my hand, letting my fingers entwine with hers. I looked at her and she smiled, her eyes meeting my own for a moment. 'I wonder what Henry's doing now?' I asked, looking away from her eyes.

'Probably curled up in front of the TV with a bottle of beer to hand,' she replied, laughing.

'Doesn't that sound like bliss? Doesn't it?'

'That's not my idea of bliss at all,' she said firmly. 'Nope, there's more to life than moping around aimlessly.'

'There's getting ahead,' I said, distastefully. She let go of my hand and I realised that I had wounded her and instantly felt sorry. If she'd been a bloke, people would still have disliked the careerist attitudes and the fanatical devotion to getting on in life, but being a woman only intensified those feelings. 'I'm sorry,' I whispered, taking her hand this time.

'There's nothing wrong with wanting to succeed, is there?' she asked, a note of hesitation in her voice.

'There is if it's the only thing in life,' I answered. 'Isn't there someone special? Someone to curl up with in front of the telly sometimes?'

She shrugged. In all the time I had known her she hadn't once mentioned a man in her life, not even as a casual acquaintance. There were rumours of course, but I couldn't believe them, Nancy just didn't seem the type.

'Well, what about . . . you know . . . at night?' I asked, smiling deviously.

Suddenly being surrounded on all sides by dense forest didn't seem so bad, it made for a nice cosy atmosphere, just right for a nice long natter.

Her face flushed pink and for the first time I saw her

turn away, her eyes unable to meet my own. She was embarrassed. Miss Perfect, Miss Jolly Hockey Sticks, was blushing! 'Come on, Nancy, you can tell me,' I whispered, drawing closer to her. 'Is there some gorgeous hunk in the background?'

'No, there isn't,' she told me flatly. 'And if your next question is about the rumours then they're not true either.'

'What rumours?' I asked, all innocent. Our eyes met again, I saw the hesitation in hers and then she smiled.

'You promise you won't tell?'

'Scouts honour,' I promised. 'And before you say it, I wasn't ever a scout but I had one once.'

We giggled at that and then she reached down into her rucksack. I watched her hand going down into the bottomless pit that she had been carting around on her back. She found what she was looking for and started to pull it out slowly, her eyes so wide with anticipation I thought they'd burst.

'This is my special friend,' she announced, red faced but somehow proud as she displayed the thick black vibrator in her hand.

'No male hormones to make you lazy,' I remarked, my eyes fixed on the sleek black phallus she held so familiarly in her fingers. The smooth surface tapered slightly at the tip, the faintest hint of a ridged glans at the top. It was big and powerful, smooth and shiny and absolutely the last thing I had been expecting.

'And it doesn't get tired,' she added, offering it to me.

It was heavier than I expected, but the shape fitted nicely in the hand, my fingers curling naturally around the base of it. Her eyes were full of expectation, and I saw that her nipples were jutting hard against the thin cotton of her shirt. I raised my eyebrows, knowing that it was my turn to go red in the face. 'It's not much for conversation,' I pointed out, strangely reluctant to hand it back.

'That's true,' she agreed, 'but then neither are most people.'

We both fell silent. No doubt she was wondering what to do next as I certainly had no idea. The thing was still in my hand and, though I hated the thought of it, I was getting distinctly hot and sticky. Already my mind was filled with images of the thing slipping smoothly into my wet pussy, stretching my lips apart as it filled me completely . . .

'Well, we're here,' she said, exhaling heavily. It was without doubt the most inane thing I'd ever heard her say.

'Small talk?' I exclaimed, more shocked by that than by the vibrator I held in my hand.

'Yes, I suppose so,' she agreed, gently prising the vibrator from my hand.

'Well, here we are then,' I agreed, watching her hold the vibrator, the shiny black surface contrasting with her white skin.

'There's a good camping spot just a few miles up ahead,' she said, changing the subject and her tone of voice. 'We can rest here for a few minutes and then hike it up the trail.'

'Good, are there toilets there?' I asked, realising that the water flow had been all one way and that my bladder was bursting. Was there a chance of a shower too, I wondered.

'Toilets? You misunderstand. When I said camping spot I meant some reasonably flat ground for us to pitch a tent and snuggle down for the night. This isn't a camping site, this is supposed to test our resourcefulness and create some team spirit.'

'Then where's the rest of the team?' I demanded.

She smiled, of course. 'They'll be here with us next week,' she said, 'looking to us for some leadership.'

I sighed; there was just no denting this woman's outsize ego and careering ambition. Not for the first time I

213

wished I was safely back at home, where the wildest thing in the house was the dirty dishes sprouting in the sink. 'Well, I'm dying for a piss,' I told her, squeezing my legs together.

'This is as good a place as any,' she said, 'or you can run round behind one of the trees.'

She wasn't joking but she was right, as usual. We were miles from anywhere and there was no point standing on ceremony. Without a word I unzipped my cut-down denims and wriggled out of them, letting them fall to my ankles. Of course the hiking boots had to come off before I could get the shorts completely off, and sitting down on the nearest available log meant that my knicks were snagged on the rough bark. I stood up suddenly and looked down to find that my panties were still sitting on the dead tree, staring up at me mournfully. I swear if Nancy had made one smart remark I would have throttled her, but as it was she wasn't even looking.

'Next week I'll wear what you're wearing,' I said, picking my panties off the tree. Ruined, the thin white lace had been ripped and the brief little garment was beyond repair.

'Yes,' she agreed, turning to face me. 'Wear something a bit less sexy and a lot more practical.'

I was standing barefoot and knickerless in front of her, clothed only in my tight denim top. Her eyes scanned me quickly, passing over my long thighs and up past the downy blonde hair between my thighs. As she watched I squatted down in front of her, knees parted, the folds of my pussy completely exposed. She was still holding the vibrator in her hand, a massive phallus in her delicate feminine fingers. It turned me on and I couldn't help it. I saw myself taking it from her and pressing it deep into my sex, fucking it into me as I exhaled slowly.

I relaxed and began to pee, a hot stream of golden liquid pouring from between my thighs onto the dark earth. A jet of fluid pouring from my body and forming a puddle in front of me, soaking the dark mulch of leaves and vegetation. Nancy watched, her eyes wide and fixed on my pussy, fascination clearly expressed on her face. Her lips parted slightly to reveal her pink tongue tracing the outline of her mouth.

I pushed out the last few drops and then stood up, aware of the electric silence between us. Her nipples were like hard points etched onto her shirt, symbols of an excitement which neither of us voiced. Did she feel it too? Somehow I was turned on, aroused by what I had just done, aroused because she had been watching so greedily. As I stood up I felt a last rivulet of fluid escape, sliding down wetly from my sex and down my thigh.

Nancy was beside me before I knew it. Her fingers were cool against my skin and I felt her fingertips skate over my flesh, tracing the jewels of silvery fluid along my thigh. An arm was around me and then she showed me the fingers of her other hand, wet from where she had touched my thighs.

'You're still wet,' she whispered, a tremor of emotion in her voice. She showed me her fingers, evidence of the natural moisture that I had pissed into the earth. She touched her fingertips to her tongue, lapping at the wetness, tasting my essence as though it were a prized gift.

'What have you just done?' I whispered, astounded by what I had just seen. I had never expected anything like that, not from Nancy, not from anyone. My pussy was flooded with sex juice, the flush of moisture evidence of the desire that stormed from nowhere. What Nancy had done was the hottest thing I had ever seen.

I groaned and parted my thighs even as I fell onto her. Her fingers were inside me, pushing roughly between my pussy lips, triggering explosions of pleasure deep in my sex. She put her hand to her mouth again, sucking at the mixture of my juices which coated her fingers. I could feel the warmth of her body and her lips touched mine and I tasted myself on her mouth.

215

'I've never done it with another woman before,' I moaned, though it was obvious from my delirium that I was enjoying every second of it. If she had done anything else I would have pushed her away. I had never been interested in making love with other women, but Nancy had gone beyond that.

'Will you do it again?' she replied, kissing me on the mouth. 'Will you squat down in front of me and ...'

I understood then what games she liked to play. The rumours were untrue, it wasn't just women that she liked, it was water games. I arched my back, letting her frig me hard with her fingers, letting her finger fuck me closer and closer to orgasm.

'Yes ... Yes ...' I whimpered, as she teased my clit with her fingers. I cried out, screaming her name as I shuddered to a climax with her fingers deep inside my sex. She kissed me hotly on the mouth and throat and then let me rest up against one of the tree trunks.

Still dazed, I watched as she began to strip off, starting with her hiking boots and working her way up. In moments she was naked, completely, pert breasts with hard nipples, long thighs and round backside, bulging pussy lips. She positioned herself in front of me, smiling all the time, her eyes fixed on mine. It was my turn to watch, fascinated and excited as she squatted down in front of me. The heavy black dildo made her skin appear virginal and white.

'Will you taste me too?' she asked, pushing the black dildo between her pussy lips. Her eyes quivered, half-closed as the pleasure surged through her. She was going to fuck herself silly with the vibrator and then empty herself for me, giving me the chance to taste the mixture of her juices just as she had done with mine.

'Yes, yes I will,' I sighed, beginning to undo the buttons on my top.

We had the whole weekend to play together, to discover the secrets we had never shared with anyone else before. The whole point of the expedition was for us to learn to work and play together, only neither of us had ever imagined we would learn to play like this.

A Taxing Service

He giggled. For a moment it seemed that he was out of
breath as his face creased up until his eyes were narrow
slits full of tears. Pausing to catch his breath, the smile
still broadening the wan features of his face, he tapped
the sheath of photocopied sheets spread carefully on his
knees.

'Do you see?' he asked, as though he had just shared
the funniest joke in the world.

Tiffany stared at him. 'No,' she said flatly. If there
had been a joke before the strangled laughter she had
missed it.

'But the figures in this section, capital allowances, just
don't make any sense if we compare with the figures for
last year, not unless we depreciate everything in one
year . . .' he began to laugh again, 'which of course we
can't do. Now do you see?'

Tiffany sighed and shook her head. No, she didn't
see. Numbers were numbers, and capital allowances and
depreciation figures were worse than meaningless. She
was sitting opposite him, her long skirt arranged loosely
around her, forcing him to sit in the armchair, papers
precariously placed on his knees, his briefcase balanced
on the padded arm.

At last he stopped laughing. He was fighting a losing
battle as there seemed to be nothing he could say that
would force a smile to her face. He coughed, clearing his
throat and settled for a deeply serious tone of voice.
'What this means, Mrs Heller, is that your assessment

for income tax has been calculated in error. And I'm afraid to say that it is far below what it should be.'

'You mean I have to pay more tax?' Tiffany deduced, eyeing him coldly.

'That is it. Precisely,' he confirmed.

'How much more?' she asked suspiciously.

For a moment she feared he was going to break out into another laughing fit. 'There is an order of magnitude error,' he said, avoiding her eyes.

'In English?'

'Add an extra couple of noughts on the end,' he said, carefully placing his papers back into his open briefcase.

She nodded. 'I can't pay that,' she stated, her voice calm and controlled.

'Are you saying that we've made an error?' he asked.

Tiffany stood up. 'All I'm saying is that I can't afford that,' she repeated. She walked across the room to the drinks cabinet, aware that he was staring at her. His eyes were fixed on her long golden hair, cascading naturally over her shoulders. 'Drink?' she asked, turning to face him.

'We're not supposed to . . .' he began to explain apologetically but she turned away almost immediately.

She caught sight of herself in the mirror at the back of the cabinet, dark eyes and tanned skin enhanced by the mass of golden curls. Quickly she poured herself a tumbler of Scotch and then turned to face him again. 'Your sums must be wrong,' she announced, staring directly at him, her wide eyes meeting his head on until he looked away.

'I really don't see how we could have made a mistake,' he replied meekly. 'Though of course I can go through all the calculations again.'

'There's no other explanation,' she insisted forcefully. She strode back across the room, her high heeled boots barely visible under the long loose skirt. She was dressed sensibly in a long skirt with a loose blouse buttoned up to the collar. The high heels were well hidden. She wished she hadn't dressed down for him, even though she could sense that he was already half-afraid of her.

'If I might suggest . . .' he ventured quietly.

'Yes?'

'If I could speak to your professional advisor? I assume you have an accountant to help you with all of this?'

'I have a man that helps,' she said. 'It's his figures you're looking at.'

'I see,' he said.

'Well, what else do you suggest?'

He looked at her, his sad blue eyes darting nervously. He was barely into his thirties but already his hair was receding and turning grey at the same time. His lips were full, slightly red, suggesting that perhaps there was more to him than plain facts and figures. 'It might help,' he suggested quietly, 'if I knew more about the line of business that you're in.'

'How might that help?' she demanded sceptically. Did he suspect, she wondered?

'Perhaps there are allowances that you can offset against income?' He was sounding optimistic, as though he really did want to save her money and not grab everything for the Revenue.

'I've told you what I do,' she replied, retaking her seat but letting the slit of her skirt do its work. His eyes suddenly bulged at the display of her long smooth thighs. Her skin was tanned to perfection and contrasted sexily with her demure black skirt and her knee-length black boots with the heels that spiked dangerously.

He scrabbled through the papers quickly, unable to decide whether to look at what he was doing or at her thighs. 'Yes, here it is,' he said finally, waving the wad of papers in front of him. 'You supply domestic services,' he read, and then looked up at her for an explanation.

'That's right,' she agreed, allowing the first smile of the day to warm her face. She was beginning to enjoy herself. The stiff drink had helped but now she was enjoying the look on his face: half fear and half hope.

'You supply office cleaning and that sort of thing,' he guessed.

'Do I look like an office cleaner?' she asked, sounding hurt. She leaned forward, letting the slit ride higher to reveal even more of her thighs.

'I . . . I didn't mean to suggest . . .' his face was slowly turning red with embarrassment. 'You employ domestic staff to look after people's houses?'

'The service I provide is far more *personal* than that,' she whispered seductively, licking her full red lips with the very tip of her tongue. He was uncomfortable and the pile of forms placed on his lap had never been more strategically positioned.

'I still don't understand,' he lied, his voice barely a whisper.

'Perhaps I ought to show you,' she suggested slyly.

'It might help me understand your finances a bit more,' he said, his Adam's apple now in overdrive.

'In that case leave your stuff here and we'll just go into my office,' she told him, standing up briskly.

There was no need to wait and she marched across the room confident that he was only a step behind her. Out in the hall her heels snapped hard on the polished floor, echoing through the house deliciously. She led the way upstairs, knowing that her heels were only inches from his eyes as he followed, the shiny black leather tipped with steel snapping like pistons on the wooden floor.

'I hope you didn't take offence earlier,' he said apologetically, 'when I said you supplied office cleaning services. I didn't mean that you personally cleaned . . .'

She ignored him and he fell silent, following her up a second flight of stairs and then a third. 'This is where I do some of my work,' she explained, stopping at the top of the stairs and pointing to the door.

'You have an office here? Have you claimed for that?'

Her smile only added to his confusion. 'It's not an office exactly,' she said. 'I prefer to think of it as my workshop.'

She pushed the door open to reveal a room shrouded in darkness. 'After you,' she said, making way for him.

'You might still be able to claim . . .' his mouth dropped open as soon as he crossed the threshold of the room.

She followed him in, trying to imagine what it was that he saw. The whipping post, the stocks, the canes and whips hanging from the walls, they all seemed so normal and functional for her, what did it all mean to him?

'Do you think I can claim for this stuff?' she asked, laughing at his obvious confusion. He scanned the room slowly, his eyes bulging, his mouth open and shocked into silence. 'Well?' she demanded.

'I didn't understand,' he admitted softly, unable to face her fully. His brow was lined with beads of perspiration and his face burned bright red with shame or embarrassment.

'I'm not sure that you do understand,' she replied. 'I was being honest when I said that I supply domestic services.'

She walked across the room to the wardrobe in the corner and pulled the door open. The strip light inside the door flickered to life and cast a pale, wintry glare on the costumes hanging neatly inside the wardrobe. Shimmering black PVC, shiny rubber, polished leathers, a collection of fetish uniforms that had cost her a fortune to collect. 'What's it to be? French maid? Naughty schoolgirl? Student nurse?'

'You'll dress up for me?' he gasped, his eyes lighting up at the prospect.

She laughed again, her hair cascading prettily over her shoulders. 'You'll dress for me,' she explained. 'You'll dress for me and then carry out your domestic duties, only if they're not up to scratch I might have to punish you for it.'

He received the news with something akin to terror. He seemed to be having trouble in swallowing, and then more trouble breathing. 'I think I've seen enough,' he managed to say, backing towards the door nervously.

'But I don't think you have,' she corrected sternly. 'It's important for you to understand the nature of my work here. Don't you agree?' He nodded wordlessly, unable to disagree with her. 'Good. Undress for me. Now.'

'But really . . .'

'Undress for me. Do as you're told,' she ordered him, her voice a hint of iron.

He obeyed though the struggle was there in his eyes and a look of denial as he began to unbutton his crisp white shirt. She watched him, her face cold and impassive as he removed his shirt and then his shoes and socks. There was a moment of hesitation that she stared away from him and then the trousers and the boxer shorts were gone too.

'Good. Now you can help me to dress too. Drop down to your hands and knees and then come here.'

'I've never done this sort of thing before,' he whimpered, crawling across the cold polished floor towards her.

'Then think of it as a learning experience,' she said. 'Now, unzip the back of my skirt.'

In moments he was at her heels and helping her step out of her skirt. She had been naked under her skirt, and now she stood before him, her sex exposed to his greedy gaze. Feet apart, heels firmly planted on the floor, she glared down at him, cowering naked by her feet. 'Have you ever kissed a woman's heels?'

223

'No, never,' he admitted.

'Then do it now. I want you to polish my heels with your tongue, lick them well, because if they're not shiny clean you'll be punished for it.'

There was no question of disobeying, no sign even of hesitation. She smiled to herself as he knelt down low and began to lick at her boots with the tip of his tongue. He squirmed in front of her, his nakedness displayed completely as he applied his wet tongue to the shiny surface of her patent leather boots. His body was slightly muscled, tanned lightly by the sun, the flesh of his backside slightly whiter than the flesh of his back.

'Enough!' she snapped imperiously, making him jump back nervously. Her boots were shiny, still wet in places but he had done a good job. 'Show yourself! Stand up!'

His cock was long and hard, the circumcised head bulging and glistening with silvery fluid. He was ashamed and lowered his head so that he wouldn't have to face her. She reached out and stroked his cock delicately, her fingers barely making contact with the velvety skin but making him sigh all the same. He was hers, she had known it from the moment he had stepped into the house.

'You'd make a lovely little French maid ...' she teased, tightening her grip around the base of his erection. 'And I bet you'd look so virginal in school uniform ...'

He started to say something but his words subsided into a sigh of pleasure as her fingers stroked against his hardness. His hot breath touched her face as she pulled him closer towards her, using his prick to steer him as she wished.

'Stay here,' she ordered.

It was difficult to decide how to outfit him, any number of costumes would have suited him, serving to both eroticise and humiliate at the same time. In the end though she decided to leave those pleasures for another

224

day. Hanging from the wall at the far end of the room were several sets of restraints from which she made her selection. He was still standing, head bowed, in the middle of the room, meek and submissive in his naked excitement.

He moaned when she snapped the clamps to each nipple in turn. The cold steel bit into his flesh. Then she snapped the last clamp to the loose skin at the base of his erection. The chains rattled lightly as she surveyed her work, the solid steel implements hanging from his body.

'Go down and pour me a drink now,' she ordered sternly. 'This is your domestic service for the day. Any mistakes will be corrected severely. Now do it!'

He winced as he turned. The chains clattered and the clamps ate into his flesh. She could see the look of pain in his eyes but also she could see that his excitement had grown; his cock was harder and the pre-come was seeping down the thickly veined rod.

While he was gone she pondered on her next step. There was no doubting his pleasure, despite the wordless groans of pain and the occasional look of defiance in his eyes. Would he survive a whipping? His pale skin would glow at the first touch of leather and she knew from experience that he was the type to scream as the lash came down.

He returned with the glass of Scotch, topped up with another shot from the decanter. Offering it to her with shaky hands, she could see his eagerness to please, the desire to have performed well written clearly in his eyes.

'You've misunderstood,' she informed him coldly, her eyes fixed on his. 'This is a domestic service, you should have gone to the kitchen. I wanted a glass of water. Go and do that, get me a glass of water.'

'But . . .' he mumbled, crestfallen.

'You'll be punished when you get back,' she promised with a smile, taking the proffered glass of Scotch.

When he returned the second time, with a drink of water in a long stemmed glass, she was sitting on a short-legged stool in the corner of the room. Her legs were parted and she was sitting well forward, her sex fully exposed, the pussy lips slightly parted.

She drank the water quickly and then put the glass down at her feet, beside the still full glass of Scotch. His eyes widened when he saw the polished wooden paddle that she picked up from the floor, the long handle connected to a flat oval the size of a hand.

'On your knees before me,' she ordered, using the paddle to indicate the spot she wanted him to occupy. He knelt down and crawled into place, his eyes never straying from the paddle. She made him kneel forward and then had him cross his hands behind his back, the chains swinging freely from the clamps on his chest.

'Do you really think I should pay that much tax?' she asked, her red lips only inches from his. His eyes said that he didn't, that he didn't think she should pay any tax at all, but unfortunately his mouth refused to cooperate.

The paddle smacked down hard across his backside, a hard slap of sound that filled the room. He groaned and bit his lips, jerking forward to escape the heat and pain that burst against his flesh. Again an explosion of sound as the paddle was brought down firmly against his backside. She stopped to admire the red flush that covered his pale backside, adding colour where there had been none, spreading a smarting pain that dissolved everything.

She beat him again and again, half-a-dozen hard strokes on his backside, each one beating out her anger and frustration. He jerked and squirmed, whimpered and cried out as the pain became more and more unbearable. But not once did he uncross his arms. Instead his backside was offered nice and pert to her biting use of the paddle.

'Do you still think I have to pay that much tax?' she demanded angrily. Her fingers explored his upper thighs and buttocks, seeking out the heat that his punished flesh radiated. He moaned deliriously as she slapped him again with her hands, her finger marks added to the redness on his skin.

'I'm wet,' she revealed, touching her fingers to her sex and then offering the evidence to his lips.

Instinctively he kissed her fingers, sucking away the honey juices of her excitement, lapping like an animal at the nourishment that was offered. He crawled forward between her thighs and began to suck her, using his tongue to pry open her pussy lips and to seek out her hard nub of pleasure.

She leaned back, letting the pleasure pass through her in waves of delight. His tongue entered her, lapping at the nectar flowing freely, her wetness sucked into his greedy mouth. She could just about see the redness of his lower back, the evidence of the punishment she had inflicted exciting her even more. She climaxed suddenly, arching her back and digging her heels into his flesh as his tongue brought her to the peak of pleasure.

He lay back on the floor, pressing his back against the cool surface and she sat astride him, offering her soaked pussy first to his mouth and then moving down further. His cock filled her, going deep into her sex as she ground herself down on him. She began to ride him, fucking him for her pleasure as she pulled on the nipple clamps, enjoying the fleeting gasps of pain that he uttered.

She climaxed again as he screamed, tried to push her off him and then subsided, spasming thick waves of come deep into her sex as she pulled hard on the chains across his chest.

She brushed the hair from her eyes as she opened the front door, the cool breeze bringing with it the

227

realisation that she was still bathed with the warmth of sex. It had been a good session, her body was still marked with the rosy flush of orgasm that had been anything but faked.

'Thank you, Tiffany,' he said, his smile attesting to the fact that he had enjoyed it too.

'That was just so wonderful,' she enthused happily. 'You were really good doing your tax inspector bit,' she added.

He laughed as he reached the door. 'I should be,' he explained, 'that's what I do for a living.'

The smile slipped from her face. 'In that case we ought to talk,' she suggested, slamming the door before he could make his escape. 'It's about my tax bill . . .'

La Tempête

He liked the look of her as soon as she came in, wide
eyed and hesitant. She looked young, if she were over
eighteen it had to be by a matter of months and not
years. Smartly dressed in fashionably long black boots,
short skirt and white blouse, she saw Nick sitting at the
corner table and flashed him a shy smile.

'Mr Moore?' she asked hopefully, her dark eyes meeting his only for an instant before turning away.

'And you must be Carole,' he guessed, rising from his
seat to offer her a place at the table.

'I know I'm early,' she apologised, 'but the bus came
early and the traffic wasn't as bad as . . .'

'Don't apologise,' Nick laughed. 'Arriving early for a
job interview never did anyone any harm.'

She allowed herself a smile, her lips parting to reveal
straight white teeth. Her round face was perfect and
when she smiled it seemed to light up her eyes, making
her seem even more pretty. When she sat down, opposite Nick, she smoothed down her skirt in a gesture of
modesty that was entirely natural to her.

'Is the job still open then?' she asked, a sigh of relief
clear in her voice.

'Yes, but only just,' he admitted. Word of the excellent salary had gone round quickly and Nick had been
inundated with calls. There had been many potential
applicants who had sounded perfect. Of the ten va-
cancies only one now remained unfilled, though he knew
that Carole looked perfect for the part.

'Thank God for that,' she sighed. 'I was sure you'd get someone else.'

'No, I don't work like that. If I've promised you an interview I'm not going to give the job to someone else while you're still waiting.'

'I really appreciate that, Mr Moore,' she beamed.

The conversation was interrupted by a harsh metallic screech that filled the entire room. Nick waited for it to die down, glad to see that the builders had resumed work after yet another coffee break. 'As you can hear,' he explained to Carole, 'there's still a lot to finish before we open.'

She nodded. The dining area was almost totally finished with the tables and chairs set in secluded alcoves and the walls decorated with *fin de siècle* scenes of Paris. There was still an atmosphere of spit and sawdust, the inevitable result of all the redecorating, but already the underlying ambience was beginning to appear. 'I think it looks really good,' she said approvingly.

'There's still a lot to do, but I agree with you, it's beginning to look the part. Which brings me neatly back to you.'

'I'm very keen, Mr Moore, you must realise that,' she assured him earnestly. The top few buttons of her blouse were undone, giving a glimpse of smooth white skin without a hint of cleavage. One more button undone and it would have been coquettish, but there was something instinctively modest about her and he was certain that it wasn't put on for his benefit. Some of the girls he'd interviewed had been practically naked, flaunting themselves shamelessly in the hope that he'd take an interest, to no avail. The restaurant he had in mind was sophisticated and classy, the last thing he wanted was a staff which was young and loud.

'Tell me Carole, how many times have you been to Paris?' he asked, formally marking the start of the interview.

230

'Four times. Two weekends and two longer holidays,' she said.

'And your French?'

'I couldn't be an interpreter but I do speak the language. I have my certificates at home if you want me to bring them in . . .'

He smiled and slid a leather bound menu across the table to her. 'Read me the menu,' he said, leaning back in his seat.

She opened it carefully and scanned through it. It was all in French of course, with no English translation. There was a separate menu for that. He listened closely as she began to read, fluently and with a pronunciation that was perfect. There was no doubt that she knew what she was reading as well, she was practically licking her lips as she went through the main courses.

'Very good,' he said, interrupting her in mid-sentence. 'I am impressed. You sound like you enjoy your food as well.'

She smiled shyly. 'Thank you, Mr Moore. I've got my figure to think about,' she added, 'but I do like my food.'

'Good, I like that. There's nothing worse than being served by someone who has no understanding of food.'

'I only wish I could afford to eat at places like this,' she sighed, handing back the menu.

He nodded. The prices in the menu were not cheap, there was no denying that, but then again *La Tempête* was not going to be just another French restaurant. 'Tell me what you know about the job,' he suggested.

She took a deep breath before beginning. 'This is going to be a very special French restaurant, very different to all the others. You've got an excellent chef, even I've heard of him.' She paused momentarily but there was no reassuring smile from Nick. 'It won't be the sort of place you come to on a whim. Every place has to be booked in advance, there will even be someone at the

231

door to stop undesirables from barging in from the pub and that sort of thing.'

'It's not so much people from the pub that I'm worried about,' he said, clarifying the point for her. 'It's just that I don't want crowds of drunken hoorays turning up and spoiling the atmosphere. Do you know the kind of atmosphere I'm after?'

'I think so,' she said uncertainly. 'Parisian sophistication, I think. You know, very elegant, smart. Am I right?'

'Partly. The missing word in your description is decadent. Visiting *La Tempête* will be an experience in more than the culinary sense. Was that not explained to you?'

'Yes, Mr Moore,' she said quickly, her eyes widening with the fear that she had just messed up her chances of working there.

'Part of that decadent ambience will be created by the girls who'll work here. *La serveuse* will be a central character; she will embody the elegant and the decadent, both in the way she looks and in the way she acts. You do understand that, don't you?'

For a moment he was certain that she was going to shake her head or burst into tears. 'I think so, Mr Moore,' she agreed softly, her voice barely a whisper of indecision.

'As you know the salary I am offering is far higher than the norm, but that salary has to be earned. Of course you'll have the added perk of enjoying some of the finest cuisine this side of the channel.'

'Yes, I hadn't thought of that,' she agreed, her smile returning slowly. Her eyes were still full of uncertainty, as though she were struggling with herself and could not make a decision.

'I like you Carole,' he told her, smiling properly for the first time. 'You have excellent French and, even better, an appreciation of the finer things in life. If it were up to me then the job would be yours, however there are the final formalities before I can make that offer.'

She looked at him eagerly, the chance of a job clearing the indecision. 'What do I have to do?'

'There's the uniform to try on,' he explained.

'The uniform?'

He laughed. 'I thought you knew. There is indeed a special uniform for the waitresses, very French and very naughty. That's what I meant about helping to create that special ambience.'

'I hadn't realised,' she said, sounding crestfallen.

'It's a French maid's outfit,' he told her, deciding to be blunt rather than trying to break it gently. 'Very enticing and sexy in a light-hearted way. If the uniform looks good on you then the job is practically yours. So far the other girls have loved it.'

She looked at him dubiously, the suspicion clouding her dark eyes. 'I wasn't really expecting this . . .' she started to mumble. The screech of the electric drill drowned out the rest of her words but the look on her face told its own story.

'May I suggest that you try it on and if you feel uncomfortable about it then we can talk about finding you some other job?'

She hesitated for a moment, weighing up the possibilities and then nodded reluctantly. 'OK, I'll try it on but I have to say that I wasn't really expecting anything like this.'

'The staff changing room is currently the scene of all that banging and screeching I'm afraid. It's the last part of the building to be finished unfortunately. However if you don't mind changing in the kitchen today . . .'

She looked shocked. 'The kitchen? But . . . Isn't there some . . .'

Nick glared at her. 'Are you always so difficult?' he demanded, suddenly angered by her obvious distrust. None of the other girls had been so suspicious, even though the uniform was a surprise for most of them too.

'I'm sorry,' she mumbled, her pretty face flushing

233

pink with embarrassment. 'If it's private I'll change in the kitchen,' she agreed.

Nick sighed. 'If it wasn't private I wouldn't have asked you to change in there. Now, please be a good girl and go and try your uniform out. It's there waiting for you, hanging behind the door. There's no mirror I'm afraid but if you give me a shout when you're ready I'll tell you how you look.'

It was obvious that she was unhappy about the whole idea but she did as she was told. He watched her cross the length of the restaurant and enter the kitchen, noting the way her long black boots accentuated the shape of her legs, and the way the tight skirt clung to her well-shaped behind. She was tall and slim but with curves in all the right places, which was just what he was looking for.

Finding the right sort of girl had proved to be a far bigger problem than he had anticipated. There were lots of pretty girls of the right age around, but few of them had the intelligence, the elegance or the personality to carry off the roles he had assigned them. Luckily once he had recruited the first four they had helped him find the others. Carole had been recommended by one of the other girls, and so far he was impressed by her looks and by her knowledge of French, however he was not so enamoured of her personality. If she were only a little more trusting or perhaps a little more relaxed then he'd be certain.

His ruminations were interrupted by one of the builders, a burly monster of a man, striding purposefully towards the kitchen. 'Where do you think you're off too?' Nick demanded, rising quickly from his seat.

'There's something needs seeing to in there,' the builder announced, his broad grin splitting his face in two.

'Very funny,' Nick sighed. 'Now isn't there some real work for you to be getting on with?'

The builder looked offended and the grin was replaced by a sullen frown. 'I was only having a laugh,' he complained. 'A feller's got to have a laugh sometimes. Pretty bit of skirt like that appreciates a joke, I can tell.'

'She might appreciate the joke, I certainly don't. Now, if you don't mind . . .'

The builder glared at Nick for a moment than turned on his heel and marched back the way he had come, muttering a litany of complaints as a salve to his injured pride. It was no surprise; the lure of pretty young women was certainly going to be one of the main attractions of the restaurant but it was also going to be one of the problems. A strict door policy sounded like financial suicide for a new restaurant, but it was the only way Nick could think of having some control over the clientele. It was a gamble and the thought always caused a shudder of fear to pass through him. His house, savings and a substantial loan from the bank were all riding on the success of *La Tempête*, which promised to be as stormy as its name.

'I'm ready,' she cried from the kitchen, her voice lacking in any form of enthusiasm.

She looked gorgeous. The black satin and white frills complemented her dark good looks and soft white skin. It was a perfect fit, from the towering black high heels to the seamed stockings, to the low cut of the uniform and the lace cap which banded her dark hair. When she moved the skirt swished slightly and he was treated to an enticing glimpse of flesh above the thick black stocking tops. The deep cleavage of her breasts was emphasised by the constricting tightness, and the apron tied at her waist served to draw attention to the roundness of her backside.

The effect was spoilt by the pensive expression on her face, her eyes flitting from side to side nervously, her lips pursed as though stifling her anger. She was standing straight, hands together in front of her, balanced finely on the high heels.

'What is it, girl?' he demanded, annoyed by her obvious discomfort. If it wasn't enough worrying about the opening of the restaurant he had to contend with the antics of silly teenage girls.

'I'm sorry, Mr Moore,' she whispered, her face flaring red once again, 'but I don't think I can handle this.'

He exhaled heavily. 'Handle what exactly?' he asked, not bothering to hide his exasperation.

'All of this,' she explained, rubbing a hand down the smooth satin uniform. 'I mean it'll hurt, won't it?'

He looked at her quizzically. 'The shoes?' he asked.

'No, not that, I can handle the stilettos all right. No, I mean, you know ... The punishment when I'm naughty.'

By now her face was bright red and her eyes were fixed at a point six inches in front of her toes. Her voice had become a strained whisper.

'I don't understand,' Nick admitted, hardly daring to let his imagination get ahead of him.

'The decadence thing ... You said you wanted us to be all decadent and naughty ...' She tried to explain, but seemed to have trouble finding the right words. 'With the high heels and everything I suppose we'll always be spilling things and so on ... It'll hurt, won't it, afterwards.'

'You mean when you make mistakes, when you're naughty as you put it,' he looked to her for the nod of confirmation. 'You expect to be punished. Physically.'

'Like in those magazines,' she added, helpfully.

He nodded sagely. Those magazines. She looked so young and naive, but obviously her education extended down to *those* magazines. He could follow her train of thought – maid's uniform, decadence, naughtiness, correction. 'Yes, I suppose it will hurt. But unless you try it how will you know?'

'I know the other girls have accepted. Did they try it first?'

He suppressed the smile. 'Yes. They were all punished by me, but only after they'd put the uniform on first. In your case I'm inclined to be extra strict, you're being very difficult about this. You either want this job or you don't.'

'But I do,' she insisted forcefully.

'In that case I think you should be a good girl and bend over the counter there.' He pointed to one of the worktops, smooth steel polished like a mirror.

She hesitated; he could see the arguments raging inside her. There was doubt there, and denial, but there was also excitement and a curiosity that could not be suppressed. Hesitantly she turned round, took the two steps to the appointed place and stopped. For a moment she stared at her reflection in the cold steel, allowing him the chance to appreciate how she looked from behind. Long straight legs, beautifully shaped by the shiny black heels, slim waist but a well-proportioned rear, and her long black hair held in place by the frilly lace cap.

When she bent over at the waist the skirt was raised high at the back, lifting clear of the stocking tops and displaying the black suspenders which pressed firmly into the flesh of her thighs. She pressed her face and chest against the worktop, wriggling slightly in an effort to get comfortable.

'Lift your skirt completely,' he ordered, enjoying the view. When the skirt was raised completely he saw the tiny black briefs were pulled up between the round globes of her bottom, the thin wisp of lace delineating the rear cleavage to her advantage. She looked good. There was no denying the enticing image her primly offered backside made.

'How many?' she asked, almost breathless with fear and anticipation.

'Six, with my hand.'

She made no reply. Instead she arched her back slightly, offering a rounder target. He stepped forward, hardly daring to believe what was happening. He touched her softly, running his fingertips over her backside, from one side to the next. She hardly dared to breathe, her eyes were half closed and her hands were clenched tightly.

The first smack was hard, landing flat on her left buttock, making a resounding slapping sound that seemed to fill the kitchen completely. She uttered a strangled gasp but did not cry or make any movement. His fingers were clearly imprinted on her white flesh, a red badge of pain that he swore was warm to the touch. He lifted his arm and brought it down again, on the same bottom cheek and with the same force. She inched forward, her knuckles white as she gripped the edge of the worktop. Her skin marked easily, the white flesh running to pink and then red at the site of impact. He touched her again, able to feel the distinct mark as well as see it.

The third stroke, and then the fourth. She cried out but, biting her lips and gripping hard, she did not move out of position. There was determination in her eyes, but with it the misting over of pain and pleasure. Her left bottom cheek was red, patterned from the top of the thigh and above. A fifth stroke, as hard and as painful as the first four. She seemed to draw her stomach down and raise her bottom higher, offering him her derrière for punishment as though it were his to do as he wished. The wisp of lace between her thighs was drawn tightly into her flesh, a black band against white skin turning pink.

The last stroke was the hardest of all, the sound of it matched by a squeal of pain that she uttered despite her best efforts. His own hand was buzzing, throbbing with pain and yet he knew it was only a pale echo of the sensations she was experiencing. When he touched, stroking her punished left buttock, he let his fingers slip lower, brushing against the sticky warmth of her sex.

'Have we finished?' she asked, hardly able to speak

238

clearly. The contrast between the two sides of her rear end was plain to see: on the left a pattern of red finger marks and the shadow of his hand on her flesh, on the right the pure unblemished softness of her skin.

'Not yet,' he told her firmly. 'There's the other side to do as well.'

She sighed, her breath misting on the cold steel on which her face rested. He looked around quickly, searching for the right implement in a kitchen full of them. There were a dozen different wooden spoons and a number of small pans which looked ideal for tanning the hide of a silly girl. The spatula looked perfect however, long, slightly curved, very strong and easy to handle.

'Six strokes,' he informed her.

'With that?' she cried, clearly alarmed by the wooden implement he had to hand.

'Seven strokes for that,' he decided. She fell silent, resigned to the facts of her punishment.

He was careful with the first stroke, bringing it down flat against the unmarked skin of her right buttock. The sound was impressive and the solid red mark it created looked good. Her eyes were wide, and he could tell that the spatula was indeed a more effective instrument of correction than his bare hand. The next few strokes fell in quick succession, each delivered firmly and with a resounding crack of sound. She was panting, breathing heavily, making little sobbing sounds as he administered her chastisement.

He stopped at number four and examined her closely, comparing each bottom cheek, touching her intimately without a murmur of dissent from her lovely lips. She was undoubtedly aroused and when he touched a finger to her sex she seemed to melt, a sigh issuing from her lips as she closed her eyes to the pleasure. He resumed the punishment, smacking hard the final strokes, the last delivered squarely between her bottom cheeks.

The punishment over, he stepped back for a moment. She seemed dazed, hardly able to move, as though she too were welded to the cold steel worktop. It gave him a chance to savour the image of her, bent beautifully over, her uniform up around her waist, her long legs stretched tautly and her bottom perfectly displayed in all its pink, punished glory.

'You can stand up now,' he told her, finally.

She seemed to wake suddenly. She pushed herself up and modestly brushed down her uniform, hiding from view the evidence of her punishment. Her chest was flushed pink and her white skin was mottled by the evidence of her pleasure just as her bottom had been mottled by her chastisement.

'Do you still want the job?' he asked, his manner cool and professional, despite the raging desire that he felt.

'Will it get any worse than that?' she asked, swallowing hard.

'Only if you're really bad,' he told her. 'Don't worry though, most nights of the week you'll just be on display, looking pretty to keep our clients happy until the food arrives. However the uniform and the punishment is reserved for special nights, when only the most select of our clients are invited.'

'You mean this,' she clutched her uniform, 'is for the special clients only? Other nights we wear something else?'

He smiled. 'That's right. Other nights you'll wear a more respectable uniform, still pretty and sexy but not like this. On our special nights however you'll have to be extra careful not to make a mistake and earn a spanking from our customers,' he paused. The entire business plan had just been rewritten, but he knew it made more sense. Act as a normal French restaurant for most nights but offer the privilege of punishing the girls on certain special occasions – and charge prices accordingly. 'So,' he finished, 'what do you say?'

She reached down and rubbed her bottom surreptitiously, as though the stinging were too powerful to ignore. 'What about if I make mistakes on the other nights?' she asked.

'I reserve the right to punish you when required, my girl,' he told her.

She nodded at once. 'Yes, Mr Moore. When do I start?'

He smiled. 'You've already started,' he laughed. 'If I were you I'd change and get home for a good night of rest, you've got a long day ahead of you tomorrow.'

'But the restaurant doesn't open for . . .'

'It's all right,' he said, stopping her mid-sentence. 'It's just that I have nine other girls that I need to reinterview,' he announced, smiling.

Changing Room

The sounds of the pool echoed around as the fluting voices and piercing squeals of children rode high above the sound of splashing water. Billie stopped for a moment to look back at the pool, the silvery blue surface rippling with light that filtered through the glass ceiling. She shivered, suddenly cold, and hauled herself out of the water. She padded quickly back towards the changing room, trailing water over the tiled floor, leaving her wet footprints behind.

The feel of wet lycra against her skin made her shiver even more. She loved being wet but only if she was naked. It always turned her on to see herself wet and nude, her body glistening with a thousand jewels of water. She loved the way rivulets of water cascaded down her skin, the way droplets gathered together before dripping down haphazardly across her chest. In the shower she loved to position herself so that streams of water ran down her face and chest, her breasts channelling the flow so that her erect nipples dripped seductively with silvery fluid.

She glanced up at the clock on the wall and cursed silently when she saw that she was already late back from lunch. It had seemed such a good idea to go swimming every lunch time, a chance to keep fit and healthy during the day rather than vegetate in the office or trail endlessly around the town window-shopping. Only an hour's lunch didn't give her much time for a proper swim. It felt as if she barely had time to get wet before it was time to go back to work again.

A quick blast of icy water under the shower was all she could take, it was enough to wash the chlorine from her hair and then she retreated to the changing room. Her swimsuit was cold and clammy, clinging uncomfortably to her body, her nipples protruding against the tightness of the lycra. She pushed opened the door to the changing room and stopped suddenly.

'Stop it . . . Someone's going to catch us . . .'

Billie waited, listening intently as the softly whispered words of protest were smothered by kisses. Should she intrude? For a moment she was inclined to back out of the room, to leave whoever it was alone, but then the thought of being even later for work made her change her mind. She let the door close softly, careful not to let it slam shut on its springs. It was quite dark in the changing room, and the narrow doorway gave her room to inch forward slowly. The sounds of passionate kisses and soft moans of pleasure were enticing.

'We'll get caught,' she heard a young woman say, exhaling heavily as she spoke, as though she were too excited to speak clearly.

When Billie chanced a proper look she could hardly believe her eyes. She hid back in the doorway, back against the wall, her heart pounding with excitement. In the single stolen glance she had glimpsed two young women locked together in a passionate embrace. Both blondes, the one with her back to Billie was naked, her bikini bottom a pretty red bundle around her ankles. She was tanned beautifully, the golden glow of her skin the same colour from head to toe, the roundness of her naked backside as golden as the firm flesh of her thighs or back.

The second young woman was mostly obscured, but Billie could see the same long blonde hair and she too seemed to be naked. A second glance saw the two young women kissing, their faces pressed together at the lips. The one with her back to Billie had her arms around the other's shoulders, and as she kissed her friend her backside was being stroked lovingly.

Billie could hardly believe what she was seeing. Her heart was pounding with excitement and she was trembling nervously, wondering what she should do. The strongest emotion of all was a sudden and inexplicable feeling of arousal. She was turned on, sexually excited by watching the two naked young women making love. Perhaps it was the taboo of seeing two women together, or perhaps the excitement of catching them at it, or perhaps . . . Her nipples were pressing hard against the wetness of her swimsuit but now they were hardening with excitement. She could feel the flush of excitement on her chest and the moistness growing between her thighs.

She dared to look again, a quick peep to see that the first young woman was still kissing her friend, but that this time she was bring fingered from behind. Billie felt the rush of excitement again, she could feel it in her pussy, in the pit of her stomach. It felt so hot and exciting, it had been ages since she had felt that turned on, that physical.

As she stood in the darkness she stroked her pussy for a moment, letting her fingers trace the outline of her swimsuit pressing against her sex. She was tempted to pull the wet material aside, to tease her pussy lips open and to stroke the warmth and moisture with her expert fingers. Only . . . only she was late for work and getting later every second. She could hear the gasps of pleasure that the young lovers were sharing, the murmur of their voices indistinct but the signals of pleasure were pure and clear.

Reluctantly, taking one last glance at the young female lovers, she retreated back out into the corridor. Her heart was still pounding and the aphrodisiac excitement was pulsing in her veins, but now the time ticking on the clock was screaming at her to hurry up.

She pushed the door to the changing room open as loudly as she could, slamming it against the wall so that the changing room shook. She waited for a single moment, heard the hurried sounds of a couple separating instantly and then strode into the room. Her face was beet red, but she marched to her cubicle without glancing anywhere else. She stripped off quickly, letting her swimsuit flop to the floor, and began towelling herself dry. When, at last, she was dry and had mustered the courage she turned and saw that she was alone in the room apart from a young blonde, looking flustered as she sat on a bench, wrapped in a thick towel.

Billie dressed quickly, looking around all the while for the second young woman, but she seemed to have made good her escape while Billie had been drying herself. The blonde sitting at the bench hardly dared look at her, which Billie took to be a sign either of guilt or anger.

Back in the office it was hard to concentrate. Even the 'why are you late again? frown from her supervisor did nothing to focus her mind. Instead she kept imagining the two young women making love, their beautiful bodies naked, mouths locked as they kissed passionately, exploring each other's body sensuously. On the way out of the pool Billie had been hoping to catch a glimpse of the second blonde, wanting to get a good look at her so that her fantasies would be complete.

In the end it had been too much, the fantasies were too strong, Billie's excitement too much. She had gone to the toilet clutching her handbag, and once safely ensconced she had used her favourite hairbrush to frig herself to orgasm, violently, brutally, driven by the strength of fantasy triggered by what she had seen. As she had climaxed she had seen the two young women naked, finger fucking each other as she watched them.

James hardly knew what hit him that night. Billie had pulled him straight into the bedroom, pushed him onto the bed and proceeded to fuck his brains out. It

245

probably scared the hell out of him, but that didn't stop him enjoying every second of it. Only in her mind his male lips had been transformed to female, his cock transformed into a woman's loving fingers. James had been turned into a young blonde female, a mirror image of Billie, and as they had made love the two of them were transported to the chlorinated changing room.

Later, when they made love again, James had questioned her, whispering into her ear as he drove his hard cock into her slick pussy. She gasped her pleasure and told him it was nothing, she just felt horny after being bored out of her mind at work. It was nothing, nothing, nothing. And then in her mind his male outline had shifted and James was honey blonde and wet from the pool.

The morning would not pass. Time dragged the more that Billie wished it forward and the work seemed duller and more mundane than usual, making it easier for Billie to escape to her fantasy again. What was it? She didn't fancy girls, not even in her dirtiest fantasies did she make love with women. And in reality the only time a woman had made a pass at her she'd fallen about laughing. Sex with women was not what she wanted, not in imagination and not in reality. Only ... only seeing the two women in the changing room had triggered something.

And then at lunch time Billie had almost broken into a run to get to the pool. The sun was out, the first real sun of the summer, and the swimming pool was unexpectedly full. Billie's heart sank as she paid for her ticket. The place was filled with school kids, office workers, pensioners and mums with toddlers. She took an age getting changed, waiting restlessly in the changing room for either of the blondes to show up. She spent a quarter of an hour in the water, swimming back and forth like one of the regulars, not speaking to anyone, scanning the entrance in the vain hope that her fantasy girls would turn up. She took an age drying off and getting dressed, knowing that she was going to be disappointed. The constant stream of people in and out meant that there wasn't even the chance of slinking into the corner to enjoy her fantasy.

The days that followed were no better, the summer sunshine bringing out the crowds and driving away the beautiful blondes that Billie longed to see again. It was worse at the weekend, the screaming school kids and James in tow meant that Billie was disappointed again.

In her mind Billie saw it all. Sometimes she entered the changing room and caught them: two beautiful young women making love, pert breasts tipped with fiery red nipples and with long thighs of glassy smooth skin. She caught them and they were embarrassed, but then she'd talk to them, tell them it was okay and then . . . then they would kiss, all three of them, soft kisses at first but then harder, deeper, until the three of them would be making love. She saw one of them squatting down, opening her pussy so that Billie could suck and lick, while the other used her mouth on Billie's oozing sex.

In her mind Billie watched them, having sex with the kind of physical abandon that made Billie climax just by watching. And then, when one of them would leave Billie would seduce the other one, mirroring the scenes she had just witnessed. Or else the two of them would notice Billie and seduce her, stroking and touching each other before doing the same to Billie. The fantasies were so strong, so erotic that Billie felt she was permanently on heat, her pussy always wet and tingly.

James was beginning to get suspicious. When they made love he'd want to know why her eyes were closed, he'd want to know what she was thinking about. When he caught her using her hairbrush on herself he felt hurt, his male pride injured as he convinced himself that he couldn't satisfy her. And her work was slipping and her time-keeping deteriorating. Her supervisor even demanded an explanation and when none was forthcoming she suggested that perhaps Billie was seeing someone every lunch time.

But they didn't understand, not James and not her supervisor. And it was so hard to explain, even to herself. Her mind was constantly filled with images of two naked women, making loving sensuously, lovingly, giving each other the most exquisite pleasure. She saw them cloistered away, always alone, hidden, in darkness, witnessed only by herself. In fantasy she had touched them, kissed them, stroked them, sucked the water dripping from their breasts, teased the honey from between their thighs.

Now, every time she saw a blonde her heart beat a little faster. She was starting to haunt the swimming pool. All the lifeguards knew her and the lady behind the ticket counter always said a cheery hello. Still she felt a rush of adrenaline whenever she went into the changing room, hoping against all the odds to find the two lovers wrapped up in an illicit embrace. Even when she was in the water most of her attention was devoted to keeping watch.

There was no point in being at the pool, she knew that for certain. The chances of ever seeing the women again was too remote even to work out and, even if she did see them again, what could she possibly hope to achieve? She could hardly march up to them and explain that she was a voyeur and that she fantasised constantly about seeing them make love. And she could hardly try to seduce them, she wouldn't even know where to begin.

But she was there still, every day, swimming back and forth while her mind brimmed with sexy thoughts that made her nipples harden and her pussy wet. God, she had even begun to secretly rent dirty films from the video shop, seeking out films with lesbian scenes in the hope that she'd find something that turned her on as much as the reality she had witnessed.

'It's safe . . . It's raining and there's no one here today . . .'

Billie froze. She stood in the doorway, hardly daring to breathe. Could it possibly be? She had given up all hope, but now, when she had least expected it she heard the voice that was stuck inside her head. There was the same tremulous protest, the same breathless excitement. Very carefully she closed the door and pressed herself against the wall, certain that her pounding heart was going to give her away.

She heard a sigh of pleasure and chanced a look. Two bodies, naked, blonde, bronzed. She recognised the long thighs and the gorgeous shape of the first woman's backside, the tan as golden as it had been in memory. The other woman could barely be glimpsed, her hands were massaging her lover's full, pert breasts, her long blonde hair obscuring her face.

Back against the wall, Billie could scarcely believe her luck. The sound of her heartbeat was deafening, obscuring the soft words whispered by the illicit lovers. She dared to look again and saw the look of delight on the profile of the first woman's face. Billie could feel the redness on her own face, she was trembling, afraid and exhilarated at the same time. There was only one thing to do.

'Please, don't stop . . .' she whispered, stepping out of the shadows.

The first woman squealed and tried to cover her nakedness with her hands. The second woman seemed to shrink back behind the first, seeking refuge from the embarrassment.

'I . . . I won't tell anyone, I promise,' Billie whispered trying to smile. She began to remove her swimsuit which was clinging uncomfortably to her skin.

'What are you doing?' the first woman demanded, obviously alarmed by what she was seeing.

'I've never seen anything so erotic before . . .' Billie tried to explain. 'Two women making love like this . . . It's so exciting . . .'

'Two women? What the hell's going on?'

The second woman emerged, stepping away from her friend at last. Long blonde hair cascaded over bronzed shoulders and clear blue eyes regarded Billie with outright suspicion. But Billie wasn't looking at that, she was looking at the hard cock that protruded from between his legs. It *had* been a fantasy, it had never been two women. He had been hidden and the long blonde locks had transformed a he into a she.

Billie closed her eyes, and there she saw them, two beautiful blondes, gloriously female, making love in the darkness.